SLA

DEREK SHANNON

CHIMERA

Slave Hunt first published in 1999 by
Chimera Publishing Ltd
PO Box 152
Waterlooville
Hants
PO8 9FS

Printed and bound in Great Britain by
Caledonian International Book Manufacturing Ltd
Glasgow

SLAVE HUNT

Derek Shannon

For Pauline, my partner, drinking buddy and best friend – thanks for the support.

Chapter One

The young woman plodded wearily along the shadowy roadside, occasionally glancing back to catch the sight and sound of an approaching vehicle, someone that might be willing to take her that much further north and save what little remained of her shoe leather. But it was Sunday night, and the traffic along her present route had inevitably lessened as the evening wore on, as she further distanced herself from her old life, and her feet ached more and more. But still she continued, ignorant of a final destination, and not really caring; anything would be better than what lay behind her.

Bonnie Jo Fisher was twenty-one, though her size and guileless looks made her seem younger, often provoking questions when visiting the more exclusive London clubs. Her chestnut hair was cut short in a pageboy that brushed her slim shoulders and framed her almond eyes. Her firm breasts were hugged by a white T-shirt, and her slim legs by blue jeans.

Perspiration ran down her back, forcing her to carry her denim jacket in one hand, trailing it along the road like a security blanket. She had nothing else to her name with her, apart from a few pounds; she hadn't any time to prepare for such a journey when she'd left London, what – only five days ago?

It seemed much longer.

She'd hitched her way north, though it felt like she'd walked most of the way. She should have stayed in

London, become one of the homeless; no one ever notices the homeless. Why she'd gone north she couldn't say, except she remembered the holidays her family would take in Scotland, how a young Bonnie would gaze with wonder at the rolling hills, the fields of heather and hedgerows, with nary another soul in sight. For a girl who'd grown up in a high-rise urban flat it was like arriving in another world, and even then she'd been able to appreciate the solitude, the peace.

She needed both so desperately now.

The road curved, bringing Bonnie to the outskirts of an alleged town, identified by a sign as Iniscay. She shook her head; she'd never heard of it, but that was hardly surprising. It was much like the other coastal fishing villages she'd passed through this week, only smaller: a few scattered stone cottages on the surrounding grey moors, with a more tightly concentrated collection of houses and shops along the main road.

The road itself was not one of the major British arteries; indeed, it was more like a capillary to a redundant organ, and it was probably this isolation that had allowed the village to keep what the tourist boards would call 'its original charm'. There were the usual thick-walled stone-built cottages, the miniature chapel with high, narrow windows and moss-encrusted grave markers surrounding it, and tiny corner shops.

Bonnie stopped to rub her eyes. She'd awakened just before dawn, sixteen hours ago, in a disused, urine-fetid gypsy caravan in a motorway lay-by, shivering despite the sweltering August weather, and had spent the rest of the day moving, just moving, ignoring the pangs in her stomach and the pains in her limbs. Moving, seeking another place for the night; it wasn't wise to remain in one place for too long, attracting unwanted attention.

It would be even worse in a place like this, where peering from behind parlour curtains at every approaching stranger was a shared pastime. She should have begged, borrowed or stolen a backpack, even if she had to fill it up with newspapers, just as long as she looked like a proper rambler.

Warm yellow lights haloed the windows of the houses around her, wherein families enjoyed late suppers or watched television; painful reminders of what Bonnie had, and lost. She discarded such thoughts as they arose, but kept looking for suitable shelter: an unoccupied house, even a garden shed or the back of someone's car. If necessary, she'd sleep on the beach.

A week ago she would have laughed at the idea. Oh, she would have fallen asleep outside, she'd have said, but only after an evening of downing expensive drinks, celebrating yet another well paid assignment. A week ago Bonnie was an ambitious cog in a London computer firm, an excellent programmer willing to go the distance to make herself noticed, respected. Already she'd earned more than her parents ever had, and co-owned a swanky townhouse with four other young high-fliers. Life was good.

Her first mistake had been Stuart. He'd seemed a decent man when she met him, a sales rep for one of her clients. And their evenings, once their relationship had extended into the bedroom, were memorable enough. How could she have known he would use her place for stashing drugs?

Her second mistake had been in running, when she saw the police surrounding her house. Stuart had been acting suspiciously all day, even erratically, and after an argument she'd left the house just to go down the road for a newspaper and give both of them a chance to cool off. Yes, she'd panicked. Yes, she should have immediately turned back, especially after she'd been spotted and pursued, before losing her followers. She'd done nothing wrong, she knew that.

But after a short while she knew it wouldn't have made a difference. Even if she was eventually found not guilty, it would have been after months on remand, locked up in some squalid Victorian cell twenty-three hours a day, with a pot for a toilet and two or more hardened criminals preying on her. Bonnie had never been imprisoned before, but she was certain she couldn't survive such an experience for long.

But was her current predicament any better? Aimlessly wandering, unable to contact her family or friends, living on the remaining money she had when she first ran? She had no street sense, didn't know the ins and outs of living rough, fiddling the system, had no connections to get her false identification and the like. She would have to turn herself in – she knew that.

But getting herself to actually do it was another matter.

She stopped outside the Causeway, a typical whitewashed country pub, seemingly little different from a hundred others she'd seen lately. Except that while the ground floor was lit, and from the sounds within, lively enough, boards covered the windows of the upper floor, as if it was in the process of being renovated. Hope raised Bonnie's shoulders as she recognised an opportunity.

She circled the building, moving around the cars parked haphazardly on the gravel lot surrounding it, as if searching for her own. The pub overlooked the beach, pebbled with overturned fishing boats, and beyond it a cove lit only by the pale cast from the rising moon. Bonnie stopped to watch a couple strolling lazily along the expanse of white sand, a lovely sight, except for the occasional wave of their hands in the air – sand midges. Bonnie grimaced; she may as well try sleeping in a pool of piranha as on the beach on a warm evening like this. She'd sooner take her chances indoors.

At the rear of the building a rusted metal fire escape stood beside a battered rubbish bin. Bottles, broken and intact, littered the area, and there was a general stench of rubbish and urine. Still glancing about, Bonnie slipped back into her jacket and ascended the steps, wincing with each creak beneath her shoes, as if it were all some Indiana Jones trap.

She reached the top, wiping the sweat from her palms on the sides of her jeans as she tried the door handle. The door gave a little; it wasn't bolted, not too securely anyway. Gently but firmly she rattled the door, the experience she'd accrued recently hinting that the pub owner wasn't as security-conscious as his urban counterparts.

There was a cracking sound from just behind the doorframe, making Bonnie wince and glance anxiously down the steps. After gathering her breath and her remaining will, she pulled at the door again, this time surprised at the ease in which it opened. She found a feeble latch, now broken, on the other side of the door, more like something a child would have for her bedroom than a man in his place of business. Perhaps with the renovations there was no way downstairs now, and thus no need to secure the upstairs more than they had.

Whatever the explanation, it suited Bonnie well enough.

Meagre outside light filtered in between the window planks. The air was still and thick with the smells of paint, cleaning fluid and sawdust, and caught in her throat. It was as Bonnie expected; a disused lounge. Dustsheets covered booths and tables, and lumber and paint tins sat or stood against the walls and the bar, also draped with sheets.

Bonnie gently eased the door shut and took a few tentative steps inward, hearing only a slight creak of the floorboards beneath the carpet. The noise from the bar below should cover it enough for her to remain undetected, at least until last orders. At the far end of the lounge the door which appeared to lead downstairs was shut, probably locked, to keep out wandering punters from downstairs. Fine. It was hardly the Dorchester, but then literal beggars couldn't be choosers.

Her eyes adjusting to the dimness, she retraced her steps towards a set of booths near the exit, for easy departure if required. She pulled back a dustsheet from a booth, stopping as she found several sets of crates resting on the vinyl cushions. A moment's inspection confirmed them to be bottles of soft drink and packets of crisps!

She helped herself greedily, only feeling pangs of guilt afterwards, as if to replace the hunger she'd felt all day. If she could resign herself to accepting breaking and entering, petty theft was hardly an extra leap further into the abyss. Only then did she begin to acknowledge what she might end up having to do in the next few days to stay free. She really didn't want to think about that.

After her impromptu meal she removed her jacket, rolled it up into a pillow, and lay back on the seat, pulling the dustsheet over her, not so much for warmth as for a reminder of happier times. Exhaustion swamped her almost immediately, and she promptly fell asleep.

The hand that clutched her shoulder also pulled her back to her feet, as well as back to a jumbled, stammering consciousness. Bonnie squinted at the potent light from the naked bulbs now burning from the ceiling, and winced at the harsh and heavily accented voice from the broad silhouette looming over her. 'You girl! What the hell are you doing up here?'

For a few bleary seconds Bonnie was disorientated. 'I… I—' she blurted hopelessly.

The figure, a bear of a man, grasped her by the shoulders and shook her like a doll. 'You broke in here and stole from me. You're a thief!'

'No—'

'I'm not blind, girl! I can see for meself!'

Bonnie recovered her senses quickly. It was obviously the pub owner. 'I – I'm sorry, I just needed a place to stay—'

'Aye, and food and drink, too.' With shocking ease he led her towards the bar, practically flinging her against it. Bonnie glanced about anxiously. The door to downstairs, now open, and the entrance through which she originally came, were now at equal distance from her, and she had little doubt that the man could stop her if she tried for either direction.

Trying to suppress her panic, she blinked and squinted in order to examine her discoverer. He was a broad bullet of a man, seemingly approaching his retirement years.

His wiry hair was iron grey, and his heavy matching beard and moustache unkempt. He was stocky but not fat; she'd felt the power in his biceps as he'd dragged her from the booths. Spilt beer and dishwater stained his red and white striped apron, and probably the white shirt and old grey pinstripe trousers underneath. He stabbed a thick, accusing finger in her direction. 'You undisciplined hellions think you can do anything and get away with it, aye? You wouldn't have in my day! We knew what to do with the likes of you!'

Bonnie could feel the perspiration gathering down her back, and she struggled to remain calm. 'I'm very sorry, sir, I didn't mean any harm—'

'Aye, your kind never means it, but you still do it,' he snapped. 'Come along then, I'm calling the police.'

He reached for her but she shrank back. 'No!' It was almost a shout; Bonnie realising too late that it gave away too much to him.

He hadn't missed it either, his eyes narrowing thoughtfully. 'You're in bother with the law already, aye? That's why you're hiding away up here like some criminal.'

'No, sir. I just don't want to get into trouble.'

'You're already in trouble.' He shook his head slowly, rage in his eyes. 'You girls are worse than the boys. If you were one of the locals I'd punish you meself the way I was punished as a lad, rather than bother the police.'

Bonnie drew in a sharp breath, finding herself saying uncertainly, 'Then… then why don't you?'

He stared with open suspicion. 'Eh?'

His demeanour had changed slightly, and Bonnie seized upon it, shocked by where desperation was leading her. 'Punish me the way you would a local. You don't have to involve the police.'

Something like a smile raised the corners of his thin, colourless lips. 'Aye, I'm sure you'd prefer that. But if I did it wouldn't be a slap on the wrist, I can guarantee. It would be twenty strokes of my belt on your bare arse.' He shook his head dismissively. 'You'll not be so willing now, I'm sure.'

Bonnie drew in another deep breath, astonished at the reserves of calm and acceptance she now found, though her mind still reeled. She was faced with the option of being disciplined at the hands of this ageing brute, or of facing the police and certain prison. Eventually she pulled her shoulders back with more defiance than she felt inside, and asked quietly, 'And could I leave afterwards?'

'Aye.'

'Twenty strokes?' she found herself repeating.

'Aye, twenty strokes.'

She nodded uncertainly. 'Okay then,' she said.

'Of your own free will?'

'Yes, of my own free will.'

He nodded, reaching beneath his apron and undoing his belt. 'Remove your clothes, girl.'

'What?'

'You heard me, remove them. Everything.' When she froze in place, so did he, adding, 'Or have you changed your mind, so I can phone the police?'

'No,' she blurted hastily, 'don't do that.' She turned her back to him as she began to undress, kicking off her shoes and supporting herself against the bar with one hand as she used the other to remove her socks. The carpet felt gritty and unclean beneath her bare feet. She

13

understood, at least on an intellectual level, that the humiliation of being naked before a stranger was an integral part of the punishment, perhaps more than the belting itself, and that being naked wouldn't in itself harm her. But why did excitement and anxiety now coarse through her body in equal measure? No, she was obviously mistaken.

She jumped, dropping her socks, as he made a snapping sound in the air behind her with his belt, his voice just as cutting. 'Come on girl, I've not got all night. Get your clothes off.'

'Yes, sir,' she said meekly, her back still turned to him as she grasped the hem of her T-shirt. Even then she was analysing why she was behaving so contritely to this man who was wanting to beat her – a defenceless girl. Was she just playing up to him, hoping to pacify him enough with this behaviour to keep him from changing his mind and phoning the police? Was she feeling the genuine need to be punished for her earlier actions; breaking in and eating and drinking his goods?

Or was she really one of those girls she'd only ever furtively read about, the so-called masochists that took great delight in being humiliated and punished like this? She couldn't imagine how anyone could derive pleasure from such treatment, let alone imagine it for herself.

The man's gruff voice brought her back to reality with a jolt. 'I told you I haven't all night for your foolishness!' he snapped.

'Yes sir.' She tugged the T-shirt over her head, and her hair swayed neatly back into place as she set the garment gingerly on the top of the covered bar. Underneath she wore only a lacy black bra, which squeezed her firm breasts together and deepened her shadowy cleavage.

Bonnie could feel hungry eyes burning into her back as she reached behind for the bra catch, fumbled with it for a moment before undoing it, and held the bra tightly against her chest with one hand as she slid the straps from her shoulders.

She gazed meekly over her shoulder at the man. His eyes flared. He was clearly eager to see her breasts – to see her naked. Bonnie felt a twinge of unexpected arousal; a part of her was actually enjoying this!

'You've not got anything I've not seen before, girl,' he assured her with a soft chuckle.

Somehow that was a perverse encouragement for her, and with a sigh of resignation she cast aside her bra and turned to face him.

Something made her stand very still as the man absorbed the sight of her delicious bare breasts. Her treacherous nipples stiffened beneath the intense scrutiny. She crossed her hands over her stomach, and meekly lowered her gaze.

The man seemed transfixed by the sight before him, the belt hanging limply from his right fist. Then he managed to pull himself together and returned to business. 'I said it'd be twenty strokes on your bare arse, girl,' he managed, his voice thick with emotion.

'Yes, sir...' She turned around again, undoing her snugly fitting jeans and drawing down the zipper. The blue denim slid down her shapely thighs and calves, and as she bent to disentangle the garment from her feet she glimpsed the man ogling her neat bum, tightly encased in black cotton knickers.

For a moment she savoured the feel of the cool air on her skin; always half afraid of being caught out as she had been tonight, she hadn't really undressed since she'd run away from London. It felt good, despite – or maybe because of – the unnerving presence of the man behind her.

Something made her pause and coquettishly draw her arms up to cover her breasts, awaiting an impatient response from her captor.

She wasn't disappointed. 'Aye, the pants too,' he said. 'I'll not treat you differently from the locals.'

Bonnie nodded and hooked her thumbs into her knickers. How many young men and women in this village had been stripped and belted here? Is that why he kept such a flimsy lock on the exit, to entice them? Did they ever come back for more, feeling as Bonnie felt now; that heady taste of forbidden fruit? She took one more glance at him, the last vestiges of her modesty cast aside.

The man swung the belt into his open palm, not even flinching as the brown leather connected with his callused skin. 'If you keep me waiting any longer it'll be thirty strokes!' he warned.

That, Bonnie didn't want. With blushing cheeks she lowered her gaze and her knickers, gingerly rolling them into a ball as if ready for the laundry, and setting them with the rest of her clothes. To her shame she'd felt the dampness in the gusset.

'Turn around, girl.'

She obeyed, trying to meet his eyes and keep him from gazing lower. But he was feasting on her nubile body, now fully exposed to his scrutiny. And his lewd attention engendered a measure of anticipation within her. Not that her face failed to blush further as he stepped forward, smiling with satisfaction, though the tone and content of his words retained their earlier impatience. 'And about time too. Now turn around again.'

Bonnie did so, flinching as she felt the cold brass tip of his belt buckle touch the soft area of flesh at the apex of her cheeks. When he spoke again his voice was softer, almost reverential. 'Have you not been beaten before, girl?'

Bonnie gulped, 'Once, sir, yes.'

'By whom?'

'By my mother.'

'How?'

'With her hand.'

'Where?'

Her heart skipped a beat before she answered, 'On my... my bottom, sir.'

'And was your lovely bottom bare?' he persisted.

Bonnie just shook her head.

'Then this is long overdue,' he said huskily. 'Bend forward, grasp the edge of the bar and spread your cheeks.'

She obeyed without another sound. The distance from where she stood to the bar was such that her arms were fully stretched in order to support herself. She stared down at the worn crimson carpet, her breasts swaying gently and her heart pounding in her chest. She listened anxiously as he moved this way and that behind her, unfurling his belt to its full length until the tip dragged along the floor.

She jumped again as his hand, large and rugged, grasped and roughly squeezed her left cheek, his thumb almost pressing on that most private spot between her buttocks. 'I said spread your cheeks,' he snapped. 'Wider!'

Bonnie struggled to obey the order, aware of how even more exposed and vulnerable she would be to him, how her sex opened to the cool air of the lounge. She could faintly smell her own arousal; a betrayal of the feelings she wanted to keep hidden from the man.

His words confirmed the futility of trying to maintain her secret. 'You're wanting this, despite your fears, aren't you?'

Bonnie's voice had fled with her resistance. She could only nod.

Smack! The vicious blow came without warning, making her yelp and almost straighten up.

'Yell all you want, girl, there's no one to hear but me. But don't move, or I'll double me efforts.'

Bonnie fought to maintain her position as the broad belt made sharp bursts of contact on her poor stinging bottom. Tears were running down her face. His aim was good, never striking in exactly the same place twice, never straying higher than the tops of her cheeks, never lower than the tops of her thighs.

She tried counting the blows as they fell, but got confused after the first dozen. To her immense surprise, though the pain was undeniable, she also felt a warm glow spreading from her backside, bridging and heightening points of arousal in the rest of her body. She yelped with each swipe, but a secret part of her admitted that maybe it was more because it was expected, rather than from the actual severity of the blows. Indeed she wriggled slightly, keeping her bum high, well displayed and aching for more, despite the wetness she could feel seeping from her sex.

In the distance he was speaking, and she drew forth from herself enough to listen. 'Aye, a wicked girl like you needs a regular beating, don't you? Regular beatings on your bare arse.'

Somewhere closer she could hear someone replying, 'Yes! Yes! I'm wicked! Beat me!'

It took a heartbeat to acknowledge that it was her voice. It took less than that to acknowledge that it was said not to assuage him, but because, for one mad moment, she meant every shameless word.

When the final blow fell waves of bliss rushed through her trembling body, and she cried out, burying her face into her shoulder and her fingernails into the bar top. Dimly, she felt her bladder give way, as a meagre stream of urine trickled down her inner thighs. She tensed immediately and held her breath. A part of her feared he'd beat her some more for losing control.

Another part of her hoped for it.

Her body was shaking, chilled despite the furnace her backside – and her sex – had become under the intense punishment. But she remained still as ordered, until he said otherwise. She felt instinctively that he would give her leave when he was ready.

After a moment he did so. 'Stand up, girl.'

She straightened up, limbs trembling and aching, her hands covering her breasts and pubic thatch, her face shame-reddened and tear-streamed, and the insides of her legs wet from her loss of control. She stared at him with clouded vision as he re-looped his belt back into his trousers and buckled it up again beneath his apron. He was breathing as heavily as she was, and was clearly excited too. Had he seen how his chastisement had made her climax, as no one or nothing but her own fingers had done in the past?

She ran her tongue over her dry lips, wetting them

before gingerly asking. 'May... may I leave now?'

He smiled. 'Not just yet. Straighten this place up, and you can spend the rest of the night here and leave in the morning. I might even fix you a proper breakfast before you go.' He moved towards her. She backed away, until she realised he was retrieving her clothes and shoes.

'W-what are you doing?' she stammered.

'Insurance.' He grinned lecherously at her. 'You're hardly likely to be running off as you are.'

The large man picked up the phone in his untidy private accommodation, dialled, and waited for a few seconds. 'It's MacTaggart, Mr Castlewell,' he said when the recipient of his call answered. 'Aye, I know what time it is, but I've got a new girl for you here... Aye, she's had the usual treatment, and she responded very well indeed, sir... It'll be the usual fee, and I'll deliver her tomorrow.' He hung up without another word – the deal done.

There was a dusty mirror mounted on the wall over one of the booths. Having woken from an uncomfortable night's sleep, Bonnie noticed it for the first time as she yawned and stretched, and was drawn by an irresistible curiosity. In the early morning light that crept in through the shuttered windows she stood before it and twisted to view her backside. Her cheeks were scarlet, angry stripes melted together into a diffuse area of pain... and pleasure. So it was true; she did enjoy being punished. How bizarre, to make such a monumental discovery in such a squalid place. Her hands crept between her legs and she lightly touched her clitoris. She shuddered deliciously.

She wanted more. It was amazing.

Heavy steps on the outside fire escape brought her back to her senses, and she hastily snatched a dustsheet from an adjacent booth and wrapped it around herself like a toga – after all, it might not be the same man.

But it was. Bonnie squinted as the door was wrenched open and bright light flooded the room and hurt her eyes. His bulky silhouette lumbered in, and he was carrying her clothes. 'Here,' he said, as he placed them on the bar and settled back against it to watch, arms folded and an amused look in his eye, as she managed to dress without losing the cover of the dustsheet – as only a female could.

'Thanks,' she mumbled, once she was fully dressed again and the sheet had been discarded.

'My name's MacTaggart,' he said. 'You did well last night.'

'I did?' she gasped, surprised at the strangely matter-of-fact compliment.

'Aye. I've seen some, lads and lasses both, blubber and plead their way through their beatings. But you took your punishment well, girl. I respect that.' He studied her closely, before adding, 'You're are on the run, aren't you?'

Bonnie nodded. There seemed little need to pretend otherwise now.

'I thought so,' he said. 'I'd like to help you, if I can. If you're looking for a place to hide, that is.'

Bonnie's eyes widened as she sensed her fortunes might at last be about to change for the better. 'Where?' she asked eagerly.

'Iniscay.'

She frowned. 'What, here in the village?'

21

MacTaggart shook his head. 'Och, no. I mean Iniscay Island, just outside the cove.'

'An island?' She was a little dubious. She knew she'd been foolishly heading further and further into remoter parts, but to go to an island seemed the height of lunacy; if the authorities discovered where she was she'd be trapped.

'Aye,' he continued. 'It's a nature reserve, no trespassers, and with the rocks surrounding it hardly anyone can make it there anyway. There's shelter and supplies waiting for the scientists that arrive twice a year, but their next visit's not until the Autumn. I can get you there in my boat, and pick you up again once the police have scaled down their search for you. They'll soon think you've made it abroad somewhere.'

Bonnie's pulse quickened. He was offering a secure sanctuary where she could get her head together and think things through. Granted, she'd be alone, but she didn't mind that; at this stage, especially after what she'd been through, she'd accept anything rather than prison.

Bonnie made her mind up, and pulled her shoulders back determinedly as she looked at her unexpected benefactor. 'Okay… thanks,' she said. 'You don't know what this'll mean for me.'

A glint flickered in his eyes as they furtively crawled over the delicious sight of her lovely young breasts straining against the tight white T-shirt. 'Oh, I do know…' he said quietly, 'believe me.'

Chapter Two

Bonnie hadn't been in a boat since she was a child, visiting the seaside during her summer holidays. She'd never liked the way they constantly rolled back and forth with each paddle stroke, with every shift of her body on the bench seat, or even at the capricious whims of the wind and sea.

Little had changed since then, and her stomach was making her regret having the fried breakfast MacTaggart had cooked up.

He took the short voyage in his stride, of course. He'd probably been born in a boat, reaching for the oars before his mother's breasts. He sat in the prow, keeping as steady a beat with the oars as he had with his belt some hours before. Occasionally he'd indulge in a little shanty or dirty limerick, to break the silence that had descended between them since pushing out from the village beach.

Perhaps she wouldn't feel so bad if she'd been better able to see where they were going. A morning fog clung cold and damp over the water, restricting visibility to only a few metres. She found herself anxiously gripping the sides of the tiny boat, her knuckles white.

She needed to take her mind off things. 'Are you sure no one visits here – apart from the scientist?' she asked, fighting the urge to gag.

MacTaggart's great mop of wiry grey hair nodded in answer.

'And how big is this island?'

'You could walk round it in a few hours,' he answered. 'Best not to, though. Dinna be seen by any passing boats.'

'And there's shelter there? And supplies?'

There was a trace of annoyance creeping into his voice. 'Aye. The three lighthouses are automatic now. But the keeper's cottage still stands, leeward side. Scientists use that. Gas stoves, cots, blankets. Powdered food and milk. Fresh water. Birds' eggs in the stacks and fish in the streams, if you've a mind to catch them. You'll not starve,' he added. 'You'll be left alone, too. Isn't that what you wanted, girl?'

'Yes.' Bonnie's own annoyance matched MacTaggart's; she had no desire to mull over her decision to exile herself. Then her attention was drawn to the sounds ahead, of water lapping against sand, and a moment later the dark silhouette of the island loomed into view. The boat rocked and Bonnie gripped more tightly as MacTaggart drew in the oars, rose, and leapt out, the water lapping up to the tops of his boots as the boat hissed to a stop against the shingle beneath. He stretched, then turned round to face her. 'If you're expecting to be carried you'd best think again.'

Bonnie struggled to her feet, then tried unsuccessfully to keep from getting her shoes and socks wet as she stepped out onto the undergrowth and tree-fringed beach. She turned to MacTaggart for some sort of advice or direction, only to find him already pushing the boat back out into the gentle waves. 'Wait,' she called. 'You're not leaving me already?'

'Aye.' He climbed back aboard and extended the oars again. 'I've done my bit. You're on your own now.'

'But – but where's the cottage?'

'Have a look round, girl,' he called as he floated away from the shore. 'You've got plenty of time now.'

She nodded in mute agreement. As he disappeared into the fog she called uncertainly, 'Thanks... thanks for your help...'

Bonnie stood there for long minutes, feeling strangely empty, and waiting for something to happen. What a mad old codger he was! After the beating he hadn't made any sexual advances, as she'd expected. Perhaps the pleasure of punishing her had itself been sufficient to make him come. After all, it had been enough for her.

Eventually she started along the shoreline for a while, the salt air filling her lungs and the mist cooling her face. There was hardly any surf at all, though the small waves did roll in relentlessly, crawling up the slight incline to her right. Above and around her the cries of gannets and terns kept the silence from becoming too oppressive.

A noise to her left made her jump, and Bonnie was stunned to see two young-looking roe deer standing at the edge of the undergrowth, in the mouth of some natural pathway through the trees. She froze, staring back with amazement; she'd never seen such beautiful creatures out in the open like this. She realised she was the intruder in their world, and felt the absurd urge to ask their permission to remain. But then something made them shy away back into the woods.

A giggle of delight escaped her lips. It was all so pristine, so primitive! And it was all hers – at least for a short time. Bonnie knelt and removed her shoes and socks, cast them aside, and squeezed her toes into the

25

soft silt carpet beneath, filled with a sudden urge to run, to drive her leg muscles to their limits. And she did, balling her hands into fists as she kicked up wet sand behind her. She breathed in deeply through her nose and filled her lungs with crisp fresh air.

After a short while she slowed, then stopped, wiping the sweat from her reddened face. With some alarm she found she'd nearly run into a collection of tiny jellyfish, laid out on the beach like mismatched tiles; grey with pink and purple centres. Too insubstantial for even the gulls' voracious appetites, it seemed, they awaited dissolution in the morning sun. Bonnie was more careful as she crossed over their graveyard, tiptoeing around them like they were sleeping wolves.

Perspiration was trickling down her back, so she removed her jacket and T-shirt, casting these aside too. The mist was lifting and the breeze cooled her bare arms and midriff, and for the first time in a long time she felt wondrously free. Now she truly felt as if she were on a deserted island, and only the sporadic appearance of weather-beaten metal signs proclaiming: RESTRICTED TERRITORY – TRESPASSERS WILL BE PROSECUTED, spoiled the illusion of purity.

This stretch of beach was a wider crescent of white sand, striped with lines of shattered seashells and larger families of rocks extending outwards. They were constantly battered and sprayed by the ferocious waves, and she could now see what MacTaggart had meant about the difficulty in arriving here by boat, unless you knew the right stretch of ocean to navigate from the mainland.

Bonnie had never felt so isolated. She was a modern-day castaway on her own island. She could do anything she wanted.

A whim crossed her mind, and she acted upon it, immediately shucking off the rest of her clothes – pausing only once, in a moment of vestigial inhibition, to glance about before lowering her knickers – and standing naked in the open air for the first time ever.

It felt glorious!

She kicked aside her clothes and waded into the rolling sea, avoiding the rocks. It was so cold – but so refreshing, too – and by the time it reached up to her waist she'd grown almost accustomed to the numbing temperature. She took a deep breath, sank back, and closed her eyes, allowing the waves to gently lift and lower her. The gulls circled above, occasionally cawing as if to protest her presence in their feeding grounds.

It was an experience conducive to relaxation and reflection, and Bonnie's mind began to drift with her body. Introspection never came easy for her; she had grown accustomed to living each day as it arrived, understanding and accepting her place in the grand scheme of things, and making only the most basic of plans for the future. Perhaps that was why she had been better able to adjust to her fugitive status than another might have, under the same circumstances. She'd even allowed herself to be beaten last night, something she'd never have considered possible before it happened, let alone... enjoyable. Why had such degradation made her climax? It had gone against everything she'd believed about sex – about herself.

Perhaps it had just been a fluke; the novelty of the experience, her fatigue, and fear of the police eroding her normal inhibitions?

If so, then the memory of last night's experiences

shouldn't evoke anything now in her but shame and regret.

Except it didn't. It warmed her, softened her outside and in, as if this were a hot intimate bath and not a chill ocean dip.

Bonnie felt herself being carried back to the shore. Steadily the support beneath her shifted from the mild rolling of the waves to the firmer foundation of the sand, until the water was no longer able to move her, and became content to work at the silt around her supine body, as if slowly burying her like some playful lover. Bonnie's body acknowledged it, though she remained faithful to the caress of the water, and above her the sun as it struggled through the mist to reclaim its mastery of the sky. A beam finally pierced the morning veils to reach down and stroke her, the sun god descending to seduce a mortal woman. She warmed, and ran her hands lightly over her body, as if to drive away the last of her chills so as not to insult her divine lover, so powerful with his touch, so mercurial with his moods. If he grew angry, how would he chastise her?

And why did that notion excite her now? Had MacTaggart helped awaken a hitherto unacknowledged facet of her sexuality?

What would it be like to experience last night again? To be made to strip, stand for inspection, to be made to prostrate oneself and be punished for crimes real and imagined?

Her pussy pulsed in response, agreeing to the direction her musings had taken, as did her nipples, no longer able to use the cold as an excuse to stand to attention. Almost of their own volition, Bonnie's hands reached up to her breasts. Gently she kneaded them, nibbling her lip at the acute pleasures her touch generated.

She'd previously had two lovers. But neither had given her satisfaction, and not even her past fantasies, the ones she read or crafted herself, were able to match the intensity she felt from her memories of last night.

Without her realising it, one of her hands had sought purchase between her legs, fingers running though the wispy down covering the tender mound of her sex. Her left leg rose until the foot was flat against the sand and her knee pointed skyward, and her thighs parted further, ever so slightly.

Her sex opened like an oyster to the eternal waves, and her fingers tentatively sought the expectant nub of her sex. She gasped aloud, and not because of the water still rushing up to lap at her entrance. The intimate movement of her fingers and her body's responses to them were no longer cautious or inhibited, but were part of a graceful, natural cycle. Bonnie, once a conventional city-born-and-bred girl, had become part of a greater environment, the loss of her former individuality and status now paradoxically balanced by a newfound freedom.

Thus, when her fore and middle fingers dove between the lips of her sex, there was no propriety guilt, but the perfectly natural swell of pleasure rebounding outwards from the source of her actions, to radiate throughout her body. She gasped aloud, her voice not lost in the choir of seabirds and the orchestra of waves, but a part of it.

Her mind soared, drawing upon memories and imagination to forge a new fantasy image: the mighty sun god, powerful and terrible in his majesty, descending from the heavens towards the helpless mortal woman.

He would take her... but she would be punished first, for her arrogance in seeking to love a deity. New images appeared: the woman, bound naked and spread-eagled upon the rocks, the sun god standing before her, a long ebony whip clasped in one hand like a snake, its tongue hot and fine and eager to taste her flesh – virginal in so many ways.

The waves of bliss she felt as she envisioned each subsequent lick of the whip churned within her, building like some great tidal force of ecstasy. Bonnie's climax swallowed her whole. She let out a cry of submission and triumph. She reluctantly withdrew her fingers and twisted to lie on her front, arms supporting her head and eyes closed. The sun, formerly her lover, was now a reassuring cloak on her back and buttocks.

The birds woke her. By rights they shouldn't have; she thought she'd grown accustomed to their incessant calls. But perhaps her short time in her new home had attuned her to the change in their patterns. Or maybe it had been something else.

She crawled over to her clothes and glanced at her watch. She had only been asleep a few hours, but her swim and... other pleasures... had stimulated her appetite again. She was now looking forward to those powdered rations she'd turned her nose up at only a short while ago.

The fog had lifted completely and the sun – her former lover – was high. The stretch of emerald she had crossed that morning with MacTaggart was now visible, the distant village a tight collection of white speckles against a grey-green backdrop. Could she swim back if required? Possibly. But MacTaggart had spoken of tide rips, whirlpools and other mysterious dangers lurking out there. Stories, perhaps? Would she risk it anyway?

With a graceful twist Bonnie rose to her feet. To her right black craggy rocks obscured her view of the rest of the beach still unexplored. Above and beyond them she could see the squadrons of birds wheeling in tight circles, as if something on the ground were scaring them into the air. It must have been some other island animal, like those deer. How delightful, to find her paradise so lively! Forgoing her clothes, she scampered around the weather-beaten rocks—

And pulled back just in time, to safely witness unobserved something that could only be a nightmare.

The beach beyond the rocks extended in more or less a straight line, though the shoreline trees had been replaced by unscalable-looking rocks woven together by marram grass, and decorated with scores of the bobbing white heads of birds in their nests. Closer to the water stood the haggard lighthouse, a dirty pillar in the distance.

This was all absorbed in the blink of an eye, then ignored. Bonnie's attention was drawn to the beach itself, or rather, to the four naked women running along it – in her direction!

She was at once alarmed and captivated by the vision. They were indeed four young women: a statuesque blonde, an equally tall brunette almost at her side, a powerful-looking black woman directly behind them, and a shorter redhead bringing up the rear, one arm clasped over her ample breasts to keep them from bouncing too harshly. And yes, they were indeed naked.

Only when the fifth woman appeared behind them did Bonnie react. This one was clothed, her hair a blonde mane flowing behind her as she sat astride a saddled white horse. The powerful animal's hooves kicked up clouds of sand, and the woman's shouts were echoed by the cracks of her short whip. She did not pursue her quarry with any great haste, sometimes pulling back as if giving them a false sense of hope for escape. Only when one of them tried to dash towards the trees did the horsewoman break her stride, herding the recusant back into the group.

And they were still heading in Bonnie's direction!

Unwilling to accede to her mind's wish to consider all this as part of her earlier fantasies, she dove back to where she had left her jeans and underwear, quickly gathering up the scant bundle. She'd left her jacket, T-shirt and footwear further down the beach, but she hadn't time to retrieve them. She'd dive into the trees for cover, get dressed with what she had, and reassess her situation.

But she had time for none of these, as a second figure on horseback appeared, this time from the closer trees themselves, almost immediately descending upon her. She shrieked and crouched down behind a small grey rock, her clothes pressed against the front of her body.

This second figure was a man, tall, broad-shouldered, his mare jet black. Bonnie assessed him in a split second. He looked to be in his mid-thirties, green-eyed, his sandy hair swept back into a neat ponytail, and with an aquiline nose over a neatly trimmed moustache and beard. He was handsome, though in a cruel sort of way. The clothes he wore – white, high-collared man's blouse with billowy sleeves, black leather waistcoat, sturdy black jodhpurs and high black leather riding boots with pointed toes – were like something out of a Gothic novel.

But they suited him, as did the black riding-crop he carried like a Marshall's baton.

The eyes, like the thin lips, held an aristocratic certainty, a superior power and grace. And when he spoke his voice was cultured and cold, but strong enough to be heard over the surrounding noises without him actually seeming to shout. 'You're not one of the others. Who are you?'

Bonnie began to answer, but stopped when she saw him reach into his waistcoat and withdraw what looked like a tiny radio, an unexpected intrusion on the illusion of antiquity. He raised it and barked, 'Paige! Take the hares back to the house, on the double!' He pocketed the radio without ever taking his eyes off her, and Bonnie could feel his full attention bearing down upon her again. 'I said, who are you?'

Bonnie gulped, shivering with trepidation even as she felt an additional measure of *déjà vu* at being caught and questioned. 'Nuh-nobody—' she stammered.

'Obviously,' he sneered openly, his voice and features quickly softening to cruel amusement. 'It's been a while since I've encountered anyone with the audacity to trespass on my island.'

Bonnie gawked. 'Your… your island?'

'My family's. We own it, as we own most of the houses and buildings in the village – and the villagers themselves, of course.' He spoke with a frightening sincerity; his boasts weren't meant just to intimidate, but were to him bald statements of fact. 'But they've learned to leave us alone, to ask no questions, or they'd find their rents trebled and their businesses closed down.' His eyes narrowed as he peered down at her. 'You're no villager. But you've broken the ancient laws, nevertheless.'

Bonnie, still crouching behind the rock, tried to back away, succeeding only in tipping backwards into the sand. Panicking, she scuttled like a mouse trapped by a cat, dropping her clothes and making a mad scramble to her feet in order to escape. It took but a moment to realise her legs were carrying her to the ocean. It took less than that for the man to come about and block her.

'Stand still!' he demanded.

Bonnie obeyed instantly, though retaining the presence of mind to cover her breasts with one arm and stooping slightly to cover her pubic triangle with the other.

The man trotted around his prey, his eyes inspecting her more blatantly. The horse stopped behind her. When she turned to glance over her shoulder the man barked, 'Stand still, I said!'

Bonnie tried desperately, but she couldn't stop shaking beneath his continuing scrutiny. Two strange men assessing her naked body in less than the span of a day; what was it about this part of the country? For that matter, why did she respond so readily to their orders? And who were those other women? There were too many questions to be answered.

But her attention was immediately drawn back by the man's voice. 'Fresh marks, but amateurish. Did MacTaggart bless you with those?'

With an embarrassed start Bonnie realised he was speaking of the marks on her bottom. With a blush she admitted meekly, 'Yes… MacTaggart did them.'

'Mmm, I could recognise his crude efforts anywhere,' he said thoughtfully. 'But I'm sure he made you come... Well?'

Anger welled up within Bonnie like a pot on the boil. 'Look, there's been some mistake here—'

'Let me guess,' the urbane man interrupted, 'you're on holiday, you wanted to visit one of the islands to see the bird colonies, and MacTaggart brought you here, right?'

A glimmer of hope lifted Bonnie's spirits a fraction; there may be a way she could salvage the situation after all. 'Yes – yes that's exactly what happened,' she said enthusiastically.

'After all,' he continued, 'out of the five hundred plus islands in the Hebrides, less than seventy are inhabited. How could you know there would be people here?'

'Yes, that's right.' She started to turn for the rest of her clothes, but the look she caught in his eyes stopped her. And her hopes dashed altogether as he continued.

'No, that doesn't sound particularly plausible. Let's try this: MacTaggart caught you in the midst of some petty misdemeanour, punished you, then, pretending to be your newfound friend, offered you sanctuary here on this deserted island, which you gratefully accepted.' He paused, as if to marvel at his own powers of deduction. 'How does that sound?'

Bonnie could feel her anger returning. Yes, that pig MacTaggart had lied to her. He'd tricked her, used her, and deserted her. And this man knew it all along. She couldn't help but let her feelings erupt to the surface. 'Bastard!' she hissed vehemently.

'I'll assume you're referring to our mutual acquaintance,' the stranger said casually. 'I don't begrudge you your anger at the deception. But how you arrived here is irrelevant. The fact remains that you are here, in blatant violation of the ancient law.'

'The ancient law?' Bonnie's head was in a spin.

'Yes.' The man nodded and gazed out to sea. 'Laws dating back to earlier, purer times, before all this nonsense about equal rights for all. When the divisions between those who commanded and those who obeyed were clearer and more honest. Under ancient law, peasants caught trespassing in the estates and hunting grounds of the local lord were subject to serve that lord, body and soul, until such time as the lord saw fit to release them from their bond – if such a time ever arose. That law was never repealed in the Iniscay territories.'

Bonnie was reeling. She felt as if she'd followed Alice down the rabbit hole, into a twisted, topsy-turvy shadow of the world she once knew. Was this man insane, to think he could treat people in such a manner?

'Now, get dressed,' he finished, climbing elegantly from his horse and reaching inside a saddlebag. 'We must return to the house to have you properly prepared.'

Bonnie moved over to where she had dropped her remaining clothing, unwilling to possibly meet his gaze while she faced him naked, but paused as she was bending down for her knickers. 'Prepared?' she said.

He glanced up, his expression casual. 'For servitude, of course.'

Panic welled up in Bonnie once more, and without a second thought she grasped the remainder of her clothes and bolted back the way she'd come.

There was a whistle, and suddenly the man's black mare – riderless – cut her off. She yelped, turned around, and faced the man once again. He carried what looked like a long leather cord, looped several times, a pair of handcuffs, and an impatient, if somewhat amused expression on his face. 'Keep resisting if you wish, but it'll be that much more difficult on you. There are laws endemic to Iniscay, laws a slave must remember at all times. You'll not be told them all, not at once, but will learn them... the hard way. The first law is this: *A slave must obey the orders given to her by a master, obey them without rebellion, question or hesitation.*' He let one end of the leather cord drop from his hand to the sand.

Bonnie stood breathing heavily, aware that she had little choice but to do as she was told. She began dressing again, but she still only had her knickers, jeans and brassiere with her. Would he let her retrieve the rest of her things?

'What's your name?' he asked.

She hesitated, for a moment contemplating giving him a false name. But as usual the truth came forth; she'd always been too honest for her own good. 'Bonnie, sir. Bonnie Josephine Fisher.'

'And where are you from... Bonnie?'

'London, sir.' In such a predicament it seemed sensible to be polite to the man.

'And your age?'

'I... I don't see—'

'Answer me,' he snapped.

'T-twenty-one,' she stuttered.

'Good girl.' He smiled thinly. 'Now don't move.'

She obeyed. He was directly in front of her now, reaching forward and bringing a thick black leather collar towards her vulnerable throat. She backed away one step, but his glare halted her. The collar, attached to the lead, was locked snugly in place. Bonnie was so absorbed by this primitive thing around her throat that she barely acknowledged the metal cuffs the man clicked around her wrists, until they were tightly secured.

She looked up as he moved away to remount the horse, still holding his end of the lead. 'And I am Kane Castlewell, eldest son to Lord Victor Castlewell, Baron of Iniscay,' he announced arrogantly. 'My proper form of address is Lord Kane. But you may call me master. Do you understand?'

Bonnie nodded with the resignation of a condemned prisoner – which she was, she supposed.

He leaned slightly closer to her, the leather saddle creaking. 'Let's hear you say it, to ensure you understand.'

Bonnie braced herself, fighting back her pride to bring her voice to bear. 'Yes... master.' It didn't come easily, but it hadn't been as impossible as she thought it might be.

Kane leaned back and sat tall on his mount. 'Good girl,' he said.

Chapter Three

Bonnie was a prisoner, and the irony that in escaping one type of confinement she had pushed herself into another, did not elude her notice.

She led the way along a winding, unmarked path through the woods, although she was on the lead like some dog, being directed by Kane who was immediately behind on his horse. 'To the left I said, stupid girl!' he snapped.

Bonnie grit her teeth and held her tongue, stepping barefoot through the lush greenery; Kane hadn't let her collect the rest of her clothes or her shoes. The trees were verdant with leaf, and the crackling of twigs and rustling of leaves revealed squirrels and birds overhead. The gentle scent of wild flowers hung in the air, and had she not been so distracted by her current predicament, Bonnie might have been better able to appreciate the rich colour and vivaciousness around her.

She felt parched.

As if reading her thoughts, Kane said, 'To our right there's a stream.'

Bonnie took that as leave to change course, and moved towards the refreshing sound of cascading water. The land began to slope away slightly, and in her wish not to trip over, she nearly stumbled into the narrow stream itself; a meandering ribbon that sparkled over mossy stepping stones with a playful gurgle.

Bonnie knelt beside it to drink, but froze when Kane

snapped, 'Stop!'

She looked up at him, dismounted and guiding his horse towards the stream with an open hand on its ebony mane, though he continued to hold Bonnie's lead with the other. 'My mare drinks first,' he announced.

'But—'

'She carries Lord Victor Castlewell's eldest son,' he interrupted. 'You're a slave. Whom do you think has a greater right to drink first?'

Bonnie trembled with sheer outrage and disbelief at his audacity. He, in turn, seemed quite nonchalant, as if his directive was most reasonable. He stroked the horse's head, and whispered reassuring compliments to it.

His back was to Bonnie now. She stared a moment longer, then defiantly scooped up a handful of the water and drank deeply. It was crisp and cold, clearing her thoughts and refreshing her immensely.

'You will regret disobeying me.'

Bonnie glanced up sharply. Kane hadn't moved as he spoke; he might have been threatening the animal, if Bonnie didn't know better. Her stomach sank at the thought of what he might do.

But she refused to be upset by his intimidation. There was currently far more to be upset about, so she continued to drink, recalling the old saying about being in for a penny...

She decided it might be wise to appear confident, so once she'd quenched her thirst she asked, 'Who were those women on the beach?'

'If you wish to ask something of your betters, you respectfully request permission first,' Kane responded without turning round.

Bonnie struggled to clamp a lid on her simmering temper. 'May I ask a question, *please*?' she finished sarcastically, and heard his impatient sigh.

"'May I ask a question please... master,'" he prompted.

Bonnie's fists struck the water, timed with the explosive gasp of anger and frustration which escaped her lips.

Kane finally turned to face her. It had suddenly grown quiet in the woods, as if nature itself had been silenced by the open defiance in the face of undeniable authority. Shafts of light from the midday sun played on the water. One shaft made a Jacob's Ladder between them.

Bonnie was able to appraise Kane as a man for the first time, as the sun illuminated the sheen on his leather waistcoat and boots, the muscular frame beneath the shirt, the biceps burly silhouettes in the sleeves, the curve of his thighs within his tight jodhpurs. He was definitely a masculine man, a strikingly handsome figure. The voice, the stance, all supported the role he played. But she sensed he didn't act in this fashion for her amusement, but his own.

His eyes, bright as suns themselves, burned down upon her, the sun god made flesh, and she had to fight the impulse to avert her gaze. His voice, as always, hinted at entertainment – though never at his own expense, of course. 'You're a pleasing mixture, Bonnie Fisher. You have spirit, but it's balanced with the good sense not to let it get you further into trouble... or so I hope.'

Crouched before him, Bonnie fought the rage building within her. Power-mad or not, this man seemingly held all the cards for her future. 'May I ask a question please... master?' she asked in a taut voice.

Something too cruel and triumphant to be called a smile lifted the corners of his lips. 'You may.' He was going to make her go through all the paces.

'Those women, were they…?'

'Slaves, like yourself?' He emphasised the word 'slaves', smirking at her bristling reaction. 'As a matter of fact, no. They are guests of my family, here of their own free will.'

Bonnie frowned. They were here voluntarily? Made to run naked down the beach, while a woman on horseback herded them along? She couldn't believe it. 'Mr MacTaggart said this was a nature reserve. He said it was deserted—'

The man laughed generously. 'I'm sure he did, dear girl! I'm sure he did!' His mocking laughter gradually diminished. 'He was half right, I suppose, in his own plebeian fashion. Flora and fauna are preserved here. But so is an ancient worldview, a recognition of a pecking order of sorts. On this island there are predators and prey, the dominant and the submissive. Of all species.' He seemed to loom closer, without actually moving, and a chill settled over Bonnie. 'Which one do you think I am?' he said.

He was mad. He had to be mad.

'Now, we must be off,' he said without awaiting an answer, his mood suddenly brisk. 'We have a long way to go.'

They walked in silence through the woods for quite some time, when suddenly the undergrowth parted and Bonnie gazed upon an expanse of manicured gardens. It was a beautifully kept area, dotted with ornate fountains and stone benches, all linked by serpentine pathways.

But her attention was immediately drawn to the two storey Tudor manor which dominated the scene. Fronted by a terraced section of garden, the rectangular building was both resplendent and imposing, with its slate-grey patterned brickwork of dressed granite, groups of rectangular oriel windows crossed with lead lines, and high, sharply angled gabled roofs and intricate chimneys. Immediately behind it were smaller, humbler buildings, but equally old and equally well kept. It truly was as if Bonnie had stepped back in time to a bygone age.

Kane dismounted with ease and stood beside Bonnie. He smelled of fine cognac, Cuban cigars, and sheer power. His eyes were fixed ahead with obvious pride. 'The Castlewell Manor. You will enjoy your servitude here.'

'Master Kane!'

It was a man's voice, and Bonnie saw the owner of it approaching rapidly from around the house. He looked young, perhaps not much older than Bonnie, dressed in a dirty grey shirt and trousers. He was stocky, broad-shouldered, with copper hair and a square chin. For some reason concern was etched on his ruddy face. Concern for her? Would this man, whomever he was, assist her?

The smell of hay and manure clung to him as he stopped before them and raised a quick pair of fingers to his forehead, an informal salute if not a tugging of forelocks. 'You need help, Master Kane?'

Kane still held the lead in one hand, and idly rested his other on Bonnie's bottom. He cupped and squeezed the soft flesh possessively, with clear intent to humiliate her before the servant. Her anger simmered, but she knew it would be wise to ignore the blatant goading. 'No, Tim,' he said smoothly. 'But you can take Shohan back to the stables.'

'Aye, sir.' There was another indecisive half bow and salute, and then he led Kane's horse away, never sparing Bonnie a second glance at any time. Kane leaned closer to her, maintaining a firm grip on her buttock. 'You belong to us now,' he hissed. 'I hope that message is forever branded in your mind.'

'But—'

'Ancient laws decree that you are now a slave,' he continued, unchecked, 'and that you are bound to obey, or be punished. However, as undeserving as you are, I will give you this one chance before we enter the manor and your new life: you may return to the mainland, or you may stay here and serve.' He touched her shoulder and turned her to face him. 'But you must choose now.'

Bonnie knew she couldn't return to the mainland – not for a while yet, at least. All she wanted to do was cry. This was unfair – so unfair! A week ago she'd been on top of the world, with money, status, possessions – a future! What kind of future could she have here, at the hands of this madman?

On the other hand, what kind of future could she have on the mainland? It was a terrifying example of the devil she knew, and the devil she didn't. 'Do… do I have any choice?'

Kane smiled confidently. 'That's for you to decide. But be quick about it.'

Bonnie knew she was trapped. Her chin sank and her eyes misted with tears. 'Okay…' she whispered. 'I'll stay.'

'You'll stay...?' His voice trailed away into an expectant note, as if Bonnie hadn't quite finished her answer.

And she knew what was needed. 'I'll stay... master.'

He chuckled softly. 'You may not believe it now, but you'll come to look back on your old life with sheer disbelief at how you endured such banality as you did.' Then he slapped her bottom. 'Now, get going,' he ordered brusquely. 'You must be readied.'

The reception area was spacious, with tapestries on the wood-panelled walls, high ceilings of oak beams, and floors carpeted in plush burgundy. The grand staircase dominated, an ascending bridge of ornate, highly polished wood, its steps rising halfway, then splitting into two and climbing further in opposite directions. A tall grandfather clock ticked authoritatively in one corner.

Close to it, scrubbing at a dark patch in the carpet, was a young blonde in a short black uniform. She seemed utterly absorbed by her task, until she looked up and saw Kane. Then she rose quickly, rushed over and curtseyed reverently. 'Good day, Master Kane,' she said hastily.

Kane removed the leather lead and handcuffs from Bonnie, but left the collar in place. 'Good day, Janine. I trust everything is in order?'

'Yes, master.' She glanced at Bonnie. 'Picked up a stray, have you?'

Bonnie rubbed her wrists and stared back, her attention divided along several lines. There was the girl herself: barely out of her teens, slightly shorter than Bonnie, but with an extremely shapely figure, and a confidence as tight as her bun of cornfield blonde hair.

Then there was her outfit. Less practical than decorative, it consisted of a black leather collar, just like Bonnie's, a lustrous leather bodice which moulded itself to her generous contours, and which closed at the front by a series of quick-release silver catches. Her milky breasts threatened to spill out of the garment at any moment. She wore leather knickers, a leather garter-belt and suspenders which held up seamed stockings, dainty black shoes, and thick leather wrist and ankle bands with silver studs.

But what Bonnie found most disturbing of all was the naked devotion with which she gazed upon Kane Castlewell.

'Yes, a stray.' Kane gently but firmly clasped Bonnie's bare shoulder, as if she were an unruly child caught shoplifting. His touch was like fire. 'This one's name is Bonnie. Take her to the Playroom and prepare her.'

Bonnie wanted to shake off his grip, but recognised the futility in such a minor rebellious gesture. She blinked when Janine asked, 'Another hare, master?'

Kane seemed to consider the question, to Bonnie's confusion, before shaking his head. 'No, I think not. At least, not yet. Perhaps later, if she proves herself worthy. For now, though, she knows nothing. Keep it that way. Make her a house slave.'

Janine glanced at Bonnie with a look of malicious opportunity. 'I'll train her well, master.'

'I'm sure you will.' Kane spared Bonnie one final glance and smile, before sauntering away.

Janine watched him leave, then turned again to Bonnie, suddenly harsh-looking, her voice clipped. 'Follow me,' she said.

They climbed the grand staircase, Janine speaking along the way like some impatient museum tour guide hurrying her last crowd through the premises before closing up for the night. 'There are four levels to the house: cellar, ground and second floor, and the attic. All have been renovated over the years, but the family likes to keep the visible modernisation to a minimum. The cellar contains the gymnasium and related rooms, an infirmary, and various utility and storage rooms. The ground floor consists of the formal and informal living and dining rooms in the west wing, and the games room, library and offices in the east wing, with the kitchens and servant's quarters in the rear behind the main staircase.'

They'd reached the second floor. Janine never stopped speaking as she briskly made her way towards another, narrower and less grand, flight of stairs. 'Here you'll find the apartment suites for Lords Kane and Martin, and Lady Paige, in the west wing. The guestrooms are in the east.'

Bonnie silently followed the girl further up, until they reached the extensively renovated attic. Paintings of various rural settings in all seasons hung on the walls, and tall potted plants filled corners.

'Lord Victor's apartment suite and office is up here,' Janine continued. 'Along with his trophy room, Lord Martin's studio, more storage areas, and the Playroom.' Delight crept into her voice, but she continued before Bonnie could question her. 'What else?' she pondered. 'Oh yes, outside there's the stables, groundskeeper's quarters, the generator house, helipad and greenhouse. But you'll mostly be working within the manor.'

It was all going so quickly Bonnie could hardly take

any of it in, but hoped she could ask more later.

'You will directly address each of the family members as master or mistress, or lord or lady.' Janine continued, stopping at one unmarked door. She produced a key, from where Bonnie didn't notice. 'Guests and staff are directly addressed as madam or sir. You, however, do not receive that privilege.' She opened the door and entered, and Bonnie followed obediently.

The so-called Playroom was large, lit by a single naked bulb, and bereft of windows and carpets. The whitewashed walls, ceiling and floor lent an illusion of spaciousness and detachment. A small basin was built into the far corner, and there was a tiny grill beneath it by the external wall, as if to drain water after the floor had been washed. Strange objects of varying lengths and with varying attachments hung on pegs on one wall.

But Bonnie's attention was focused on the chains: thick, heavy-looking grey chains built into the walls, the floors, and the ceiling. The latter were further attached to strong pulleys that seemed to allow the chains to be lowered or raised. Each of the chains ended in manacles, for wrists and ankles. There was even a metal plate on the floor, with manacles built into the four corners.

Bonnie divined the sort of play that took place here, and shuddered.

Janine, of course, took it all in her stride, moving over to the basin and starting to fill it up with water. 'Lord Victor is lord of the island. Lord Kane is master of the hunt. Lady Paige is mistress of the house. I'm chief housekeeper. There's also Isobelle, another slave like yourself, Delilah the cook, and Tim the groundskeeper, stable-hand and general dog's-body. You'll be up before dawn and work until after dusk. And you'll treat all the staff with the same respect and obedience you would the family and guests.' When the basin was filled she turned off the taps and finally faced Bonnie. 'Now take off your clothes,' she ordered coldly.

Bonnie blinked at the girl. 'Excuse me?'

'I said take off your clothes,' Janine repeated. 'Are you deaf? You have to be washed and dressed in an appropriate uniform. You certainly won't be allowed to remain in what you have on.'

Bonnie reached up to cover her breasts. 'Look, I can take care of washing myself, thanks. Just give me a uniform—!'

Janine closed the distance between them with such speed that Bonnie was unable to adequately defend herself as the younger girl slapped her with the back of her hand. Bonnie staggered and gasped with shock and hurt pride, clutching the assaulted cheek.

Impatience and anger vied for dominance in Janine's expression, and she stabbed an accusing finger in Bonnie's direction, her voice threatening; too much so for someone so young. 'Listen you bitch,' she hissed. 'As much as I'd love taking my time to discipline you, there's still a great deal of work ahead of us. Remember, I'm chief housekeeper, and you take orders from me. I'm one of the last people in this house you want to annoy. Understand?'

Bonnie was so shocked at the speed and ferocity of the strike that she could only nod dumbly.

'Good.' Janine took a step back. 'Now get undressed, and put your clothes on the floor in front of you.'

Not wanting to risk being on the receiving end of another attack, Bonnie undid her jeans, slid them down her legs, and stepped out of them. Then she unhooked and removed her bra, and dropped it to the floor. Her knickers followed and, finally naked, she stood before the girl, coyly trying to cover her breasts and downy bush.

If Janine objected to this slight display of modesty, she said nothing as she returned to the basin. She clicked her fingers and Bonnie followed. 'Stand still and lift your arms up,' she instructed, as she soaped a flannel.

'Please,' Bonnie urged, 'let me wash myself.'

'That's not an option. Lord Kane ordered me to wash you.'

'But he doesn't have to know—'

Janine raised her free hand, as if to strike Bonnie again. 'He is my lord and master.' Her tone was sinister. 'I will not deceive him. I will not deceive any of the family. And if you have a lick of sense, you too will not deceive them.'

Bonnie realised she had underestimated the depth of feeling the girl had for her masters and mistress. It wasn't fear, or even a facade of devotion for their benefit. She truly believed in them, and accepted her position as perfectly natural, even desirable.

And why not? Kane himself had said a pecking order existed here among the humans, as it did the animals. Janine seemed able to not only accept domination from a supposed superior like Kane, but to revel in it. And her attitude seemed equally applicable to making a supposed inferior like Bonnie submit to her authority. Why shouldn't Bonnie accept it, too?

Why shouldn't she revel in it, too?

She was pulled back from her jumbled thoughts by Janine grabbing her wrist. 'Come here,' she said.

Suddenly, despite all her prior rationalisations, Bonnie resisted. Was it all too much, too soon? Was it that her episode with MacTaggart really was a one off, and being stripped and dominated in truth disgusted her? Was it because another female had made her strip, eyed her naked body, and wanted to touch her, albeit only to wash her? Whatever the reason, Bonnie found herself lashing out, knocking the flannel from Janine's hand.

Janine, in return, grappled with her, snarling and cursing, as each of them sought superiority. Bonnie snarled and cursed in return, as if she'd been fighting other women all her life. An intense rush of excitement had displaced her fear. Now the little bitch would get hers!

So intent were both of them on hurting the other, that they failed to hear the door open, or see the looming figure enter and close the door behind her. They only stopped as the figure moved towards them with a speed that belied its size.

Bonnie just caught sight of the huge black woman, tall and round like a sumo wrestler, with arms as large as thighs. She wore a dirty apron over a sleeveless vest that hugged her massive breasts, and trousers that hugged her legs – and a black leather collar. Her hair was a cropped raven burr, and her eyes were twin coals of determined fire as she approached Bonnie.

Bonnie didn't know who she was, but in that split second she knew enough to want to avoid her. But it was hopeless. The woman slipped her arms under Bonnie's and pinned them back, easily able to lift her off the floor despite the poor girl's kicking and screaming.

Now with assistance, Janine approached, wiping a

trickle of blood from her lower lip before grabbing Bonnie by the ankles, restraining her further. 'Damn you!' she spat. 'Help me get the little bitch into the floor stocks, Delilah!'

Bonnie wasn't listening. Rage and panic had clouded her senses even as they had galvanised her limbs into action. But with the realisation that her struggle was effectively over, she went limp, convulsing into a sobbing fit that didn't involve actual tears. A part of her still registered her captors' subsequent actions, as if for later recall. They flipped her over, her breasts swaying as they carried her over to the metal plate. With adept motions they fitted her wrists and ankles into the plate's four manacles, each locking with a solid click.

It was only then, when they no longer needed to hold her, that Bonnie's full awareness returned, and with it, fresh panic. She was fully confined, on her hands and knees and with her thighs parted enough to feel the air on her inner flesh. She was unable to rise or lie down. The manacles offered no give, and the metal plate was chilled and harsh against her open palms and knees.

Reluctantly she glanced up at the two tormentors who had restrained her into such a shameful position. Janine clearly seethed, pacing in tight circles, as if stirring her fury into tighter and tighter coils. 'Bitch! Bitch!' she cursed. 'She was warned!'

But Delilah seemed suddenly bored. Her slight continental drawl seemed laced with apathy. 'Then beat her and get it over with. You'll have to get the table ready soon.'

Janine nodded, and strode to the objects on the wall. She chose what looked like a short leather belt. It had rows of ominous-looking studs along one side of its length. She eyed it with immense satisfaction, then turned her gaze to the trembling source of her annoyance.

Unable and unwilling to contain herself any longer, Janine approached and began laying the studded belt across Bonnie's proffered backside, sending jolts of pain through the restrained girl's body. The belting continued; swift, rhythmic, charged only by Janine's unfettered fury.

Bonnie recognised this, as she recognised the thrilling surge each strike sent through her body. It was like it had been with MacTaggart, but... even better. Was it because another female was administering the chastisement? Or because she was this time restrained? Or both?

Whatever, the strikes induced charges which hardened her nipples and dampened her further between her legs.

She fell silent, head arched back and eyes squeezed shut, allowing the waves of pain and pleasure to build within her, the moist heat of her open sex a sweet distraction that made her want to touch herself... or even better, have one of her captors touch her. She didn't even have time to question how she could feel that way about her own gender, after her rage and panic of moments before. The pressure of her climax was building, reaching the point of release, like a champagne bottle shaken until its contents were ready to burst forth.

'Stop that,' she heard someone – Delilah – saying.

'Forget it – I'm enjoying this,' Janine hissed back.

'So's she.'

That observation did make Janine stop the beating, and caused Bonnie to open her eyes and look up at them with mixed emotions of anger and frustration. She was close – so close. How could they stop now? She tried and failed to find her voice as Janine turned away and replaced the belt, before looking back. 'I'd best get started on her,' she said.

'No,' Delilah retorted, shaking her head. 'You go down and get the table prepared for dinner. I'll see to her.'

Janine thought for a few seconds, and then, probably realising that she'd overstepped the boundaries of her jurisdiction, agreed with what Delilah was suggesting. Bonnie watched her leave, her own anger gradually dissipating.

Delilah waited until Janine had left the room before picking up the flannel from the floor. She dipped it back into the basin, reapplied the soap, and began to wash Bonnie's back and shoulders.

The warm soapy water soothed. There was a rich flowery fragrance to the soap, and a gentle, maternal manner to the woman's touch, as she ran the flannel over Bonnie's back, around the curve of her stinging bottom, and down to her tensed thighs and calves. It was a lovely, sensual act; one which Bonnie adored.

Delilah was singing softly to herself, pausing only to chuckle and comment, 'Girl, you've got a backside made for beating, and you know it. That's why you act up like you do, to get in trouble. I can see that for myself. No wonder Master Kane sent me along.'

Bonnie said nothing in reply, but trembled slightly under the delicious caresses, her treacherous desire mounting again.

Delilah paused in her ministrations. 'You didn't come when Janine was beating you.'

It was a statement rather than a question. Bonnie

remained silent, not wanting to break the spell she was under.

'But you wanted to,' Delilah concluded. Setting aside the flannel, she set one hand in the dip of Bonnie's back as if to steady her, and felt with the other between Bonnie's blotchy cheeks. The woman's touch was not gentle, but Bonnie didn't mind. Already she could feel her arousal returning, given another chance to overwhelm her. The thick fingers teased and stroked the tender outline of her sex, finding her swollen clitoris. Bonnie sighed and fell into the rhythm, her climax approaching again, until it burst and overflowed from her. She moaned softly, unable to collapse despite the sheer bliss running through her.

'There, there…' Delilah purred as she lifted the flannel and continued washing her beautiful captive.

Chapter Four

Martin Castlewell's office, like the rest of the manor, was lavishly accoutred with brocaded drapes and couches, and imposing examples of hardwood furniture. The gabled windows behind the mahogany desk overlooked the gardens at the rear of the manor.

But the room was dominated by nine large television monitors, set into the wall facing the desk. Beside these hung a detailed map of the island. Computer terminals and keyboards sat on another, slightly smaller desk. These were rare examples of modern technology in the Castlewell manor, apart from those examples which could not be so easily seen.

Such as the fibre optic microphone, sensors and camera, hidden in the Playroom. The camera's wide angle, high definition lens provided a panoramic view of the room and its occupants, bringing it all into focus on one of the television monitors. The sounds and images of Bonnie, Janine and Delilah were almost as clear as if they were being spied upon through a window.

In a chair facing the screen like some avid cineaste, Kane Castlewell raised a snifter of brandy to the scene of Bonnie being brought to an orgasm by Delilah. 'Such a spirited thing, isn't she? And with so much to learn.'

'Aren't you getting a little ahead of yourself, brother?' Paige Castlewell stood close by, staring with feigned interest at a painting, as if the scene in the Playroom did not hold as much fascination for her as it did Kane.

She was a tall, lithe woman in her early thirties, with large hazel eyes and full lips. She had showered after her afternoon run on the beach with the hares, and changed to a sleeveless black dress, its V-neck unbuttoned just enough to boast an enticing cleavage. Although purposely mirroring much of her older brother's tastes, she favoured Kentucky bourbon to his brandy. 'It seems a tad too propitious that MacTaggart should happen to find a girl so ideal to our philosophy, and so close to the hunt.'

'There is such a thing as good fortune,' Kane replied with a shrug.

'And it seems a tad too reckless of you to take her in before she's even been cleared.'

'You didn't see the look in her eyes. She's afraid and angry – not of being dominated, but of loving it.'

'She may just be a good actress.'

'You worry too much, little sister. Our brother is checking her identity even as we speak.' Kane turned his head, though he was unable to see past the curved back of his chair. 'Well, Martin?'

'Give it time, Kane.' Martin Castlewell sat behind the desk of computers, absently tapping a pencil against his chin as he watched the hourglass cursor blink on the terminal monitor. 'You expect too much, too quickly.'

'And often, that which isn't good for you,' Paige added. 'It'll be your downfall someday.'

Kane smirked. 'And if that day comes, I'm sure you'll be wringing your hands with worry, won't you, little sister?' He returned his gaze to the television screen. 'Such a glorious creature. Oh, how I'll savour bending you to my will.' He twisted his head again and snapped,

'Well, Martin?'

'It's almost finished, Kane,' Martin replied, exasperation at his brother's impatience creeping into his voice. 'I wanted to double-check the capacitance scans I took of her body and clothes for any hidden tracking devices or microphones.' Martin was a tall man, and the youngest of the three siblings. 'And in case you're interested,' he continued, 'I found nothing on her. Now the identity trace is almost done.'

'Is that safe?' Paige asked as she pointed at the computer.

'You mean, is it traceable back to us?' Martin smirked, never looking up from the flow of data onscreen. 'You've never bothered to ask whenever I've checked on a potential hare.' He cleared his throat, awaiting a witty comeback. When none was forthcoming, he continued. 'As you know, I personally wrote this program. It's thoroughly shielded and tamper-proofed, with encrypted and untraceable random sequence codes that activate search procedures through Interpol, the FBI, credit, tax, benefit and military records, domestic and international.

'For instance, as far as those databases are concerned, this is a routine background check on a prospective employee of the French Consulate General. The next inquiry I conduct will be disguised as an RAF security inspection. There's also a scan for any connecting references on the Internet News Websites, also shielded and tamper-proofed.'

'In not so many words, then, it's safe,' Paige mocked.

Martin ignored her, reading from the screen. 'Bonnie Josephine Fisher, Londoner, age twenty-one, just as she told you, Kane. Computer programmer with Datamax, second-level education, good credit rating. Mmm... she's currently wanted for questioning by Interpol and Scotland Yard in connection with a drug smuggling operation. They're keeping an eye on her bank and credit cards in case they're used anywhere.'

'Does the story appear legitimate?'

Martin shrugged. 'I'll do some further investigation. But if it's not, then someone has gone to an awful lot of trouble to make it look legitimate.'

'Drugs,' Kane remarked, with a mixture of surprise and awe. 'Not what I expected of the little spitfire.'

Paige finished her bourbon and moved to the drinks' cabinet. 'Well, what did you expect?'

'Oh, some petty misdemeanour that an impressionable mind would blow out of all proportion. Perhaps no crime at all, in fact. Perhaps pre-wedding jitters, a fear of facing a bourgeoisie suburban purgatory of once-weekly sex and snotty children's noses. Perhaps a youngster seeking adventure, out in the big wide world—'

'Are you taken with her?'

All eyes turned to the large chair facing the windows. A thin ribbon of cigar smoke rose from behind it.

'Of course he is,' Paige scoffed.

Kane shifted a little awkwardly. 'I'm only taken with the idea of shaping her into something new, something different, something more suitable – and then giving her to you.'

'Will she be part of the hunt?' the voice asked.

'Perhaps,' Kane answered. 'We'll not reveal too much, too soon, to her.'

'But the hunt's only a week away,' Paige objected. 'She'll spoil it for the rest of us—'

'I said perhaps,' Kane interjected, throwing a harsh

glare in the direction of his sister. 'We'll see how she responds to the conditioning.' He returned his attention to the back of the chair and the rising cigar smoke. 'But whatever the outcome, father, she'll be yours. I've never let you down before, have I?'

'No, you've never let me down before,' the voice behind the chair agreed.

'Yet.' Paige added, *sotto voce*.

Kane suppressed a retort; there was little value in engaging in petty bickering with his bitch sister, with their father present. He returned to the monitor. Delilah had released Bonnie from the floor stocks, briskly rubbed her down with towels, and taken her into the adjacent wardrobe room for her uniform...

'Just like Janine and Isobelle,' Delilah was saying.

Bonnie acknowledged the woman's words with a nod, but remained transfixed by her own reflection in the full-length mirror, and by the feel of the new outfit on her body.

The black leather corset was hardly practical, and like Janine's it threatened to expose her breasts to anyone lucky enough to see her thus attired. Always most comfortable in T-shirt and jeans, she'd never worn anything quite like it. As she posed and twisted, she felt so much more aware of her body than she ever had before. 'H-how do I look?' she asked timidly.

'You look lovely,' Delilah said.

Bonnie ran a finger underneath her collar. 'Do you think I could take this off for a while? She asked.'

'It doesn't come off.'

'What?'

Delilah tapped her own. 'Not for you, not for any of

us. The family holds all the keys. Rules of the house, I'm afraid.'

Bonnie could barely believe it. What a potent reminder of her new lowly status.

Within half an hour, the kitchen – a humid room with a huge stove, several sinks, and pots and pans hanging on hooks over a free-standing wooden table marked with years of knife strokes – was a storm of activity. Delilah was the calm eye in the centre, casually directing Bonnie and the other house slave, Isobelle; a red-haired local girl with an unconventional prettiness. Delilah handed Bonnie serving spoons and a dish of vegetables. 'Go through and serve. Don't speak unless spoken to.'

Bonnie nodded, took a deep breath, and went through to the formal dining room. It was more or less as she'd expected; paintings and tapestries and classical piano background music. The table was long enough to generously accommodate those sitting around it, and was draped with immaculate white linen and decorated with shiny silverware and crystal wine glasses and decanters.

The diners themselves were equally immaculate. And as she began serving each of them in turn, she recognised the four so-called hares from that morning; it would be difficult to forget the image of them running naked along the beach. There were also a few young men, one of them a particularly handsome black lad.

And they all had something in common. They were all smartly dressed, but wore collars too – like the staff, but theirs were earth-brown rather than black.

The family, however, seemed uniform only in their aristocratic airs and utter disregard for Bonnie's presence, acknowledging her only with a dismissive wave. Even Kane, who had shown so much interest in her earlier, now treated her like some anonymous waitress in a restaurant. She wanted to catch his attention, make him acknowledge her, then thought better of it. There was something else; a fresh resurgence of the attraction she initially felt for him. It warmed her insides, and she couldn't wait for the time when they would be together again, with perhaps the intention of getting to know each other on a more intimate level.

At the head of the table, of course, sat the lord of the manor. Victor Castlewell was a silver-haired, gaunt-faced, wiry-looking man. He was ageing, but still impressive. And there was a detached manner about him. He had a similar arrogance to the other Castlewells, but more intense, as if the years had made him more certain of his superiority.

'Hey! Hey, you!'

Bonnie blinked, glanced at the woman beside her, Paige Castlewell, and realised with horror that whilst serving Victor Castlewell she had inadvertently allowed a steamed baby carrot to roll off the dish into Paige's lap. 'Oh, I – I'm so sorry,' she stuttered.

The woman snarled. 'Not yet, you're not.' Her napkin was in her lap, and she scooped it and the carrot up and slammed them down on the table. 'Damn it, this half-witted bitch has ruined my appetite!' She pointed to the dish Bonnie was holding. 'Set that down on the floor!' She indicated her own plate, only partly covered with food. 'And this one beside it!'

Bonnie, trembling under the hateful look she was receiving from Paige, obediently set the dishes down as commanded. 'I'm really sorry…' she repeated pitifully.

Paige glanced in disbelief at the others around the table. 'And she speaks out of turn, and without the proper form of address!' She turned back to Bonnie. 'Get down on all fours and eat, and I don't want to see you use your hands!'

'Y-yes, mistress.' Bonnie knelt and lowered her face to the vegetables, bending until she hovered over the dish. She hesitated – to be made to eat like this, on the floor like some animal, was utterly degrading. But as she thought more about it, that those on her side of the table could look down and see her hunched forward, her buttocks hugged by her panties, her degradation twinned with excitement. She began to eat.

And as she did she listened to the various conversations around the table, and none of them were about her. It supported her suspicion that a punishment such as this was to be regarded as fairly normal.

Then she heard Paige. 'This new one of yours doesn't show very much promise, Kane. Perhaps your instincts are waning.'

But he remained casual in his response. 'Housekeeping skills are teachable. I chose her for her more natural capacities, which may be considerable.'

Bonnie felt a surge of pride. He supported her. And now she wanted to make the man she'd hated only hours before actually proud of her. So she began eating enthusiastically from the dish and the plate.

Back in the kitchen Bonnie continued working with the others, washing and drying dishes and performing other such chores. It was tiring, but not intolerable, and no one mentioned her punishment in the dining room, though she sensed this was more because it was nothing special than because of any embarrassment.

But Bonnie couldn't help but mention it, or at least, the part that played most on her mind. 'Kane supported me in there,' she said to Isobelle. 'He actually stuck up for me.'

Isobelle was drying and storing silverware in a drawer, and she chuckled. 'I know what you're thinking,' she said.

'And what am I thinking?' Bonnie asked defensively.

'You're thinking he's got a soft spot for you.'

'I am not,' Bonnie sulked.

'Of course you are,' Isobelle persisted, 'I did. We all did. Anyone who's ever been under his influence did. And he loves us, but only as a master loves his slaves… He has only one true love.'

'Oh.' Bonnie was still none the wiser. 'His father?' she fished.

Isobelle laughed. 'Oh aye, he loves his father,' she said, once she'd recovered from Bonnie's amusing naivety. 'He loves thinking about the day when he inherits everything from the old man.'

'But wouldn't him being the eldest son mean the title and estate must all be passed to him anyway?'

'The money and businesses aren't connected with the title. The title means little to the children, except for the pleasure they get from flaunting it. But it was just something else the family bought.'

'They bought it?'

'Aye. Victor Castlewell's some Italian publisher. His real name's Castliogne. He bought the island and village twenty years ago. They just act like they've been here for generations.'

Bonnie was stunned. Up until now she felt she'd been following some centuries-old tradition on the island, accepting the Castlewells' snobbery and treatment of her. Ancient law indeed! What a fool she was! Nevertheless, when she considered it, things really didn't change much. She was still there as a willing slave.

'So,' she said, changing the subject, 'Victor favours Kane?'

'Aye,' Isobelle confirmed, 'though Paige is always vying for her father's favour.'

'And Martin?'

Both Isobelle and Delilah sighed, suggesting that Martin Castlewell was a favourite of theirs.

'Well now,' said Isobelle, 'there's something about Martin. He doesn't try to dominate us like the others. I don't think his heart's really in it.'

'He's definitely the white sheep of the family,' confirmed Delilah.

Now Bonnie had the two talking, she wanted to know more. 'So what's all this about calling their guests hares?'

The joviality vanished from the other two, and the atmosphere changed immediately. 'We've been ordered not to discuss that with you,' Delilah snapped. Her expression darkened as she turned her attention back to her work.

Just then Janine entered the kitchen, and increased the uneasy silence that had permeated the room.

'Bonnie,' she said, 'Lord Kane wants to see you in the study. Come with me.'

Bonnie's pulse quickened as she set aside the plate she was drying. Kane wanted to see her!

With the curtains drawn to the evening, only a desk lamp illuminated the study. Most of the room remained in semi-darkness. Kane was leaning against the desk, pensively smoking a cigar. Bonnie stood near the door, not really sure what to do.

Eventually, after watching a particularly thick plume of silvery smoke twist up to the ceiling, he motioned to her. 'Come here,' he said smoothly.

He studied her for a moment, before saying. 'When a slave is summoned by a master or mistress, the slave is expected to kneel before them, head bowed, hands clasping thighs, awaiting further instructions.'

Bonnie dropped to her knees, positioning herself as he described. Her knickers were a little damp, and had been from the moment she heard Kane wanted to see her. She could feel his eyes burning into the top of her head, and she held her breath, wondering what would come next.

'So, Bonnie, I know it's only been a few hours, but what do you think of your new life?'

'It… it…' She faltered, hesitant to express her true feelings, not knowing what would please him most; to think she was suffering, or enjoying. In truth it was turning out to be a mixture of both, but she settled for the more neutral answer. 'It's different, master.'

'What an imaginative answer.' There was mirth in his tone. 'Yes, I'm sure it is *different*. And how did you feel about Mistress Paige's orders in the dining room? Were you humiliated?'

'Yes, master,' she answered truthfully.

'You'll have to watch her,' he advised, 'she can be spiteful. But for now I own you, unless and until I wish to give you away. Do you understand?'

Bonnie nodded.

'And now,' he went on, 'I should acquaint myself more with my new possession.' He took another long draw on his cigar. 'How experienced are you?'

'Master?'

'Tell me about your sexual history.'

Bonnie faltered, not expecting such a forward question. Knowing that further hesitation could prove damaging, she struggled for an answer. 'There's... there's not much to tell, really.'

'Oh, I'm certain of that.' He paused, and she could hear him enjoying his cigar, before he continued. 'When did you first have intercourse?'

She knew she had little choice but to answer truthfully. 'I was... I was eighteen.'

'A late bloomer,' he noted with gentle amusement.

'I've always been shy,' Bonnie added, feeling obligated to explain further.

'And how many lovers have you had? Men and women, that is.'

His reference to women brought back memories of a few hours before, when another woman had first touched her, and she felt herself blushing, even as her nipples rose. 'Three men... master. No women.'

'Until this afternoon,' he pointed out, with a chuckle.

Bonnie gasped; Delilah must have told him! How could she? But then, how could she not? Kane probably demanded a report from her. Perhaps he'd even ordered her to seduce Bonnie.

'Well?' he prompted.

She understood he was awaiting confirmation; just to hear it from her own lips. 'Yes, master.'

'Good,' he said, looking down at her. He was in total

control; control of himself and control of her – his plaything. 'And now…' he said slowly, 'I want you to demonstrate your devotion to me.'

Bonnie dared to look up at him, her cheeks burning. She knew exactly what he demanded, and she knew she had to obey.

Without another word she reached up to the front of his trousers, uncoupling his belt, then finding buttons where she'd expected a zipper. She undid the buttons, then paused to glance up at him timidly. He still looked down at her, cigar poised between manicured fingers. She took a deep breath and drew his trousers down to his ankles. She stared at his muscular legs, then at his underwear; tight briefs that outlined his penis. Slowly, she drew them down too. She could feel his heat and smell his maleness.

His penis began to rise from beneath the hem of his shirt, a small drop of pearly fluid gathered at the tip of the engorged helmet. It reared up from a cluster of black curls, above a sac firm and dark.

Amazingly Bonnie had never done such a thing for a man before, but for a fleeting second it occurred to her that because she had no choice, she found herself able to cast aside her inhibitions, able to indulge in activities she'd only fantasised about before. Was that the secret to enjoying life as a slave to others?

'Oh please, take your time,' Kane said sarcastically. 'I have all night.'

Bonnie reached up tentatively and clasped his penis at its base. It was a solid stalk of male flesh. She hesitated for a moment, but not wanting to annoy him, she parted her lips and tentatively took him inside. His penis swelled and pulsed further, hotter and thicker...

and incredibly powerful.

She leaned forward experimentally, accepting more of him until she had to remove her hand, and his wiry pubic hair brushed her nose. Then her tight lips moved slowly back up his gnarled length, and she began to grow a little more confident. He seemed to approve, making little grunts of pleasure. This bolstered her, helping to cast aside the last of her doubts.

When she felt assured enough to establish a rhythm, she moved her hands to clasp his hips, just under the tails of his shirt. The ridge of his member pulsed, and she worked against it, running her tongue along the underside, his pre-come mixing with her saliva. She felt him shudder slightly and heard him groan, and the fact that she could assert so much control over a man while still being a slave to him made her pussy pulse within her tight knickers.

Growing more and more assured, she pulled back just enough to lodge the bulbous head of his penis between her wet lips, and gripped his shaft again, slowly masturbating him. Kane responded, groaning loudly. Bonnie smiled triumphantly to herself. Her pussy ached and she tried to rub her thighs together, but it was no good. But Kane would take care of her shortly; she was sure of that.

Her forehead dampened with perspiration. His breathing quickened, and he began to shake. She knew what was imminent, and wanted to surprise Kane with how prepared she would be. But still, as he ejaculated in her mouth, she underestimated the force of it. His seed erupted into her throat, then again and again, in gradually decreasing bursts, as his knees quivered against her breasts and his balls rose in their sac. She swallowed valiantly, struggling to take all he could offer.

When she felt his spasms die away, Bonnie withdrew and leaned back, exhausted, on her haunches. His penis, already beginning to soften, hung twitching before her face. She looked up at him, awaiting the praise she felt she deserved.

But all he did was nod and say, 'Not bad. But you'll need plenty of practice to match the ability of Janine and Isobelle.' Ignoring the stunned look on his slave's face, he stubbed out the remains of the cigar in an ashtray on the desk, reached down and raised his briefs and trousers, and refastened them.

'Now,' he said, his clothes neatly straightened once again, 'you would like me to satisfy your own cravings, wouldn't you? You'd like me to take you to my bed and fuck you all night long.'

Bonnie felt utterly deflated and humiliated, by her own traitorous body, by his hurtful words, and by the ease with which he was able to read her. But she couldn't help but confirm her desires with a tentative nod.

'And would that sate your lusts, my dear?'

Her pussy was hot and moist in its aching anticipation. 'Yes, master… it would.'

He smirked, looking down on her, in every sense. 'I'm sure it would. But now you must learn the second of the slave's laws on Iniscay: *A slave exists to satisfy her master's needs and desires; there are no limits to what she must do to accomplish this. But while a good master must keep his slave, as a prized possession, from being permanently damaged, the idea that a master must consider his slave's needs and desires is ludicrous.*' He paused for long seconds, letting the consequence of the statement sink in. 'You may,' he eventually said, 'relieve yourself now before me.'

Bonnie flushed with anger and frustration. He wouldn't touch her. He was going to test her obedience to the limits. What kind of man was he to treat her like this?

But she already knew the answer. He was a master, as she was a slave. What other answer could she truly expect?

Summoning what little resolve she had left, she ignored the urge to accept his offer and rose from her kneeling position. 'Thank you, master, but I won't. Will that be all?'

He nodded. 'You may leave now. And you may thank me again, for granting you the privilege of serving me.'

Her voice was taut, but remained sufficiently contrite. 'Yes, master. Thank you, master.'

As she left, though, Kane called after her, 'You'll really thank me soon, you know, and mean it. You'll reach a point when you'll be begging to masturbate before me, begging to do anything for my attentions.'

Bonnie didn't respond to his taunting words, or the mocking laughter that followed.

She rushed to the rear of the house, to the servant's quarters she'd been shown earlier. Her assigned room was tiny, bleak and windowless, a naked bulb illuminating a single bed and a chest in which were outfits similar to that which she wore, plus some more conventional clothes for outdoor wear, and make-up and toiletries.

Bonnie flopped onto the bed, trying to stem the flood of emotions swirling inside her, threatening to burst forth in a scream or a tantrum, or something that would undoubtedly get her in trouble. Instead, she desperately groped for the waistband of her knickers, reaching inside, unwilling and unable to delay even long enough to remove them entirely. Eager fingers worked over her throbbing clitoris. Her limbs stiffened in response. She could still taste Kane in her mouth, could still feel his come strike the back of her throat.

She felt her orgasm coming quickly and easily. Her body tightened and her back arched as the waves of pleasure struck and she gasped for breath. She felt as if she were floating, and she let her senses revel in it.

As the wonderful orgasm subsided she lay exhausted and breathing deeply, but was cruelly wrenched from her drowsy state as the door crashed open, and Janine stomped in. 'What the hell are you doing here?' she demanded.

Bonnie struggled up onto her elbows. 'C-can't you knock?' she stammered.

Janine glowered aggressively. 'You play with yourself in your own time,' she snapped. 'And you've still plenty of work to do before you've any of that!'

Bonnie knew it would be unwise to antagonise the belligerent girl too much, so she rose quietly and moved towards the door. But Janine thrust out an arm, blocking her way, and hissed, 'I've seen plenty others like you before: naïve, presumptuous, arrogant.' She sneered. 'They all learned, and you'll learn, too.' She snatched Bonnie's wrist with surprising speed and strength, her sharp nails making Bonnie wince as they dug into her flesh. 'Remember what I said in the Playroom: I'm one of the last people in this house you want to annoy. Understand?'

'Yes!' Bonnie gasped, eyes squeezed shut.

'Yes...?'

72

'Yes, Miss Janine!'

Janine smiled victoriously and released her wrist. 'Good… now get moving.'

Chapter Five

When Bonnie first saw the list of chores to be completed each day, she'd thought it was actually the weekly list. As soon as Janine happily quashed this notion, she began to understand why they had to start before dawn. There was something like twenty rooms to dust and sweep, meals to be prepared and served, windows to be washed, floors to be scrubbed, clothes and sheets to be laundered – none of which seemed to involve the use of any modern equipment.

And though most of the work was divided among Delilah and the three maids, with a short break for a scant mid-morning meal, by noon Bonnie was exhausted, and didn't know how she'd be able to manage to rest of the day. How the others managed to keep up the pace was a mystery to her.

She stood before one of the kitchen sinks and poured herself a glass of water, staring out of the window at the rear gardens, a quiet haven she wished she could visit, even for a short while, just to get away from the house and its family. Not that she'd seen much of the latter; they were either out on their horses with their guests, or not even up and about – Kane included.

She didn't know if not seeing him – them – was good or bad.

The events of yesterday resonated in her head like a song her mind refused to put aside. So much had happened to her in so brief a period of time. In the span of less than two days, others had conspired to peel away so many of what she once would have considered inviolate inhibitions, like the veils protecting the modesty of some harem girl. Is that what this place was doing to her; stripping away her most treasured standards?

No, she amended. If they had been that treasured by her, they would have remained inviolate; she would have opted for the sort of detention offered by Her Majesty's Constabulary and Prison Services. And the only real reason she'd chosen the devil she didn't know was because of that first taste of extreme pleasure she'd received at the end of MacTaggart's belt. All subsequent experiences, though they may have seemed initially degrading, were found to be worth the cost, to reach the heights of bliss she had achieved – and had yet to achieve.

Indeed, if she were truly honest with herself, she would admit that she even looked forward to how much further Kane, his family, staff, and way of life here could take her. Was there anything Bonnie might consider too extreme?

She pressed her thighs together with anticipation. She couldn't wait to find out!

Janine appeared from behind and held a plate of piping hot steak and kidney pie before Bonnie, who set aside her glass and accepted it, holding it carefully by the outer, cooler edges. 'Thank you—'

'It's not for you, you stupid bitch,' Janine hissed. 'Take it out to Tim in the stables.'

There was a coolness to the air, or perhaps it was being outside in such a revealing outfit. The grounds to the rear of the manor were as well kept as the front, with the added attraction of vibrant flower displays flanking the winding paths. Bonnie had been told that Tim was the groundskeeper and stable-hand, among other things, but such was the size of the grounds in question, and the care and detail in evidence, that she had to doubt Tim could manage it all on his own. Did the house slaves assist? Or perhaps some of the so-called hares?

Right on cue two of them – the powerful-looking brown-skinned woman Bonnie learned was named Hannah, and the pale French redhead named Annette – jogged by, clad in matching grey T-shirt and shorts. Patches of sweat darkened their backs and under their arms. Neither acknowledged Bonnie as she stepped aside to let them by, though she suspected they were merely intent on their training, rather than contemptuous of her.

Training, Bonnie repeated to herself, though she couldn't say for what. Kane and the others continued to refer to them as hares. What did that mean exactly?

'Hey, you!'

Bonnie turned in the direction of the voice. It was Paige Castlewell, on horseback, as natural in the saddle as her brother. The look on her face suggested anger, and the tone in her voice confirmed it. 'Stop enjoying the scenery, you lazy bitch, and get on with your work!'

'Yes, mistress,' Bonnie blurted, and wisely headed briskly for the stables.

The stable building, without as much overt renovation and restoration as the manor, appeared far older. It was dark, and the smell of hay, oats and manure filled the air; an earthy mixture that wasn't as unpleasant as

Bonnie had expected. The walls were thick and the windows narrow, keeping the interior warm and dry.

The stable consisted of two rows of horse pens with half-doors, facing each other, and a hay-strewn stone floor separating them and leading to another room. The ceiling was high, supported by a skeleton of thick wooden rafters that held bales of tightly packed hay. There were several horses within their pens, and Bonnie stood for a moment and listened to them whinnying and clomping their hooves on the floor, but heard no human sounds. Had Tim gone out?

'Hello?' she called.

From the far end a gruff, familiar voice called back, 'Here!'

Bonnie hurried along, hoping the meal would still be hot enough for him, then stopped when she turned the corner. Tim was there, standing over a saddle mounted on a small wooden bench. He was bare-chested and was hunched over, putting all his strength into polishing the saddle's surface into a fine buff. He never looked up, but said, 'Over there.'

Bonnie turned, realising he meant his meal and the table behind her. Then she faced him again, suddenly transfixed by the sight of him. His arms and torso were perfectly proportioned, and so inviting, glistening with sweat and grime. A light thatch of hair covered his chest, between the toned contours of his pectorals. Bonnie also acknowledged the scent of his body as he straightened up and stretched his arms, revealing soft copper down beneath them.

But Bonnie felt she was lingering, and was suddenly uncomfortable, not wanting someone from the manor to come looking for her. 'If that's all, sir, I should be going–'

'Wait.' He never looked at her as he turned to an open wooden barrel filled with clear water, cupping handfuls from it and splashing it over his head, torso and arms.

Bonnie could now see pink stripes on his back; prior punishments from one of the Castlewells, no doubt. Or perhaps it had been a reward for something? Nothing about this place would now surprise her.

Her eyes were also drawn to his buttocks, firm and tight within dirty jeans. There was a raw, candid hardness about him that caught not only her attention, but her active interest.

She smelled him as he walked past her to the table, setting himself on an adjacent barrel and tucking hungrily into his meal. Bonnie stood nearby, hands clasped together for wont of anything better to do with them, continuing to watch him eat. For a while there was only the sound of Tim's fork clinking against the plate.

Bonnie glanced around inquisitively. Over her shoulder she saw a wooden ladder leading up to a loft. She turned back to Tim. 'Do you want something to drink with that?' she asked, nodding at the food. 'I could go to the house and get you some milk, or water.'

'No.'

The silence hung awkwardly between them, so she tried to make a little light conversation. 'Have you worked for the Castlewells for long?' she asked.

'Aye,' he grunted.

'Do you like it?'

'Aye.'

Bonnie frowned. He wasn't much for conversation, was he? Well, she'd better think about making her way back to the house before she angered Janine again. 'They're probably looking for me—'

'Up top,' he grunted between mouthfuls.

'Pardon?'

He stopped eating long enough to look at her and jab his fork towards the loft. 'Up top.'

It wasn't an aggressive or demanding tone, but Bonnie knew she had to obey; even Tim was of a higher station in this bizarre world. Without a word of objection she turned and climbed the ladder.

Once up in the loft Bonnie looked about. The arched roof was just above her head now, and large bales of hay were stacked against the walls. There was also a simple bed with pillow and blanket, and several corked and uncorked jugs nearby. Did Tim sleep up here?

She wasn't kept waiting long. Tim climbed the ladder briskly. He dusted his hands on his jeans as he looked her over once again, and then pensively picked a piece of meat from between his teeth. 'Take your panties off,' he ordered gruffly.

Even as she found herself obeying, Bonnie couldn't help but wonder at the rightness of it all, and she voiced her concerns. 'Should we be doing this? I mean…'

Her words trailed away as she watched Tim quickly and efficiently strip, casting aside his boots, socks and jeans. He wore no underpants, and had a sturdy frame, with thighs like pistons. His penis, long and thick even at rest, was slowly throbbing to life, the shaft thickening, pointing at her like some turgid diving rod, its head emerging from its hood. His balls hung beneath, gently swaying between his thighs.

Bonnie had only met him briefly yesterday, traded a dozen words since, and though she'd never screwed a virtual stranger before, since her old life had already been cast aside, why should she wait? She could use him as much as he clearly intended to use her.

Under Tim's bold scrutiny her arousal, already simmering deliciously, flared into life. Her nipples were hardening inside the corset, and as she posed before the stable-hand, she arched her back and pushed her breasts towards him. She licked her lips and whispered huskily, 'So, do you do this often, or is it just with the new girls?'

'On the floor,' he said, ignoring her comment and moving towards her. He clasped her around the waist, his hands feeling huge and calloused even through the leather of the corset, turned her around and brusquely pushed her down to the loft floor.

Bonnie had an idea what he wanted when he moved her onto her hands and knees. She remembered being confined in those floor stocks yesterday, but ignored the memory, more intent was she in the wetness seeping from between her thighs and the knot of tension in her stomach. Out of sight now, she could only imagine his shaft, anticipating how it would seek out her entrance, filling her with determined male flesh. In response to this image, the throbbing between her thighs grew insistent.

Shifting in position she presented Tim with a view of her rounded bottom, still bearing pink stripes from her previous beatings. She parted her thighs a little further, and waited for him.

Kneeling between Bonnie's legs, Tim grasped her hips and lifted her up slightly, making her pussy more receptive. Bonnie moaned as she felt the head of his penis meet the wet folds of her sex, moistening him as he gently but firmly slid his entire length into her. His pubic hair pressed against her bottom, and sheer bliss thrilled her to the core. She was climaxing already!

If Tim perceived her surging and pulsing around him, he said nothing, drawing almost fully out of her before plunging back in, again and again, his hands firm on her hips, supporting her easily. Bonnie braced herself, meeting his driving thrusts, her breasts swaying free of the corset, feeling as if he would split her in two. She groaned aloud, savouring the oncoming rush of another orgasm. 'Yes, *Tim*…' she urged, 'that's it…'

'I'm sure it is,' answered a male voice from nearby. And it wasn't Tim's.

Bonnie froze, her orgasm on hold as she opened her eyes to see Kane, standing on the ladder so that only his head, chest and arms were visible. He glanced at Tim. 'See to Shohan,' he said.

Tim nodded. 'Yes, sir,' he said, and withdrew from Bonnie. If he felt as frustrated as she did, his still-erect penis didn't show it.

Bonnie simply knelt where she was, feeling flustered and abashed.

The annoyance she felt at Kane's intrusion must have shown in her eyes, for he smiled at her devilishly. 'Ah, sweet Bonnie...' He glanced at the stable-boy, who was reaching for his jeans and boots. 'Your lascivious behaviour is hardly fair on young Tim, now is it?' He looked back at Bonnie. 'Finish him off with your hand.'

Bonnie sighed with dismay. Kane was going to humiliate her as best he could.

His grin widened. 'Get closer, Tim, and she'll finish you off. It's the least the little hussy can do.'

Bonnie couldn't take her distraught eyes off Kane,

her cruel tormentor, until Tim's erect and glistening penis bobbed in front of her face. So she turned her attention to it, reaching up slowly and curling her fingers around it, and began stroking, the foreskin smoothing back and forth over the bulbous glans. As she became more involved in her task and less conscious of Kane's presence, she pulled at the throbbing penis with more vigour, watching with wide eyes as the turgid helmet looked fit to burst.

'That's it, Bonnie,' Kane goaded, breaking the steamy silence and threatening to put her off. 'That's a good little slave.'

Bonnie gritted her teeth and looked up. Tim, arms at his sides, looked down at her, a faint smile on his lips, his expression dreamy, clearly unperturbed by his master's presence and involvement. He would come soon, she knew. With her free hand she reached up and cupped his heavy balls, holding them carefully. Her own excitement was increasing, compounding her unrelieved need.

Tim moaned and tensed, and his spunk arced into the humid air and spattered the bales of hay beside Bonnie. She watched, spellbound, her fist still clamped around the base of the spasming organ, absently stroking back and forth. Tim reached down and stroked her hair, in an unexpected display of affection.

Kane ruined the moment in his own inimitable fashion, clapping his hands in mock applause. 'Very nice, my little slaves. Very nice. A welcome minute or two of plebeian diversion. Now, Tim, get dressed and see to Shohan. And you, my dear girl, make yourself presentable and meet me outside.' He disappeared without further ado.

Bonnie rose and slipped back into her knickers, as Tim again reached for his own clothes. She felt empty and ashamed, and deeply unsatisfied. Was Kane determined to keep her unfulfilled indefinitely?

Kane stood quietly as Bonnie emerged from the stable. She remembered the procedure when being summoned, and knelt before him, buttocks resting on her heels, head bowed, legs slightly parted, hands flat on her thighs.

If he approved, he never said so. 'Quite a charming scene in there, my little Bonnie. Like something out of a *DH Lawrence* novel.'

She looked up at him, annoyed that she had to justify her behaviour. 'He ordered me up into the loft. I was told I have to serve everyone here equally, master.'

'Not equally, my dear. There is a pecking order, as I explained yesterday in the woods. The orders of your masters and mistress take precedence over guests and staff, and the orders of our guests take precedence over staff. But in this case, I don't fault either of you; Tim deserves his desserts.'

She looked up at him boldly. 'Then why didn't you let him...'

'Finish? You mean, why didn't I let you finish?' His grin faded. 'Rise and follow me back to the manor.'

She obeyed, instinctively keeping one step behind him. He continued speaking, without looking at her. 'What do you think of my home, Bonnie?'

She looked about, unnecessarily; her opinion had already been formed. 'It's lovely.'

He nodded. 'Yes, it is. Everything is as I want it to be… except you.'

'Me, master?' She was shocked by the comment.

'Yes, Bonnie. You're a natural slave.' He glanced back at her, as if sensing her reaction. 'Don't take that as an insult, my girl. I mean it as the highest compliment. People are made to either command, or serve, and the outside world gets it wrong so many times. People who should be leading are forced to work under those who are better off following. Why do you think so much goes wrong in the outside world? Quaint, unrealistic notions of equality for all merely serve to destroy potential. But not here on Iniscay. Here, everyone realises their full potential... as will you.

'But you are untrained, and I don't mean only in the domestic arts. You may be a natural slave, but like a born athlete, you still need the proper conditioning to help you reach peak potential. That's when you'll begin to truly enjoy your role.'

Bonnie said nothing. A day before, his words would have been dismissed as the ramblings of an eccentric. Now, however, she had begun to see what he meant, not only through her own experiences here, but in the eyes and words and actions of others. People really did seem to settle into the role of natural leader or servant. But what did he mean by conditioning? Was that what the other women were doing here? Being trained to serve others? Or being trained to be leaders?

'Are there aspects of your new life here which you have enjoyed, Bonnie?' Kane finally asked.

'Yes, master.' She couldn't deny it.

'The punishments, perhaps? The sexual interludes?' He smirked. 'Ah, but they're only part of the full spectrum of pleasures on offer as a slave. And under my tutelage, you will learn to fully value your part in the order of things here. Have Janine show you to my suite at nine tonight. And don't touch yourself before then; I want you primed and ready for me.'

Bonnie blushed and nodded.

'Now, run along and report for work.'

He stopped and watched her hurry along towards the manor, and stood there long after she had disappeared through the kitchen door.

Bonnie was barely able to contain herself in the intervening hours, wondering what the coming night would bring. She nearly dropped several dishes and glasses in the kitchen, and missed a number of places in the living and sitting rooms where she should have dusted. But she ignored Janine's harping, and continued to glance at the clocks.

At last the hour arrived, and Janine led her to the west wing. She left her charge outside Kane's suite, and departed without a word. Bonnie straightened her outfit once, then again, smoothed back her hair and tried to control her breathing, before knocking on the door and calling softly, 'Master?'

'Come in, my dear girl,' he responded from within.

She entered. The interior was dim, illuminated only by candlelight, but Bonnie was aware of the immense space in the private lounge, with several plush chairs, a desk, bookcases, and several doors leading to other rooms. One of the doors was open, and Kane stood there, leaning against the frame, arms folded across his chest. He was bare from the waist up. Candlelight flickered across his muscled skin. His voice was soft – softer than she'd ever heard before. 'Close the door behind you.'

She obeyed, then walked on trembling legs to kneel

before him and assume the expected position. He acknowledged the submissive posture. 'It's not as difficult as it had been the first time, is it?' he said.

'No, master,' she admitted.

'Of course it isn't. Now rise, and remove your clothes. You won't need them for a while.'

Bonnie stood up and slipped out of the corset. Already her nipples were stiffening with anticipation. Her fingers worked quickly, removing her shoes and stockings, her garter belt, and finally her damp knickers. Now naked apart from her slave collar, she pressed her thighs together, trying to quell the desire burning in her sex and threatening to overwhelm her.

He appraised her boldly, then stepped back and held out an arm in invitation into the next room. 'Go in and lie down on the bed, Bonnie.'

She entered. The room was smaller than the private lounge, with a huge four-poster bed dominating its centre. Warm lanterns flickered on bedside cabinets, casting moving fingers of shadow and light over the pale sheets and the fringe on the canopy.

Bonnie reached out. The bed was almost waist high, and the mattress firm.

She lay down, shifting to the centre of the bed. She looked over to where Kane remained by the door, watching her squirm into place.

Eventually he moved effortlessly towards her, and she wet her lips and closed her eyes, ready to accept him. But he stopped at her legs, and pulled her left ankle out towards the nearest post. She opened her eyes, but was rendered unable to move by the tension in the still air. 'What are you doing?' she ventured to asked.

Seemingly intent on his work, he never looked at or

corrected her for speaking out of turn, as he answered, 'I want you tied. Do you have a problem with that?'

Excited but confused, she could only stammer, 'N-no, of course not.'

'Glad to hear it.' He finished with her left ankle, then moved around the foot of the bed, to her right. She looked down at where she was tied; the bond was bizarre and unexpected.

Kane confirmed what she saw. 'Tissue paper, my dear. Simple tissue paper.'

'But… but I can tear that easily.'

'I know,' he replied cryptically. 'But try not to.' He finished with her ankle, then moved up to take her wrist and pull it towards the right post of the headboard. Bonnie watched, bewildered, as he straightened her arm and tied her wrist to the post, as he had done with her ankles.

'I don't understand,' she finally confessed.

'I know you don't.' He walked around, saying nothing further until her left wrist was bound as well, and she was spread-eagled on the bed, the lips of her sex ready to part at his merest touch. He sat beside her, his hands lightly tracing a line down her front, from the soft valley between her breasts, and orbiting around her flat tummy. 'This is all part of your conditioning, dear Bonnie. Conditioning in discipline. It is the third law of a slave on Iniscay: *Without her master, a slave is nothing. Acts of independence, whether of thought, word, feeling or deed, are acts of rebellion against her master, and must be immediately and ruthlessly suppressed and punished.*

'A slave cannot successfully serve without discipline; discipline in controlling their own emotions, their own reactions. I saw the look in your eyes when I interrupted you and Tim today. A less forgiving master or mistress would have beaten you for showing such emotion.'

'But that was…' she protested, without conviction. 'I was…'

He hushed her, his hand stroking her stomach lightly, sending shivers through her body. 'Yes, you can easily break your bonds. But you won't, no matter what I do to you for the next hour.'

Bonnie's breathing quickened. An hour? What was he planning to do to her?

'Should you show enough self-control to resist my touch,' he continued smoothly, 'you will be given leave to tear your bonds, and I will join you in my bed for the rest of the night. Should you lose control, and break even one bond, you leave. Do you understand, my dear?'

Bonnie took a deep breath, and nodded.

He smiled, and raised a lean forefinger. She watched, spellbound, as it lowered to her chest, to her right nipple, stroking both it and her aureole. His touch was cool and light, and Bonnie struggled to keep calm as she felt her bosom swell, her nipples peaking. He moved to the other, and repeated his actions.

Bonnie sighed and gently arched her back, as the finger was joined by another, and another, their collective touch growing firmer, more insistent, no longer caressing but kneading her tender flesh.

She moaned softly as the fingers left her.

He took something from the bedside cabinet. It was a white feather, as soft and delicate in the candlelight as a snowflake. Holding it between his fingertips, Kane lightly ran it around the circumference of Bonnie's breasts, in ever-decreasing circles until it reached her nipples. She gasped and shuddered, her spinning mind still conscious of not put any strain on the delicate bonds.

She tried to concentrate on something else. She opened her eyes and tried to study the play of glimmering candlelight and shadow dancing on the lace canopy above. She tried to absorb the mingling scents of lavender and honey from the candles themselves. But it was all hopeless, such was the intensity of the pleasure he was creating as the feather descended from its conquest of her breasts, orbiting her navel several items as if assessing its potential for sweet torment, then drifting further to the border of her pubic hair, idly trailing through the dewy curls, and then tickling the lips of her yearning sex.

Bonnie gasped again. It was exquisite. No prior lover had ever shown such patience – or cruelty – in stimulating her like this.

Kane's voice, when he spoke, was so soft and intimate it seemed to dilute his taunting. 'Ah, little slave, you've shown remarkable self-control… so far.' The feather disappeared and he reached for something else from the bedside cabinet. 'But the hour is far from over, and I have only just begun,' he added, ominously.

He brought into view something that, with a dreamy first glance, might have been another candle; white, long and narrow. Only when Kane twisted one end and a slight buzzing hum displaced the silence in the room, did Bonnie recognise it as a vibrator.

Kane held it in the air like some magic wand. 'Do you like it, sweet Bonnie?'

Without waiting for or requiring an answer, he lowered the buzzing implement until its tip sank smoothly into her deep cleavage. She'd only ever seen such a thing in magazines before, and certainly never used one. Now she was being given a first-hand demonstration, but under such humiliating conditions!

Bonnie's attention focused on her lower half again, as the vibrator followed the feather's trail down to her pubic curls, hovering like its predecessor over her vulnerable sex, which throbbed in welcome. But while the feather's touch had been soft, ephemeral, like a gentle draught from under a door, the vibrator and its oscillations sent active fingers of sensation penetrating to her very core, their intensity so acute they could not be ignored or denied.

'No... please don't...' she gasped.

'But why not, sweet Bonnie?' Kane asked with feigned innocence. He was staring openly at her pussy, manipulating the vibrator like an artist's brush, portraying an image of barely-restrained desire on the canvas of her sex. 'You've done well to this point. Why should now be any different?'

Bonnie clenched her jaw and clamped her eyes tighter, fearing the worst. She would not allow her body to betray her. She would not!

The nose of the vibrator nudged its way between her lips, gradual but insistent. Kane set the vibrator to rest between her damp and quivering thighs, and parted her outer lips further, exposing her inner flesh to the scented bedroom air. With intricate care he gathered the dew he found there on his fingertips, tasted it like a connoisseur with a tentative dab of his tongue, and nodded in appreciation. 'Quite a delicious taste, my little slave. When the Greeks spoke of the nectar of the gods, they surely must have meant the taste of a woman in heat.'

Then he touched her clitoris, risen fully to meet his

fingers…

And Bonnie jerked and ripped the bond around her right wrist. It was a cruel sound that seemed to fill and echo around the room and poor Bonnie's head. Time stood still for a few seconds, and she anxiously awaited her master's response.

He tutted and looked at her flushed face, all feeling and interest in his eyes blown out like one of his candles. 'Oh, such a pity,' he said quietly, and shook his head. He removed and turned off the vibrator, and placed it back on the side cabinet. He stood up and turned away. 'Break the other bonds and leave,' he said wearily, as though bored with his new toy.

'But… master, I'm sorry…'

'Leave.' He moved to the window and stared out, his expression vacant. Bonnie looked at him with tears of frustration blurring her vision, but his broad back, turned towards her, told her the evening was over.

Kane stood in the flickering half light, waiting, listening, before reaching for the bedside intercom. 'Delilah, where's Janine?'

The continental accent sounded hollow through the speaker. 'Beside me, Master Kane.'

'Send her up to me immediately.'

'She's on her way, Master Kane.'

But Kane wasn't listening, more focused was he on controlling the torrent of desires within him. That young woman… with so much potential. He couldn't recall any prior slave provoking such levels of reaction within him. True, Janine came close, but he'd tamed her long ago, and while the domination of her remained pleasurable, there was something unique about conditioning a newcomer. Especially such a delicious newcomer.

It would be a waste to present her to his father.

Then he dismissed such thoughts as counter-productive. Kane had to be the heir to his father's wealth; he had to rule Iniscay. If Paige took over, Kane might as well leave and find a position among the masses of the outside world. He shuddered at the idea; it would be better to throw himself over the side of a boat and swim out to sea.

There was a knock on the bedroom door.

'Come in, Janine.'

She was naked, her clothes having taken the place of Bonnie's on the floor of the private lounge. She moved forward and knelt before him in the standard pose. 'I await your commands, Lord Kane.'

He stared down blankly at her, reaching out to stroke her flowing blonde hair. 'Do you, sweet Bonnie?'

She looked up, her cheek fitting into the bowl of his hand. 'It's Janine, Lord Kane, not Bonnie.'

But he shook his head. 'No. Tonight, it is Bonnie. Do you understand?'

Janine froze against him. 'Yes, Lord Kane,' she whispered.

Chapter Six

A helicopter arrived the next morning. Janine ordered Bonnie and Isobelle out of their normal uniforms and into more conventional jogging tops, bottoms and trainers, with appropriate underwear and socks, in order to help Tim unload the supplies and post it delivered.

The helicopter had flown off, and Bonnie was carrying the last of the packages into the kitchen, when Paige appeared and smacked her bottom harshly. 'You, girl,' she said aggressively.

Bonnie yelped at the shock and severity of the impact on her buttock, then turned to face the woman, knowing well enough not to forget the correct response. 'Yes, mistress?' she said politely.

Paige stood there in a simple yet elegant white blouse, and black jeans which highlighted her firm and shapely form. Her blonde hair was tied in a neat pony-tail, and although she wore no make-up or earrings, Bonnie noticed for the first time that she was strikingly attractive.

'When you're done with that, see me around by the stables,' she ordered. 'We'll be taking a tour of the island together.'

'Yes, mistress.' Bonnie hurried inside, not once deceiving herself into thinking this would be anything casual or friendly.

And she was right. Near the stables, Paige was standing by what appeared to be a squat horse-drawn cart. It was wooden and two-wheeled, with a bench seat in front of an open box. Extending from the front were two parallel bars, between which a pony could be harnessed. Indeed, the bridles and harnesses hung on the seat and between the bars like tangles of Spanish moss, waiting for the appropriate steed. And as she saw Bonnie approaching, Paige called over her shoulder, 'Tim! Ready my horse here!'

Bonnie stopped before her, pausing under Paige's withering stare, before realising her error, and hastily dropped to her knees, head bowed, awaiting a punishing blow from her mistress. Instead, all she heard were the impatient words, 'I don't know what he sees in you, I really don't. Now get up.'

Bonnie did as she was told, hands clasped before her, waiting for Tim to bring the animal around.

Except he showed up alone. And as he approached Bonnie, taking her arm and guiding her between the bars of the cart, she finally understood and her stomach sank.

Aghast, she spun round to face Paige. 'I – I didn't think… I mean… I didn't expect I was meant to…' But she stopped her feeble protests, knowing only too well it was pointless. And the continuing look she received from Paige was chilling in its bluntness.

Tim was brisk and efficient as he began fastening the leather straps and harnesses to a heavy collar he secured around her throat, and to her wrists. She became conscious of the increasing number of restraining devices on her body, and of the reaction they were producing within her. Her sex tingled within her panties and her nipples pulsed pleasurably.

When a metal bit was wedged between her lips she

willed herself to remain calm, telling herself she shouldn't fear anything; they weren't going to harm her, after all. She concentrated on breathing slowly and deeply through her nose, and with a slight tremble of shame, she realised her spinning emotions were a cocktail of trepidation…and excitement; excitement fueled not only by Tim's touch on her body, but by the reins and harnesses attached to her arms and shoulders and waist. It was delicious.

She marvelled at how quickly she was adapting to this regime; further evidence that it was what was meant to be, for her.

Paige, climbing onto the cart seat, lifting up the reins with one hand and a horsewhip with the other, drew her back from her thoughts. She tugged on the reins and called, 'Gee up. Let's get moving.'

Wondering what else such a pampered cow as Paige Castlewell had to keep herself busy, Bonnie grasped the bars and lifted them to a level position. As she set off into a slow trot, she was surprised at how light and easy the cart was to move, and at how quickly she picked up on the tugs on the reins, translating them into directions.

The muscles in her limbs tightened agreeably with the exercise. Under Paige's guidance she found herself heading away from the buildings and along winding paths through the woods, paths that were wider than that which led Kane and her to the manor, only days before. Perspiration glistened on her flesh, and her sex pulsed naughtily within her panties, unwilling to be ignored. That she could do nothing to assuage its needs in her present circumstances only seemed to heighten her desires.

They passed by a lake, almost completely surrounded by tightly packed trees. The ground edging the lake was bare and soft, and Bonnie found it more difficult to pull the cart here.

Not that Paige seemed to care, judging by the number of times she struck Bonnie with the whip. 'Come along, you lazy bitch! Or do you expect me to step off and help you? Well?'

Bonnie grunted and shook her head desperately, unable to make any coherent noise because of the bit and her breathlessness. Her nostrils flared with the effort, but with a final surge of adrenaline she managed to clear the soft ground and continue on their way.

They emerged near the beach, near to where Bonnie had previously left her footwear and clothes. She didn't see them, concluding that one of the staff must have since come by and retrieved them. She welcomed the cool caress of the sea breeze on her hot face as much as she welcomed Paige's order to halt.

She lowered the cart poles, and watched Paige strutting about, stretching out her arms and filling her lungs deeply, the horsewhip ever present in her grip. Then she walked back to Bonnie with a smile that was almost cordial, as if they were girlfriends and not mistress and slave. She unfastened the saliva-coated bit, and allowed it to hang around Bonnie's neck. Bonnie remained patiently silent while Paige worked at the remaining straps and bindings. Once free, she rubbed her wrists and shoulders where the bonds had left red marks on her flesh, then wordlessly followed her mistress away from the cart and towards the waterline.

The woman soon stopped and drew an uneven line in the sand with the toe of her boot, then nodded towards the black rocks a hundred metres or more away. 'We race to those, then back. Then we'll see who's fit. Agreed?'

Bonnie could have remarked that, having pulled the haughty cow around the island for the last hour, it would hardly be a fair competition. But she knew better. So she nodded and said, 'Yes, mistress.'

Paige didn't even wait for Bonnie to ready herself, but burst forth from the starting line like a young greyhound. Bonnie took after her, her trainers pounding into and kicking up the soft surface of the sand. She ignored the discomfort of her bouncing breasts and the complaints of her tired muscles and lungs.

Paige was ahead, had reached the rocks and was on her way back, just as Bonnie was making her turn. But on the return run Bonnie had the presence of mind to stay on the seaward side, where the sand had been compacted by the waves – the tide now out. Puddles were splashing beneath her feet, wetting her trainers and jogging bottoms, but with arms pumping she gained on and then passed Paige, and that was all that mattered.

And then, instinctively, she slowed. Something made her deliberately check her pace and let Paige regain the lead. It wasn't exhaustion; she could have easily held out for the additional five seconds it would have required to reach the finishing line. No, it was fear; fear that defeating the spoilt Castlewell woman would stir up a hornet's nest of retribution.

But then, too late, she realised her decision had backfired.

Bonnie's run slowed to a shambling trot, and then a walk. Then she stood still, her chest heaving, her legs aching, suddenly aware of the rasping rawness in her lungs. And of the sight of Paige, similarly exhausted, but wound up by rage. She passed the finishing line and then circled back to where Bonnie stood.

'You bitch…' Her words were punctuated by heavy pants. 'You bitch… You let me win… How dare you insult me like that…? As if I need your pity… Get down on your hands and knees!'

Without a word of complaint Bonnie obeyed. She knew what to expect, and didn't need to see Paige go back to where she'd dropped the horsewhip. She swallowed hard, her breathing gradually slowing to normal, and waited.

Paige returned, gripped Bonnie's jogging bottoms and her panties beneath, and angrily tugged them down to her knees, leaving Bonnie's cheeks exposed to the salty sea winds.

The kneeling girl glanced up, then turned away again as Paige barked, 'Eyes down, bitch!' She tensed, certain Paige would not keep her waiting long, such was the level of her fury.

And she wasn't wrong. She heard the hiss of the whip through the air, then felt the stinging blow across her clenched buttocks. She rocked forward and gasped aloud, her fingers digging into the sand, her nipples swelling within her bra and her pussy pulsating with pleasure, sensing that another climax, already sparked by the harnesses, was blossoming.

'Hasn't Kane taught you the fourth law of slavery yet?' Paige demanded, through clenched teeth.

'No, mistress,' she managed, despite the pain, 'just the first three.'

'You'll learn the fourth now. A punishment given by a master or mistress to a slave should be regarded as a gracious gift, as it helps the slave improve him or her self. Now, you're to count each strike that falls upon you, and thank me after each one.'

'Yes, mistress. One, thank you.'

'You still presume too much,' Paige continued relentlessly. 'You didn't do that when I delivered the first strike, so it doesn't count.'

'But… I didn't know I had to do it then,' Bonnie protested.

'Don't argue with me!' Paige spat viciously. 'Insolent little slut!' And she continued with the punishment, venting her rage, cutting the air with the whip and slashing into Bonnie's poor exposed bottom.

'One, mistress… thank you!'

The whip cut down again. 'Two, mistress…' Bonnie panted. 'Thank you!' She surreptitiously rubbed her thighs together, enjoying the stimulation against her aching clitoris.

'Don't move!' Paige screamed, raising the whip again and lashing it down.

'Three… mistress,' tears sprang from Bonnie's tightly clamped eyes, but whether they were tears of anguish or tears of wicked delight, even she couldn't tell. 'Thank you, mistress…' The fires building within her loins threatened to overwhelm her.

The remainder of the beating melted into one mass of pain and ecstasy. Bonnie's orgasm was upon her, threatening to burst forth like water from a ruptured dam. She was sobbing now as she counted each cutting blow and thanked her mistress for it.

But the final strike that would tip her over the edge into an abyss of pleasure never came – and neither did Bonnie. After long moment's she risked further wrath by glancing over her shoulder, and saw her assailant looking not at her, but back towards the edge of the trees, the horsewhip raised in readiness to lash down.

Kane was there, on horseback, watching the proceedings. Bonnie forced herself not to move from the humiliating position she held, as Kane drew his horse closer to the scene, sparing only a glance down in her direction.

It took Paige, mustering up some measure of bravado, to set her hands on her hips and break the uneasy silence. 'You have something to say, dear brother?' she sneered. 'Perhaps you wish to jump in and save your damsel in distress?'

But Kane remained unperturbed, in expression or word. 'From the expectant expression on the damsel's face, it's more likely she would kill me for interrupting her pleasure. But you know the laws, Paige. They are our property, we shape them to our liking, but we do not leave damage upon them. The horsewhip, and your current level of anger, are an inappropriate combination.'

'Oh, but of course, my dear brother.' She made a theatrical bow towards him, the sarcasm dripping from her every word. 'I stand corrected.'

'If you damage her,' Kane said decisively, 'standing is all you'll be doing, because you'll not be able to sit down for a month.'

'Don't worry, Kane,' Paige scoffed, futilely trying not to show how intimidated she was. 'Your little gift to daddy won't be harmed... too much.'

'See that she's not.' Kane turned his horse, and disappeared into the dense greenery.

Bonnie, feeling surprised, confused, and undeniably

frustrated, now knew that Kane was merely using her. Fine, she would obey her master and be a good slave to her master, but she would also curb any desire she had for him. That, he did not deserve.

'Complete prick though he is, he's right,' said Paige, her thoughtful words being whipped away on the stiffening wind. 'You'd make a very fine present indeed.' She crouched, and idly stroked Bonnie's hair. 'I must make a confession to you… Bonnie,' she said, the resentment in doing so evident in her tone. 'My anger at you hides my envy. You have fire, girl, as well as beauty. But you also have intelligence. Too much to think that remaining here should be an option for you.'

Bonnie was confused by the woman's eccentric mood swing.

'You don't know what you've put yourself into by choosing to stay here, Bonnie. You cannot guess what will be required of you here.'

Bonnie felt a little more confident, and, perhaps unwisely, opened up a little bit. 'But, you don't know what waits for me on the mainland.'

'Yes, I do.' Paige leaned closer, and Bonnie could smell her fresh breath. 'We checked your identity when you first arrived. We know all about your trouble with the authorities.'

'I didn't do anything,' Bonnie protested.

'Hush, girl. I believe you. That's why I'm telling you this. You may think living here is a better alternative to the law, but you'd be wrong. Still, if I can't persuade you to return to your old life, I can offer you an entirely new one.'

Bonnie's eyes widened as Paige elaborated, her words as gentle and relaxing as her fingers. 'Yes, I can offer you a completely new identity, with Martin's help. The nature of our life here necessitates such capacities. Often we and our guests require verifiable incognitos when we move about in the outside world. We can arrange a new name for you, legitimate qualifications, even a start in one of father's foreign businesses. All you have to do... is accept.'

Bonnie's eyes narrowed with suspicion. 'Why do you offer me all this?' she asked carefully.

Paige shrugged, apparently nonchalant. 'Maybe it's through pity.'

'Pity? Why should I need your pity?'

'What does it matter? Whatever my motive, the end result remains the same... freedom for you.'

Bonnie considered carefully what she was hearing. A new life, away from everything that had recently plagued her. To begin again, free from the fear of the law catching up with her. Yes, that was an enticing prospect.

But she said nothing. Why didn't she just grab this unique offer, and flee from the law and Iniscay Island? Was it because this new life, with the physical trials and tribulations it offered, was too enticing to leave behind? Was it because she suspected that Paige wouldn't really do what she said, and that Bonnie's acceptance would be one more flimsy excuse to punish her in some fashion? Or was it, that despite her denials, she was still too attracted to Kane to leave him now?

Within a few seconds Bonnie decided that no matter what Paige offered, the price would always be too high. She looked up and stared at her. 'No, I'm not going anywhere,' she stated firmly.

For the look on Paige's face, Bonnie might just as

well have slapped her. She rose, her eyes glinting, her voice cutting as she said, 'You'll think differently before I'm through with you, I promise you that. Take off your clothes… Hurry!'

Bonnie complied, casting her trainers, jogging outfit and underwear aside. When naked she was afraid again, but strangely not regretful of her decision. Paige circled her like a drooling predator. 'Oh yes, you little bitch,' she snarled, 'you'll think differently before I'm through. Get back on all fours.'

Bonnie did so, fearfully watching Paige flex the horsewhip, her stomach churning at the prospect of whatever was about to happen. The woman moved out of sight, and Bonnie's breath and pulse quickened as she sensed her hovering like a cat toying with its doomed prey. Then Paige knelt behind her, nudged her ankles apart and shuffled between them.

Bonnie gasped as the cool sea air touched the exposed lips of her sex. She cringed as Paige's hands, strong and powerful and cold like stone, crept down her back and over her tender red buttocks. They crawled to her hips, gripped her there as Tim had done in the stable, and Paige pushed forward, grinding her groin against Bonnie's raised bottom. 'You know, little slave, it may be a cliché and hardly politically correct,' she whispered hoarsely, her voice fighting against the wind to reach Bonnie's ears, 'but I envy men and their ability to dominate another simply by virtue of their external equipment. Not that I would actually become one, given the choice,' she added. 'Men are intrinsically powerful, but women are more devious. Men are blunt hammers, and go bludgeoning their way through life. Women are scalpels, able to do more damage with little effort. Able to go straight for the jugular.' Her hands moved back to Bonnie's cheeks, parting them and exposing the secretive cleft of her bottom. 'Or whatever appropriate body part would suffice.'

A finger touched the puckered opening of Bonnie's rear passage, making the kneeling girl squirm and break her silence. 'W-what are you—?'

'Now you don't really need to ask that, do you?' Paige interrupted, probing for Bonnie's moist sex, dabbing at the copious dew she found there, ignoring Bonnie's moans as the lubricated finger returned to the waiting rosebud, and then firmly inserting it, working it back and forth, wordlessly inviting the girl to open further.

And the tight entrance did just that. Bonnie stared out to the horizon, eyes wide but not seeing. She groaned aloud, as much from the shock of her body's response as from the stimulation itself. Never before had anyone, man or woman, touched her there. And her reactions to it, beyond the fear and humiliation, were amazing.

And Bonnie's inexperience was clearly apparent to the older woman kneeling between her trembling thighs. 'It's nice to find some virgin part of you,' she said softly, 'something my half-brother has not yet defiled. And you here three days already; he must be getting soft in his old age.' And then her voice was harsh again, and she returned to the business of cruel domination. 'But I'm not doing this to give you pleasure, am I, my dear?'

'I – I don't know… mistress.'

'Oh no. I'm doing this not only to punish you, but to convince you of the error of your ways. My offer still stands. Just say the word and I'll have you off this island quicker than that!' and she emphasised the promise by sharply slapping Bonnie's poor rump with her free hand, causing the girl to gasp as the action jabbed the intruding finger deeper into her tight passage. 'Kane need never know, until it's too late.'

The reminder of the offer and the stabbing digit helped Bonnie refocus from the sensations coursing through her, and she remembered why Paige was treating her so cruelly. Well, she just wouldn't give in.

'I'll take your silence as your answer.' Paige's finger withdrew roughly – and was just as quickly replaced by something harder, larger, cooler... it was the handle of the whip.

Bonnie whimpered, as much at the degradation as the discomfort. Her breath quickened, and it felt like Paige was inserting the entire length into her. But she held her ground, refusing to collapse, willing herself to relax, to accommodate this shameful violation. Eventually the slow insertion stopped, and Paige stood and moved away.

'You should see yourself now,' she laughed.

Bonnie took the taunt as an invitation, and strained to look over her shoulder. The black leather handle was firmly embedded, and the tapering whip rose from between her stinging cheeks. It was an obscene sight indeed, making it look like she'd grown a tail; Kane's damsel in distress turned into some half human creature by the machinations of a wicked witch.

Paige stood back and stared coolly, as if forming an opinion about some museum artwork. 'Yes, very pleasing to the eye,' she decided. 'But I wonder if your performance matches your appearance.'

Bonnie didn't have long to wonder what Paige meant, as the mistress approached, draped one leg over her perspiring back, and sat astride her. Bonnie had just enough time to brace herself for the sudden weight, but little more, as Paige grasped her hair like reins and ordered, 'Take me back to the cart!'

Bonnie's hands and knees sunk into the sand, making the journey back incredibly draining, even without the whip sheathed in her bottom, or Paige constantly tugging her hair and slapping her flanks to urge her to greater efforts.

Paige sat in the semi-darkness of her suite, a brooding silhouette with the moonlight shining behind her through the window. She was motionless, save for the occasional lifting of the gin glass to her lips. She was waiting.

Waiting for the knock on the door, which eventually came. 'Come in,' she called softly.

A second silhouette appeared. 'Mistress Paige?'

'Close the door, Janine.'

Whilst shrouded in almost total darkness herself, Paige was able to watch the moonlit form of the house slave kneel before her. She paused, sipped more of her gin, then spoke. 'What do you make of the newcomer?' she asked.

'You mean Bonnie, mistress?' Janine hesitated, not quite sure what her mistress wanted to hear, and not wanting to say the wrong thing. 'Well, she seems inexperienced, but well suited for her work here.'

'Yes, she is.' A wealth of emotion and meaning were bound by those three words. 'I heard what Kane did to you last night. He pretended you were Bonnie, didn't he?'

Believing herself to be cloaked by the darkness as her mistress was, Janine allowed herself the luxury of bristling at that information; Janine had told Isobelle in confidence, but she sought to keep her reply and its tone appropriate to her station. 'Whatever a master may ask of his slave, mistress.'

'Yes, yes.' Paige waved a hand dismissively. 'But it is insulting, nevertheless. Even slaves need to be appreciated for themselves.

'Recall what things were like before her arrival. Oh, Kane dallies with the hares, as we all do. But they're not around forever, are they? The rest of the time he devotes to you. But if Bonnie remains, do you think that will continue?'

Janine frowned. 'But, I heard she's being groomed for Lord Victor's personal pleasure.'

Paige leaned forward conspiratorially in her chair, until Janine could smell her perfume and the alcohol on her breath. 'Assuming Kane goes through with it. And even if he does, do you really think that'll stop him from playing around with her, even before he inherits my father's wealth and power?

Janine tried to collate the myriad of thoughts stampeding through her mind, and she began to feel a terrible uncertainty in her life again, something not felt for years, not since she was Janine Carroll, drifting through jobs and lovers, always seeking satisfaction in both, but finding it in neither. Then she'd ventured into the Scene, and there met Kane Castlewell, during one of his infrequent forays into the outside world.

And it was Kane who took the basic colours of domination and submission, bondage and discipline, and created masterpieces. An artist devoted to his work, where others before him had been mediocre dilettantes. Kane had taken her to heights of pleasure she never knew existed, then offered her a lifetime filled with such delights. All she had to give up was her identity and freedom. It was a price she readily agreed upon.

Life had been sweet for Janine ever since. She was chief housekeeper and Kane's personal slave, just as Isobelle was Paige's. But if Bonnie's arrival threatened that...

'What can be done?' she asked tentatively.

'Nothing, if things are allowed to remain as they are,' came the whispered reply from the heavily scented silhouette. 'Bonnie's continuing existence here will change things, and not to either of our advantage. So she must leave, of her own free will. Once that happens, my own plans will come into fruition. Kane will be ousted as hunt master, possibly even as heir apparent as well. And then I'll need someone to be mistress of the house.' The plotting shadow leaned even closer. 'Any ideas on who might fit that position?'

Janine smiled slowly, as realisation dawned. 'Oh yes, mistress. I know just the person you need. What can I do to help you?'

'Us, dear, help us; we're both in this together, though in secret.

'From first thing in the morning you will harass Bonnie, keep her working, criticise everything she does, punish her – but without giving her satisfaction. Be wary of Kane; he'll no doubt be watching both of us. And of course, if he asks, tell him nothing of our plans.'

'Yes, mistress.' A thrill ran through Janine at the thought of the opportunity presented to her. Of course, she knew that with Paige ruling Iniscay, Kane might not wish to remain under her authority, even with the threat of being totally disowned should he go. But still, to be elevated to house mistress, and perhaps even taking on more slaves to do her bidding. Though she enjoyed serving her superiors, she'd grown to relish dominating others, too.

She couldn't wait to get started. 'Will that be all for now, mistress?' she asked, trying to suppress the excitement in her voice.

'No…' Janine watched the dark shadow rise to her feet, 'we must seal our pact… with a kiss.'

Chapter Seven

Bonnie carried the stack of warm fresh towels to the gymnasium in the cellar. The room had no windows, and the walls were covered with mirrors, which not only fed egos but provided a constant illusion of reflection upon reflection extending into infinity. Heavy blue mats covered much of the floor area, and there were various weight benches, parallel bars, and more exotic mechanical equipment. It all reminded her of the Playroom, and the memory of it and what had happened to her there brought a stirring response from within her knickers.

Bonnie nodded politely at the two guests working out, and continued on into the locker rooms to stow the fresh towels away.

On her return the man, Rafael, called out, 'Wait. Can you stay for a while?'

Bonnie paused, aware that she should comply with their wishes. 'If you like, sir.' Then she stood uncomfortably watching them continue their work out, wondering why she'd been asked to stay.

The female was a Scottish beauty named Zoe. She was perhaps a little older than Bonnie, with a voluptuous figure and raven hair. Her sweat-soaked T-shirt and skimpy shorts hugged her shapely contours as she lay on a bench, pumping a barbell over her chest.

Rafael, on the other hand, seemed ideally suited for the leg presses he was currently performing with tireless and precise motions. He was a lean and wiry figure.

She continued to watch, listening to the controlled bursts entering and leaving their lungs, and getting fidgety; someone would miss her soon and she might get into trouble. 'Is… is there anything I can do for either of you?' she asked.

'Well,' Rafael said, 'you could put some more weights on this.' He patted the leg press like it was a faithful Labrador.

Bonnie approached, waited until he lowered the weights, then repositioned the pin down a couple of slots. 'Will that be enough, sir?'

'Yes – and you can stop calling me sir.' He smiled pleasantly at her. 'It's Rafael.'

Bonnie blushed and smiled back. 'Very well… Rafael. Thank you.'

Zoe suddenly let out a short sharp yelp. Bonnie turned, then rushed over as the beauty balanced the barbell uncomfortably on her very shapely chest, clearly unable to lift it clear. Bonnie grabbed it and, straining with the effort and wondering how Zoe had been able to bench-press such a weight, managed to lift it onto its rest. 'Are you all right, miss?' she panted, genuinely concerned.

Zoe was gasping for breath, one hand draped on her breastbone, the other swaying above the floor. 'Whoa, that was a narrow squeak,' she managed. 'My strength just seemed to drain away all of a sudden… Thanks for your help.'

'Are you sure you're all right, miss?'

Zoe smiled ineffably. 'Well, it might have left a little bruise.' As she spoke her tone grew dreamy, and she drew the damp T-shirt out of the waistband of her shorts and up until her breasts, cupped snugly within a white sports bra, were exposed to the fluorescent lighting above. 'Could you have a look, please?' she cooed.

Bonnie, to her utter embarrassment, knew she was staring at the girl's beautifully toned bosom as it rose and fell with each breath taken, but she couldn't avert her eyes from the mouthwatering sight.

But Bonnie chided herself; it wasn't right. She wasn't supposed to feel such a way about another female. It went against all conventions. The incidents with Delilah and Paige had been out of Bonnie's control. She wasn't supposed to feel attraction towards her own sex.

But then again, she countered, why not? Zoe was a beautiful, graceful, athletic creature. She was undeniably feminine, yet strong in a way someone like Paige could only envy. And if Bonnie wanted to remain within convention, she should have left this island long ago. Besides, it wasn't as if anything would come from simply admiring her. Was it?

'Y-you look f-fine to me, Miss Zoe,' she blustered, and then summoning all her courage, she added sheepishly, 'In fact, I'd say you look gorgeous.' She knew she was blushing profusely, but couldn't resist the temptation to venture further. 'Are... are you tender anywhere?'

'I am,' Zoe encouraged. And then, without taking her eyes off Bonnie, she touched a fingertip to her bra, over one clearly outlined nipple. 'Like here, for example.'

It was an invitation Bonnie couldn't refuse. She knelt beside the bench and gingerly reached out, and she swooned as their fingers touched lightly over the stiffening bud. To her delight, Zoe squirmed a little and sighed her approval. Could this possibly be the first time she'd felt this way about another female, too? Bonnie found it hard to believe; so sexy and self-assured was Zoe.

'You... you might be wise to call it a day, miss,' Bonnie suggested, her lips dry with the tension of the moment.

'It's Zoe,' the raven-haired beauty whispered, 'and I think you could be right.'

Suddenly Rafael was with them, but such was his manner that Bonnie didn't feel he was intruding on her intimate moment with Zoe, or that she should be ashamed of her behaviour. And when he placed a strong hand on her shoulder, she couldn't help but shiver with anticipation and excitement.

To have them both... Bonnie couldn't believe what was happening to her; were her experiences on Iniscay widening her sexual horizons as well as her appetites?

'You push yourself too hard, Zoe,' Rafael suddenly broke the electric silence. 'You should give your upper body a rest for once and work on your legs.' With his free hand he gently slapped Zoe's neatly muscled thigh.

'Oh no,' Zoe responded, 'I want to be all-over fit.' She raised herself and drew Bonnie close, and in a mock conspiratorial whisper, as if Rafael wasn't there, said, 'You want to watch out for him. Some day he'll end up as a pair of legs and nothing else!'

'Nothing else?' he echoed, glancing down to where a considerable bulge stretched his shorts. 'I don't think so!' He looked proudly at both girls, grinning broadly.

Bonnie felt more relaxed than she had since stumbling upon Iniscay, and she enjoyed the good-natured company of this attractive couple. It seemed a far cry from the bitching nature of Janine and the rest of the house staff. Or, for that matter, from the back-stabbing colleagues at her former place of employment in computer technology. And that thought raised a question. 'Did you two know each other before coming here?' she asked. 'It's just that the others seem to come from widely differing places, and yet…'

Her words trailed away as she noticed how Zoe and Rafael glanced at each other, as if silently gauging how much they were allowed to reveal to her. Had the guests, like the house staff, been ordered not to talk about the island and their mysterious hunt? Or was it just a general reticence to speak about such things?

She was about to retract her question, when Zoe shrugged. 'We ran into each other a couple of times, on the Scene,' she said.

'The Scene?' Bonnie probed.

'Fetish clubs,' Rafael elaborated, and then he glanced at Zoe, his eyes smiling. 'We've done more than run into each other, too.'

Zoe sat up, smiling dismissively, her shirt still rucked up over her firmly jutting breasts. 'He wishes he could get someone like me,' she informed Bonnie. 'Dream on, big boy,' she added, teasing Rafael. 'Besides,' she continued, 'I have to direct all my energy towards my figure.'

'Lifting weights won't help you,' Rafael muttered. 'Running's what you're going to have to work on here.'

Bonnie took a chance, and asked, 'For the hunt, you mean?' and immediately wished she hadn't. The atmosphere changed instantly. Rafael rose and started some stretching exercises, and Zoe eased her shirt down, covering her breasts.

'We were given strict orders not to discuss that in front of you,' Rafael eventually broke the uncomfortable silence. 'Something about your background still being checked.'

Zoe frowned. 'Mmm… you'd think this was some sort of international spy ring.'

'Well, they do have to be careful, Zoe,' Rafael pointed out, switching to side bends. 'It may not be a spy ring, but it's no knitting circle, either.'

'But still...' Zoe gestured towards Bonnie, 'we both know what she's been through here. What sort of an impostor would go through all that?'

Rafael's stretching or opinion never wavered. 'Zoe, you act as if we're fully in the know.' He looked at Bonnie, still kneeling beside the bench. 'We're probably as much in the dark as you are.'

'But not in the same dark,' Zoe corrected, catching Bonnie's attention again with a look and a touch of her arm. 'Maybe we can pool our information and gain an advantage over the others—'

Rafael cleared his throat brusquely, interrupting Zoe. He touched his tightly pursed lips with a forefinger in a gesture of silence, then pointed to the ceiling. Zoe groaned quietly, and was clearly annoyed with herself. Bonnie understood; the room might be monitored by microphones.

And then the implications of this realisation sunk in. How much of this place might be monitored, audibly or visually? Could she have been spied upon from the moment she entered this house of depravity? Her humiliation in the Playroom, and her times with Kane in the study and bedroom? Just how many unseen voyeurs might have witnessed those moments? She didn't know – couldn't know; but it was an awful and unnerving thought.

Suddenly the door opened and Janine appeared, looking as irritated and impatient as ever. 'There you are, you lazy bitch,' she snapped at Bonnie. 'You're scheduled to polish the brass upstairs. Get back to work.'

'Yes, Miss Janine.' Bonnie rose to beat a hasty retreat, but Zoe rose too and placed a protective hand on her upper arm, gently but firmly keeping her in place. And Zoe's voice remained typically cheerful, but laced with unexpected layers of steely determination. 'We've ordered this servant to assist us with our exercises,' she said.

'I hope you don't have a problem with that?' Rafael added.

'Because if you do,' Zoe concluded, offering Janine no leeway, 'then please inform Lord Kane that we wish to speak to him about the matter.'

Janine visibly shook as she struggled to compose herself in a manner befitting a staff member dealing with those above her in the Iniscay hierarchy. Eventually she nodded politely, if curtly, her tone matching her actions. 'When you're through with her, please send her upstairs so she may continue her duties, and avoid being disciplined.' She threw Bonnie a withering glare, before exiting.

Bonnie exhaled and relaxed, then smiled at Zoe and Rafael in silent gratitude. Even so soon after a stressful encounter with Janine, something stirred within her pussy, warm and moist, and she knew the source of the stimulation; it was Zoe's touch on her arm.

'Rafael,' the beauty said huskily, her gaze never leaving Bonnie, 'do you think I can find some use for this... slave girl?'

Rafael approached, and from the way each of them

spoke slightly louder than was necessary, Bonnie knew that it was more for the benefit of whoever might be listening. 'Well, we could use her to scrub our backs in the shower,' he suggested.

'Well now, what a very good idea,' Zoe purred.

As in the gym, they had the locker room and showers to themselves. And of course, it was all spotless, courtesy of Bonnie's hard work in the early morning.

Now she stood watching Zoe and Rafael strip off their damp sports gear, unsure what to do, before Zoe looked up at her with an alluring smile. 'Are you intending to get your uniform wet when you're scrubbing our backs... slave girl?'

Not wanting to appear ungrateful to the pair for protecting her from the spiteful Janine, Bonnie took off her corset, stockings, suspender belt, and knickers. Her nipples were already erect, and her vulva felt swollen – expectant. But she chastised herself mentally; this encounter wasn't for sexual purposes, she reminded herself, it was merely an opportunity for them to speak in confidence. That was why they'd suggested getting together in the showers, where the noise of the cascading water would mask their voices... wasn't it?

'Are you ready?'

Bonnie turned to the sound of Zoe's seductive voice, and instinctively licked her lips at the sight of her. Zoe was as striking without clothes as she was with them. Those mouthwatering breasts were as firm as they had appeared in the sports bra, and were budded with dark pink nipples that stood, seeking attention. Her pubic hair, deep mahogany in colour, was trimmed and only just covered the outline of her sex lips. She was otherwise silky smooth, totally bereft of body hair. Like Bonnie, she still wore her collar, but this exception seemed to accentuate rather than detract from her stunning nudity.

Rafael, too, was a perfect physical specimen; a smooth-skinned, sepia-shaded man whom Bonnie couldn't help but admire. And she couldn't help staring at his semi-erect cock; long and thick, its moist head collared by a dark ring of skin, its root nestling in a bed of ebony pubic curls.

The two of them went through to the showers and began turning them on, while Bonnie stood at the doorway, watching, feeling a little foolish without knowing why.

Soon all the showers were turned on, water cascading down onto the tiled floor, and steam rising up and filling the room. Zoe and Rafael squeezed soap from the wall dispensers and massaged it into a rich lather on their shoulders, from where it oozed down and nestled between their legs. Despite the pleasantly hot water coursing down her body, Bonnie shivered as Zoe reached out and drew her and Rafael in close. She watched Zoe's succulent lips peel slowly apart, and held her breath, hoping for a kiss from them…

'So, what's your story, Bonnie?' Zoe whispered, and Bonnie felt ashamed of her disappointment. 'How did you end up here?'

Bonnie paused, gathering her composure, and suddenly aware that it would be the first time she had really talked about the circumstances which had led her to Iniscay, since the Castlewells already seemed to know about it without her mentioning it, and the house staff showed no interest. But she still held back, despite her warm feelings for these two people. How would they react, learning she was a fugitive from the law? How did she know they weren't undercover reporters or something, just as others suspected she might be?

Maybe she finally felt she had to trust somebody, or maybe she no longer cared one way or the other, but she cleared her throat and answered, 'I'm wanted by the police. I didn't do anything, really, but I ran just the same. I ended up in Iniscay village, and was tricked into coming to the island. Kane found me, and made me a slave for trespassing. Somehow they learned my story before I even told them, but I don't think they all believe my appearance here was just a coincidence. I'm a pawn between Kane and Paige, for their father's affections. I think Kane sees me as a present for Victor Castlewell, once I've been prepared for him.' She shrugged. 'And I'm... I'm still trying to decide why I remain here.'

Zoe glanced at Rafael, their eyes meeting and exchanging ineffable messages. Then she turned back to Bonnie. 'Have you ever been involved in the Scene, Bonnie?'

'No,' she answered truthfully, 'not before I came here.'

'Well, away from the public venues, the clubs and such, there are more exclusive cabals, secret societies for those who don't just flirt with the Scene, but devote their all to it.'

'It sounds more mysterious than it really is,' Rafael admitted. 'They're mostly just people hoping to find fulfilment, while avoiding media and legal attention. That's how Zoe and I met, through one of them.'

'And at that time,' Zoe continued, 'we'd heard

rumours of a place up north, and a competition called the Wild Hunt, one that offered its participants a lifetime of fortune, or a lifetime of servitude. Rafael and I asked about it discreetly, seemingly getting nowhere. Then we were approached by a man we'd met once before, and it turned out to be Kane, though he was incognito. He didn't tell us much more than we already knew, except that the hunt was open only to those with a taste for submission, and nothing to lose: no family, no career.'

Rafael, his eyes still on Bonnie, nodded to Zoe. 'We both qualified for that, needless to say, so we accepted. Given no notice, no time to tell anyone what was happening or where we were going, they brought us up here. And here we've been this past few weeks, told to enjoy ourselves, and wait.'

'But, wait for what?' Bonnie asked.

'They won't say,' said Zoe.

Bonnie was amazed to learn about these two. 'And you just accepted coming here, risking everything, without knowing beforehand what the game was about? Am I the only one who thinks that was a bit too risky?'

Rafael shrugged, a confident grin on his face. 'Risk is part of the fun. Not just the risk of the game, but of life itself. The greater the risk, the greater the reward.'

'And what will be the reward?'

He shrugged again. 'A lifetime of fortune?' he guessed. 'At least we know they can afford it.'

Bonnie stared at Zoe through the water and steam, and saw the same gleam of opportunity in her eyes as she had seen in Rafael's. She couldn't pretend to understand either of them; to understand how they could chance their freedom, perhaps their very lives, on something unknown that may or may not be won by them, or even achievable.

Just then Bonnie was wrenched from her anxious thoughts by a familiar voice that cut through the falling water. 'She works best when under the influence of a forceful personality.' The three looked through the rising steam at the door, where a broad silhouette stood. 'Provide just enough control to keep her on track, and she'll surprise you – and herself.'

'I think we can handle her, Lord Kane,' said Rafael.

'Really?' the voice challenged. 'Then prove it. Have her thank Zoe properly for the privilege of serving her.'

No one moved. The water continued to beat upon them like a million tiny drumsticks, washing away the last of the soap to the drains near their feet.

'What's the problem?' Kane mocked. 'One would think you had ulterior motives for meeting secretly like this, which would certainly place your eligibility for the hunt into doubt.'

Bonnie felt Zoe stiffen beside her as she finally spoke up. 'It's not that, Lord Kane,' she said. 'It's just, well, with you watching…'

'Oh, I'm so terribly sorry, my dear,' Kane said sarcastically. 'I didn't realise you're so concerned about the modesty of our little slave. But have no fear, she's performed before me already. Not satisfactorily, mind you, but then she is a beginner.' He paused, waiting. 'Well? Are you going to obey me, or are you prepared to break the rules of the house? Rules, may I remind you, that you hares agreed to abide by when you arrived here? When a Castlewell gives you an order…'

Bonnie looked uneasily at Zoe and Rafael, wanting both of them, but not under Kane's watchful eye, or conditions. Zoe was breathing more rapidly than before, and not from any unease about Kane's possible suspicions. A glance at Rafael confirmed him to be in the same condition, as did a movement from his groin, where his penis stirred, brushing against Bonnie's thigh. They were clearly turned on by Kane's dominating presence.

'Oh, I see now,' Kane admitted grandly, cutting the uneasy silence between them. 'You await direction. Ah, the burdens of being superior, they do weigh so heavily upon one. Bonnie, I want you to kiss Zoe. And convince me you mean it.'

Bonnie's nipples stiffened at the thought of what she was being ordered to do. She reached up and lightly traced her fingertips along the line of Zoe's smooth jaw. She glanced quickly over her shoulder at the figure watching them, and then drew forward and pressed her lips to Zoe's. Their breasts moulded against each other, and Bonnie thought she was sure to faint away with sheer pleasure, as Zoe's tongue slipped between her parted lips and thrust into her mouth. She relished Zoe's taste, wormed her tongue into her mouth, and gasped as she began sucking on it. They clasped each other, refusing to let the other go.

'Very nice,' Kane interrupted their mutual pleasure, offering skimpy applause. 'Now, Rafael, pull the slave her away.'

Bonnie opened her eyes and looked into Zoe's, twin fires which mirrored her own excitement. As she was pulled from her, she could still feel the intensity of their kiss, an intensity echoed in her sex. She became aware of Rafael's strong fingers, clasping gently but firmly on her shoulders. She also became aware of his erection, nudging bluntly into the cleft between the cheeks of her bottom, as if asking for entry. Maybe... if Kane allowed it.

'Of course, anyone can kiss lips,' Kane continued. 'Even our demure little slave, virgin to so much before her arrival on Iniscay, had no problem with that. So let's see how she deals with something more... fundamental. Get her on her knees, Rafael.'

Rafael hesitated, and Bonnie turned her head and caught his gaze, trying to communicate her acknowledgement of the situation, that she wasn't really being forced into this, any more than Zoe or he were; they were all turned on by the scenario, as Kane intended.

'Eyes front, Bonnie.' Kane was relentless. 'Or we'll be keeping you after class for remedial work.'

Bonnie obeyed, seeing Zoe sway slightly with the heady anticipation of further pleasures. There was an irrepressible pressure on Bonnie's shoulders, and she sank slowly to her knees.

Her own body was hot and excited, consumed by a desire to become intimate with the woman in ways she wouldn't have dared only weeks ago. She wouldn't have been ready then. She was now, though, reaching up and resting her hands on Zoe's hips, momentarily at a loss as to how to proceed further.

Kane, thankfully or not, was there to help out. 'You'll find it's slightly different from performing on men, sweet Bonnie. Zoe, open your legs wider, and Rafael, offer any support required.'

Bonnie looked up. Zoe seemed so statuesque, her breasts standing proudly, water dripping from their erect tips onto Bonnie's upturned face.

Now Bonnie could detect the humid fragrance of the other girl, so much like her own.

'Nothing quite like the female sex, is there, Bonnie?' Kane chimed in from a million miles away, as if unwilling to be forgotten in the heat of the moment. 'The poet John Farrell described it as "the Gates of Heaven", four hundred years ago. No one's ever been able to sum it up more aptly.'

Bonnie could understand that. As she peered closer at the wet treasure, she could see the tip of Zoe's clitoris, protruding from the folds of flesh encasing it. She could feel the heat radiating from within Zoe's body as she drew closer, finally burying her face into the other girl.

Zoe moaned and clutched Bonnie's head, as the kneeling girl sought out the tiny bud she'd seen waiting for her, and reached round to clasp Zoe's hollowed buttocks.

Unexpectedly quickly, Bonnie felt Zoe's muscles contracting sharply against her face, and her whole body shaking with rapturous release. Bonnie sighed against the delicious girl with a deep satisfaction, stroking the smooth flesh of her taut buttocks, delighted that she'd been able to give her such a special orgasm.

Once again Kane mocked them with applause. 'Not bad,' was his verdict. 'Better than I'd anticipated, in fact. Yes, much better.'

Trying to ignore him, Bonnie sank back a little, feeling Zoe's juices coating her face and tasting them on her lips. Zoe slumped back against the tiled wall, looking totally replete as the water washed down over her limp body, her breasts rising and falling as she breathed deeply. Oh yes, Bonnie had done a good job indeed.

Gradually she became aware of Rafael, still behind

her, still awaiting release, just as she did. Without permission or direction from her watching master, she twisted round, and took Rafael's erection into her mouth. She heard Rafael groan, much like Zoe had done, as she ran her tongue around the velvety rim of his cock, and then along the whole length to his gently swaying testicles.

Bonnie wanted to touch herself, to stroke her engorged nipples, or between her legs, where her sex lips pulsed, soaked with much more than just shower water. She needed to steady herself against Rafael as she continued to suckle him, loving his taste, his feel, loving the way his hard flesh filled her hungry mouth. She pulled back again, keeping just the throbbing head within, sucking strongly at it, tasting the salty pre-come. She furtively rubbed between her thighs, and as Rafael grunted and her mouth filled with his copious emission, she came too, whimpering softly, vainly trying to keep the fact from Kane's attention.

The slowly softening stalk of flesh plopped from her mouth, and as her shoulders sagged and she knelt, exhausted, Kane's harsh tones again penetrated the hissing of the water around her ears.

'I am not amused,' he said. 'I am disappointed with you all, but mostly I am disappointed with Bonnie – our slave. I did not give you permission or instruct you to perform such an act. Your punishment, therefore, will be severe.'

Bonnie was bent over the dining room table, naked, her clothes scattered around her feet, her breasts squashed against the linen tablecloth, her arms outstretched until they almost reached the other side of the table. The diners remained, their untouched desserts still before them, watching Paige. One of Bonnie's shoes was in Paige's hand, and she was forcefully smacking Bonnie's vulnerable bottom with the flat sole. Bonnie stared ahead, not wanting to look at the others; unwilling to catch any silent shows of pity or solidarity.

It had been a calculated set up. The family and guests had been nearing the end of their dinner, when Paige loudly noted the spotted state of the dessert spoons. Janine helpfully informed her that those had been Bonnie's responsibility that morning, after the brassware. Bonnie protested her innocence, and that outburst earned her an additional ten strokes, on top of the dozen Paige had already decreed. Bonnie was ordered to undress and bend over the table, and dessert was forgotten as everyone could do little else but watch the execution of the sentence.

Each smack drove blistering shocks through Bonnie's system. She couldn't help but note the vicious power behind each blow, and the sadistic delight that had engulfed Paige. Bonnie was gasping heavily, and thought she might wet herself on the table linen. How many further blows would that earn her? It was becoming too much.

Suddenly Kane spoke up, breaking the silence that had settled over the room and its occupants. 'That's twenty-four now, Paige,' he pointed out. 'You've applied two too many.'

Paige stopped, glaring at Kane for interrupting her pleasure, but aware of their father's silent presence, still at the figurative head of the table, watching everyone and everything, his thoughts unreadable. 'Yes,' she panted from the exertion, 'I did say twenty-two, didn't

I? How considerate of you to point that out, *Kane*.'
Transparent hatred for her brother dripped from her
venomous retort.

Bonnie rested her forehead on the table, relieved that
the torment was at last over, but concerned about how
far Paige may go in the future. But then her heart sank
as she heard Kane add, 'I only point it out because I
want you to give her a further ten from me. She was
most insolent today.'

'Oh, it'll be my *pleasure*,' drooled Paige.

And so the beating continued.

Later, her buttocks still burning within the cool leather
of her knickers, Bonnie was serving drinks. She
delivered Kane's to his study, where he sat alone. She
was determined to say nothing that would give any
indication of her true feelings. She was determined to
be the stoic slave he demanded and expected.

He grasped her arm as she turned to leave, his eyes
never leaving the blood-red colour of his brandy. 'You
feel betrayed, don't you?'

She stiffened at his touch. 'Acts of independence,
whether of thought, word, feeling or deed, are acts of
rebellion against her master, and must be immediately
and ruthlessly suppressed. Your third law of slavery,
master. Of course, you can order me to feel betrayed.'

He squeezed her arm further, quickly downing a
mouthful of brandy, before snarling, 'Being a master
has its restraints, too, in case you didn't know. The
things he feels... the things he wants to say to a
woman...'

Bonnie stared down at him, and he realised he'd said
too much. Slamming his glass onto an occasional table,

with such force that it nearly shattered, he hauled her down across his lap and delivered a frenzy of jarring blows onto her unprotected bottom. This violent outburst seemed to calm him, and allowing her up, he smoothed his ruffled hair back into place and ordered her to leave him.

Cupping her abused buttocks she hurried from the room, angered and confused, and leaving Kane in much the same mental state.

Chapter Eight

'Bonnie, I'll be needing your help this afternoon.'

Bonnie had grown accustomed to hearing such announcements, not just from Martin Castlewell, who in all the time she'd been employed on the island, had said barely a word to her; a record of non-involvement surpassed only by his father, Victor.

Oh, she'd listened to the jokes from the others, how Martin was the white sheep of the Castlewells, how he never seemed to indulge in the same perverse games as his brother and sister, and, by implication, their father. But to Bonnie, he just appeared to be the less ostentatious type, that surely he couldn't escape without at least some of the Castlewell traits of sadistic debauchery. Still, when he approached her while she was scrubbing the hallway floor and announced his requirement for her presence later in the day, she thought perhaps she could be forgiven for not replying in the manner befitting a slave, just nodding and saying, 'Of course.'

He nodded back. 'I'll inform Janine you're to be excused from other duties from one o'clock. Report to my studio in the attic at that time.' With that he nodded again and walked away. Bonnie returned to her scrubbing, puzzled by the exchange. What could Martin want with her?

Janine, annoyed by Martin's announcement but unable to do anything about it, revealed nothing to

Bonnie, and the others were too busy or disinterested to help her out either.

The appointed hour arrived, and Bonnie, as usual, knocked and awaited an answer before entering. There were still a number of rooms in the manor that she'd not yet seen; the studio being one of them. Consequently she didn't know what to expect – but was still unprepared for what she found.

It was a cluttered area of blank and painted canvases stacked together, some on easels, incomplete and aborted works of oil and charcoal. There were sheets piled into one corner near a couch and other props. There were shelves crammed with tins of paint and thinners, and jars of brushes, some dry and unused, and others soaking in dirty fluid. Smocks, some clean and some smeared with vivid colours, hung untidily from wall pegs, and delicate particles drifted like gold-dust in the shard of afternoon sunlight that pierced the grimy skylight. Spanish guitar music filled the air, as did the scent of the oil paint and cleaner.

It took a moment for Bonnie to actually notice Martin. He sat in one corner, crouched over a laptop computer. He was dressed as casually as she'd ever seen him, in a paint-flecked T-shirt and jeans, and he didn't look up from the laptop screen as he said, 'Come on in and close the door. I'll be right with you.'

She approached, slightly hesitantly. Technically, he was Lord Martin Castlewell, and as he had summoned her, she was surely expected to kneel before him, head bowed, awaiting further instructions. Something told her he wasn't the type to expect such subservient behaviour, but preferring to err on the side of caution, she approached and adopted the posture.

'Damn,' he finally cursed.

Bonnie risked a glance up, suspecting the expletive was not directed towards her or her decision. 'Master? Is there a problem?' she asked.

He ran a hand through his mop of dark hair, tapping at the screen in distraction, still not glancing away from it, as if afraid whatever difficulty he had would only increase when his attention was diverted. 'Sorry to keep you,' he said, with an unexpected politeness that threw her a little off balance, 'but I thought I'd have this glitch corrected before now, and father's expecting it to be done before he attends a shareholder's conference at six.'

Bonnie relaxed a little, his apology increasing her confidence, but she was still a little unsure of how to address him. 'Does he do a lot of conferencing... master?'

Martin grinned wryly. 'My father wouldn't know a RAM from a sheep. Hell, none of my family would, for that matter. But he appreciates what the information age can do for him, hence he attends more international investors' and shareholders' meetings via electronic proxy since his official retirement than he did when he was jet-setting around the globe. And all without leaving the safety and security of his self-made paradise.'

Bonnie thought she detected a little distaste in the last few syllables, though her attention was drawn more to the machine Martin was working like the piano of a frustrated composer. 'Excuse me, but is that an eight six eight?'

Martin nodded. 'It's networked to the house computer, a twelve hundred Supermini.'

Bonnie gasped with transparent awe. 'A Supermini?

With the RAM-intensive algorithms and AI Risk Chips?'

Martin nodded again, grinning with satisfaction, perhaps even solidarity, knowing Bonnie, of all people on the island, could properly appreciate it.

Bonnie's mind reeled at the processing power at this man's fingertips, power Bonnie had only ever flirted with on assignments, on other people's company equipment. But did the Castlewells, with all their investments and such, really need that much computer? She was so in awe she couldn't help but mutter, 'You're so damned lucky...'

Instead of chiding her for speaking out of turn, he smirked. 'I feel many things, but lucky isn't usually high on my list. This was a prototype when we got it, and I've been debugging it ever since. Communications with the outside world, energy efficiency and environmental maintenance for the house, internal and external security, father's business holdings, blah, blah, blah... I can't even call in help because father's understandably paranoid about any of our secrets leaking out.'

And no wonder, Bonnie thought, her mind filing away these unexpected snippets of information. Internal and external security; cameras and microphones, perhaps?

'It's amazing how glitches will appear in the most obscure and unlikely of places,' he continued, leaning back and stretching. Finally he seemed to notice her subservient position. 'Sorry, you can stand up,' he said. As she did so, he keyed in a few final strokes, then shut down the laptop and rose. 'It's no good, he'll have to settle for a less than perfect image for the Koreans.'

'Umm... perhaps I can take a look at it?' Bonnie

offered carefully, somehow keeping herself from bouncing up and down like a child with the prospect of raiding a toy chest of goodies.

'Not permitted,' he declared flatly, before adding more sympathetically, 'Unfortunately.' He stretched again and stepped away, the floorboards creaking underfoot. 'Perhaps I should tell you why you're here. Basically, father wants a portrait of you.'

'Me?' Bonnie was shocked.

'Father likes sketches and portraits of all his new... employees.'

'Oh.' Until now, the enigmatic and elusive Victor Castlewell had given no direct hint of any interest in her. 'And you'll be painting it?' she asked.

Martin nodded, moving an easel and blank canvas to what looked like a familiar, well-worn area of the floor. 'My mother was an artist,' he explained. 'Father encouraged it in me, as well as computer sciences. Fortunately I turned out to have a talent for both.' He paused for a moment, as though recollecting. 'He always did have a gift for exploitation,' he concluded quietly, a hint of bitterness in his voice.

The more Bonnie learned about the Castlewells, the more she knew there was no real love lost amongst any of them. Unlike the others, however, Martin could elicit some measure of sympathy from her. Perhaps because of their shared interest in computers. Or perhaps, more simply, because he'd done nothing against her, and seemed genuinely nicer than the others.

'Now,' he interrupted her thoughts, 'take off your clothes, please, but leave the collar on. You can put them on the couch.' He indicated the piece of furniture in the corner. 'Father had specific instructions as to how

133

you should look in the picture.'

Bonnie did as he instructed, and said nothing. What was there to say? She was a slave, there to obey the orders of her masters without question. Her eyes followed him as he stooped by one of the sheets and pulled out something that looked like a large cat's scratching post. It was a waist high wooden post as thick as a man's thigh, and mounted onto a square board covered with red carpeting. Attached to the top of the post were two short chains with leather cuffs dangling from their ends, and a longer chain between them, with a clip on its end.

As she placed her folded clothes on the couch, she silently watched him position the post in front of the easel, where the sunlight bathed it. He stood back, walked around it, rubbed his chin pensively, and carefully readjusted its position a fraction. 'Sorry,' he murmured, without glancing up, 'I should have had all this ready for when you arrived.'

Why was he so damned polite with her? It was unnerving. She instinctively tried to cover her breasts with one arm and her sex with one hand, and realised that Martin's gentlemanly behaviour had reawakened her sense of modesty.

She waited quietly until he seemed satisfied with the post's placement, then motioned for her to approach. 'Right, just kneel on this,' he indicated the carpeted base, 'and lift your arms.'

Bonnie obeyed, demurely keeping her thighs together, and watched Martin secure the soft cuffs around her wrists, and then take the longer chain and clip it to a ring on her collar. His hands were cool and gentle, and there was a scent like cinnamon or some other dry spice about him.

Bonnie's modesty grew more pronounced with his close proximity. To her immense chagrin her traitorous nipples crimped and stiffened, making her blush.

But Martin said nothing, and seemed to pay no attention to her body's response to being chained to a wooden post. When happy with his subject he moved to the easel, and appraised her without any sign of emotion. Although apparently nicer than the rest of his family, Bonnie found him disturbingly detached.

Then he shook his head a little. 'Can you move your right knee to the other side of the post?'

Bonnie did so, and was suddenly aware, with her thighs now parted, that her sex was clearly exposed, and she groaned inwardly because she just knew it was open and wet.

Martin held up his hand, silently telling her to adjust her position no more. 'Good,' he decided. 'That's just how I want you. I think we'll try the charcoals first, and if I'm not happy with that we'll go for the oils.' He opened a narrow tin box and set it beside the easel. Then he regarded her again. 'Grip the wrist chains,' he directed, 'as if you could break free from them. Keep your head high, your gaze proud – defiant.' He scrutinised his model some more. 'Now, I want you to imagine you're a princess from a faraway land, captured by wicked slavers and sold into captivity. They've stripped you of your clothes, your title, but not your dignity or your pride. They've chained you in the marketplace to be auctioned away to the highest bidder, but you refuse to be defeated. You have plans, schemes of your own, ambitions that show in your expression. You know you're more dangerous than your captors have accounted for. Now, you simply wait for the opportunity to seize power from them.'

Bonnie listened to him, the intoxicating image his words created painted as clearly in her mind as it would soon be on the canvass. It was an image of some fantastical bygone age, where all men thought as the Castlewells did now. It was an age where lives were bartered for, used, and cast aside. Where she'd be chained naked in public, under the derisive eyes of the crowds, to be sold like cattle and used in whatever fashion her owners deemed fit. Perhaps to be beaten, whipped further into submission, enjoying the bitter taste of the leather on her back, her buttocks, her thighs. But still a part of her would remain free, planning to take control. To escape, or to give others a taste of the pleasures she'd sampled.

'Now that's perfect,' Martin said, wrenching Bonnie from her strange thoughts. He reached for the tin of charcoal. 'It seems you had little difficulty in imaging the scene.'

Her mind raced. Was he right? Was she subconsciously planning something? If so, what? To escape from Iniscay? She could have easily done that by accepting Paige's offer, and she still could. If not that, then what? Was it simply to learn the secret of the hunt and the hares? Did curiosity alone drive her on?

Or would she try to seize some sort of power, as her imaginary princess would? And if so, how could she possibly do that? She was hardly the revolutionary type.

Information is Power, stated a poster that had hung in her former company's office. Perhaps that was the key. Study the full program, understand the parameters, find the bugs, and fix them.

Or exploit them.

'May a slave speak, master?'

Martin smirked, either out of amusement or embarrassment at her deferential tone. 'You don't seem to have much of a problem in that department. What is it?'

Bonnie started, then paused, careful in selecting her words. 'This seems like a vast operation your family runs here,' she said. 'Bringing people to the island, arranging to find suitable hares, presumably checking their identities...'

'Your point being?' Martin asked.

'Hasn't anyone made any investigations? The government, the media, the authorities looking for missing persons?'

'Do you know how many thousands of people go missing each year?' he asked. 'Mostly of their own free will, to escape creditors or bad marriages?' His eyes absorbed every detail of her lithe body as the charcoal reproduced her beauty. 'Look at your own situation, for example. You're wanted by the police—'

'But I didn't do anything—'

'It doesn't matter,' he interrupted. 'The fact remains that they're looking for you. Yet you've managed to evade them, and no boys in blue have come knocking on our door, now have they?'

Bonnie shook her head; what he said was true.

'And even if someone is looking for those that come here, it's easy to leave a false trail. Nothing that appears too much like a false trail, you understand, but just a few clues. For instance, when the authorities check your credit card records again, they'll find you tried to use them in a clothing shop in Paris yesterday.'

Bonnie's jaw dropped. 'What?' she gasped.

He grinned. 'I arranged it, via a judicious application of electronic muscle.'

Bonnie's shock remained. Martin was right again. Unless someone came here, saw her and was able to identify her, she was truly safe from the law. But she remained dubious. 'But surely people still ask questions?'

'Even before my help, father knew how to survive,' Martin said. 'He learned from the mistakes of others. He never seeks media attention. He lets most of his business contacts believe he's an invalid on Iniscay, rather than purposefully reclusive. He never plays politics. He never courts controversy or invokes debate through his business dealings. He pays his taxes, and so never leaves himself open to investigation or blackmail. Of course, he maintains a wealth of blackmail on a host of assorted authority figures, should the need arise, but never abuses what he knows... And of course,' Bonnie thought she detected a hint of resentment creep into his expression, 'he keeps his loved ones close at hand, to help support and maintain his philosophy.'

She knelt, absorbing what she was hearing, her modesty cast aside by the implications of Martin's words. Was that Victor Castlewell's secret of survival, in a world where everyone seemed to be under someone else's scrutiny? He had built his own little universe here, where he ruled over his family and his slaves, retaining absolute power over them all. What if she left now and told the outside world what she'd seen here? Assuming she was even believed, assuming the authorities didn't just lock her up and throw away the key, assuming the Castlewells didn't cover themselves with alibis... There were far too many assumptions. No one was here against his or her will, and she was sure no crimes were being committed – no major ones, anyway. If she did get away, it was more than likely that Victor Castlewell would use his considerable influence to ensure she never saw freedom again.

Suddenly, the idea of being a slave here wasn't just some isolated fantasy that could be burst like a bubble with a thought of the outside. It was set in concrete, a reality as strong as that she once held in her old life. Now, it made the choice given her by Paige that much more pertinent; leave, or stay.

She wanted to stay, to drink more from the exotic wellspring of pains and delights this little world offered. Kane had been right that first day, that the outside world would be far too mundane for her now. But Paige and Janine would keep harassing her, of that she was certain. So she had to consolidate her position here; fortify it against her opposition.

Which led her back to her quest for information.

'I take it you believe I'm really a fugitive, then,' she fished, 'and not some reporter or spy?'

The charcoal stopped moving for a second as Martin considered her question. 'Yes, I do believe that.'

'Then, can you tell me about the hunt?' she probed.

'No, that I can't do,' he said firmly. 'Your background is no longer an issue. But your telling the hares anything that might alter the game beforehand, is. And especially if—' he checked himself, and closed his eyes as if mentally kicking himself.

'If what?' Bonnie pushed.

Martin's expression grew resolute. He was clearly determined to put aside that line of conversation. 'Your determination to triumph is evident on your face,' he stated. 'But you're missing the lust that still drives you, heedless of your ambitions.'

So engrossed was Bonnie by her curiosity, that she'd forgotten she was supposed to be posing erotically. She gathered her thoughts, and then did her best to readopt the required sultry look.

With less than satisfactory results, judging from the look he returned. 'Think back to my earlier description. A proud woman, stripped and shackled, displayed to the crowds, any thoughts of modesty or position cast aside with her old life. They all want you, men and women both. They want to use and abuse you, but only some are prepared to pay the price. The very thought of what could happen to you fills you with lust, doesn't it?'

Bonnie blushed and lowered her eyes. Like his siblings, Martin's voice had a seductive quality to it, ensnaring her, demanding her full attention. She gripped the chains more tightly and proudly lifted her chin, secretly savouring the slight pull of the chain on her collar. She felt warm, intense, her nipples dark and puckered, her pussy tingling, seeking indulgence.

'Then someone buys you,' he continued, the charcoal now moving more swiftly, with more purpose. 'Maybe it's a man, maybe it's a woman. You don't care, so long as they know how to treat you. You may have been a princess in your own land, but the lessons you've learned as a slave have ignited fires within you that can no longer be ignored or denied. Do you see yourself, under their possession, taken away on a lead like an animal?'

'Yes,' Bonnie whispered hoarsely, her throat

tightening, the heat increasing between her thighs.

'Perhaps you'll be made to work in the fields, or the stables. Perhaps within their house, cooking and cleaning. Or perhaps you'll be their plaything, required to satisfy their basest lusts, to feed their insatiable carnal appetites. Perhaps they have a string of lovers, of both sexes, all demanding your body. There are so many of them, Bonnie. Can you satisfy them all?'

'Yes,' she murmured, unable to look up at him any more. Yes, she felt she could, she could satisfy them all: Kane, Paige, Victor, Zoe, Rafael, Tim... and Martin, too. Yes, she could, and her clitoris pulsed deliciously at the very idea.

'Are you wet, Bonnie?' Martin asked softly.

'Yes,' she confessed, surprised by his boldness in asking such a thing; it didn't suit him. And she couldn't tell if he asked just to elicit the appropriate response on her face, or if there was something more.

She wanted more.

She wanted Martin to cast aside his work, and to torture her flesh into submission with deeds and not just words, like his brother and sister had done before him.

'Prove it,' he challenged, his voice barely more than a whisper. 'Spread your legs further.'

Without thinking twice, Bonnie leaned back further on her heels and exposed her glistening pubic down, the swollen lips of her sex parting for his gaze. She could feel her dew escape from within, seeping down between her buttocks. She looked up dreamily at Martin, hoping for a favourable response. She wanted him to drop the charcoal, rush to her, and take his pleasure from her in any way he chose.

141

But Martin continued to sketch, seemingly unaffected by her unspoken invitation. 'You crave relief, don't you, Bonnie?'

'Yes,' she gasped, possessed by a feverish spirit that hungered for more than could be assuaged by thought alone.

'But there's no one or nothing to give you that relief, is there?' he teased. 'Not even your own hands, bound as they are, out of reach of the treasure between your legs. What would you do, princess? What would you do if your hands were free?'

Caught up in her own desires, in the siren spell of his voice, his woven fantasy which had mixed truth with reality, Bonnie drew herself towards the post and rubbed against it. The cool polished wood was a balm against her throbbing clitoris.

Despite a flicker of anguish at such a wanton display of degradation, the reaction of her body erased all other concerns from her mind. The room was silent but for the melodic guitar in the background, the rough stroke of charcoal on canvas, and her own moans as her pussy and thighs lubricated the post, spreading her scent, marking her territory.

It wasn't that long since she'd last masturbated, but until now she'd never done it in the presence of another. It was a novel occurrence, a twist on a familiar theme. She could have masturbated before Kane, that first night in the study, but had been too angry and ashamed and afraid to do so. Now that precious moment was lost, but something like it could be recaptured before Kane's younger half-brother. And if she pleased him with her performance...

Her back arched, her arousal mounting. She rubbed

her clitoris against the post with increasing urgency, further encouraging the approaching orgasm.

She whimpered as she climaxed, shuddering helplessly with her head thrown back; and it was not a show for her audience of one. Gasping for breath, still reeling from the wonderful but subsiding waves of her orgasm, she looked over to Martin, her eyes pleading along with her weak voice, 'Please... please free me...'

Martin, who had watched her seductive performance in rapt silence, set aside the charcoal and knelt beside her. He released the chains from her wrists and collar, and she feverishly drew him into her arms, kissing him hungrily, trying to force his lips apart with her avid tongue.

'Bonnie—' he gasped, trying to extricate himself gracefully. 'No, please don't—'

She ignored him, clawing at his back, trying to tear away his shirt. But he was still resisting. With surprising force he grabbed her forearms and pulled them away. Then he let go and stood up, backing away from her, looking ruffled, his expression one of pained disappointment. 'I – I'm sorry...' he stammered. 'I like you, I really do. I like to talk to you, to be with you... but...'

'What do you want from me?' she pleaded, confused. He was so different from the others; a kindred spirit. She wanted to be worthy of him, like no other. 'I can be anything you want me to be, Martin.'

He shook his head hopelessly, his shoulders slumped as though his strength had drained completely away. 'Can you... can you be a man, Bonnie?' he asked wearily.

The games room was all leather and mahogany, with burgundy carpets and drapes. There was a snooker table, chess table, card table, glossy potted plants in the corners, and the smell of fine cigars in the air. It could have been any typical evening in a men's club.

Except for the sight of Bonnie in her slave's uniform, serving drinks. She felt drained, exhausted from her afternoon with Martin and the revelation it had brought. Only the sparkling smile from Zoe as she handed the gorgeous girl her drink cheered her.

Paige was at the snooker table, having just potted the black with a resounding clack. She held her hands high as if to accept applause, and announced, 'And Paige Castlewell wins the Iniscay Cup once again.' She looked around at the indifferent gathering. 'Anyone want to play a frame or two with me?'

Bonnie was still close to Zoe. 'Must be tired of playing with herself,' she whispered.

It was meant as a quip for Zoe's ears only, but the gentle background music decided to pause at that moment, and everyone heard the remark.

'You cheeky little bitch!' hissed Paige, totally unable to contain her fury.

Bonnie inhaled sharply, wishing she'd not been so cheeky, or so careless. 'Forgive me, mistress–' But she had no time to complete her apology, as a hand gripped her shoulder from behind and pushed her forward. It was Janine, and the little vixen took great delight in shoving Bonnie over to the snooker table.

Paige stood waiting, slapping the thin end of the cue into her open palm, her face taut. 'Tell me you're stupid, slave,' she spat. 'I'll believe that. Because if I thought you were being deliberately abusive, there wouldn't be an inch of skin left on your rear end.' She pointed the cue at Bonnie. 'Slaves exist at the suffrage of their betters, and I'll be damned if—'

'Sufferance,' Bonnie corrected, and immediately cringed and wished she could bite her stupid tongue off.

'I beg you pardon?' Paige said slowly, clearly taken aback by the slave's audacity.

Having gone this far, Bonnie decided she might as well put the spiteful bitch in her place. The situation couldn't get very much worse, after all. 'I think you meant to say sufferance, and not suffrage,' she said, gradually feeling better for standing up to the woman. 'Unless, of course, you intend to give slaves the vote on Iniscay.'

There was a smirk and then an embarrassed cough from one of the guests.

'Is that right?' Paige said, the venom dripping from her voice. Then, in an alarming display of temper, she slammed the snooker cue on the edge of the table with such force that it shattered with a loud crack, and a section spiralled across the room. Gripping what remained of the cue, she pointed at Janine.

Janine knew what to do, turning Bonnie and forcing her forward until she was bent over the table, her rear in the air, then holding her there. Paige was around to Bonnie's side before the latter even registered it, and without further ado began laying the remains of the cue across Bonnie's bum. Her knickers were scant protection. Shards of pain shot through her body with each blow, the pain eclipsing any pleasure she might have experienced alongside it.

'Thank your mistress!' Paige bellowed. 'Haven't you

learned anything by now?'

Bonnie began thanking her after each strike as best she could, but they were coming with such speed that she hardly had time to catch her breath and speak.

And then unexpectedly, through a haze of pain and confusion, she heard Zoe's sweet voice. 'What can she learn from this?' she said. 'What can any of us learn?'

The beating stopped. Paige pulled Bonnie back up by her hair, then pulled her over into the centre of the room. Hot waves radiated from Bonnie's bottom, but she had little time to decide whether they were enjoyable or not, as Paige confronted her newfound friend.

'So, Zoe, you'd like to play questions and answers, would you? Well, I didn't bring my blackboard, so...' She tugged Bonnie's hair with a viciousness that made Bonnie squeal, and hissed through clenched teeth. 'Pull your knickers down to your knees and put your hands behind your head.'

Fighting her mortification, Bonnie obeyed, and could feel all eyes in the room feasting on her exposed sex and buttocks, while Paige, broken cue still in hand, walked slowly around her, addressing the room's occupants with a detached manner like a lecturer teaching her students. 'Now, perhaps I should tell you all a little more about punishment.' She paused for a few moments, checking she had the full attention of them all, before continuing.

'Those in favour of set corrections will have detailed numbers and types of punishments set for their slaves, depending upon the slave's particular grievance and past record. They feel it lends an established air to their role-playing – assuming you only play roles and not live them, as we do here.

'For instance,' Paige continued, resting the cue on Bonnie's shoulder as though indicating a specimen, 'this little brat insulted me. That earned her a dozen strokes, and if I take into account her dismal record for the past week, she might deserve another dozen.'

Bonnie gazed at Zoe, her eyes a little blurred by tears of humiliation, but she knew Zoe couldn't risk interfering much more without risking being removed from the hunt, with its promise of fortune.

'However,' Paige proceeded, resuming her orbit around Bonnie. 'I differ from that philosophy. I believe that uncertainty is as potent a weapon of discipline as a good leather strap. Knowing what can be expected from the breaking of a particular rule can lead a slave to bargain with him or her self, believing the punishment worth the crime. But if they have no idea how stern or lenient their master or mistress will be... well; just imagine what the crime rate on the outside world would be like if criminals believed that when they went to jail, they'd have no idea when they'd be released? Masters and mistresses must never be seen as predictable.'

There was a murmur among the attentive group.

'So, think about what's going through this pathetic slave's mind, such as it is. How many more strokes will she get for her error? None? Five? Fifty? Will her past errors be taken into account? Will I use the cue again, or my hand, or—'

'Or maybe you'll just talk her to death.'

All eyes turned to Kane, standing in the doorway with a stern expression on his face. Paige pointed at him with the cue. 'Stay out of this, Kane,' she snapped. 'This is a lawful punishment. I have witnesses to the slave's misdemeanour.'

Kane approached, never looking at Bonnie. 'Yes, I'm sure Janine will corroborate that.' He stared bluntly at Janine, still by the snooker table, her head now bowed, out of either deference or chagrin, if not both. 'I really must speak with her about recent developments.'

Paige exhaled heavily, from outrage or anxiety, it wasn't quite clear. 'If you're accusing Janine and me of collaborating in any way—'

'Then I'd probably be right,' he interrupted, regarding Bonnie once, but revealing little beyond his superior airs.

'Do you intend to intervene in this slave's correction?' Paige demanded.

'Oh, not at all,' Kane replied dryly. 'By all means, go ahead.'

'Good. Now, if you'll excuse us.'

'Just one thing, though.' He finally faced Bonnie directly. 'Will you keep thanking Lady Paige for each strike she gives you?'

'Of course she will,' Paige insisted.

But Kane ignored the interruption, his eyes still on Bonnie. 'Well, Bonnie? Will you?'

Bonnie's voice was taut as she responded, 'If Lady Paige wishes it so, then yes.'

'She knows the slave's fourth law, Kane,' Paige informed him unnecessarily. 'I had to teach it to her the other day, on the beach. *A punishment given by a master to a slave should be regarded as a gracious gift.*'

'Don't quote the slave laws to me, little sister. I helped father forge them when you were stuffing tissues in your training bra.' He moved closer to Bonnie, his voice low as he said, 'I'm going to ask you something now, Bonnie,

148

and I order you to give me a truthful answer. When you're thanking your mistress for the punishment, will you be meaning it?'

Bonnie surprised herself with the resolution in her answer; whether it was actually true or not was another story. 'No, master, I won't.'

Kane grinned as he backed away again. 'No, of course you won't.'

Paige scowled dubiously. 'Why should I care if she means it or not? As long as she says it.'

Kane shook his head. 'That's the difference between you and me, Paige. And that's the difference between you and a true master of slaves.

'She's forgotten the fifth law, Bonnie,' he concluded, the hint of a wry smile in his eyes, and then he turned and sauntered from the room.

A fifth law? Bonnie thought. How many laws were there for slaves on Iniscay?

'Pull up your knickers and wait for me outside my suite!' Paige snarled into her ear. 'And move it!'

Chapter Nine

Paige didn't keep her waiting long. She soon arrived with two assistants, and of course, they had to be Zoe and Rafael.

She pushed Bonnie into her private suite and turned on the light. Unlike Kane's, this one was not divided into two rooms, but was open plan. Her bed was just as large, of course, but there were also similarities to the Playroom. There was a wall rack of various punishment tools, and a pair of adjustable chains were suspended from a ceiling pulley, and another mounted to a round metal plate on the floor, directly below the ceiling chains, just in front of the bed.

Paige left them standing in the centre of the room as she reached for a box of cigars on a dressing table, lighting one up as she glanced with affected indifference at them. 'You two – undress your little plaything, then yourselves.'

They obeyed, but at one stage Zoe leaned close to Bonnie's ear and whispered, 'I'm sorry.'

Paige, lounging in a large leather chair, tapped grey ash into an ashtray and murmured, mocking Zoe's whispering, 'Not as sorry as the slave's going to be. And don't speak to her unless I give you permission.'

When they were naked Paige stubbed out the cigar although it was barely smoked. 'Good,' she said. 'Now stand together, to attention.'

Paige rose as they obeyed, like raw recruits to some

perverse military boot camp. Indeed, Paige, in her billowy olive blouse, pearl-coloured jodhpurs, and shiny black riding boots, and the way she deliberately paced before them, could have been a drill sergeant inspecting her troops.

Bonnie watched from the corner of her eye as Paige stopped first before Rafael, smirking at how he kept his body as still as possible, his eyes ahead, even as she reached down and took his penis in hand and held it as it stirred. 'I know all about you, dear Rafael. Never held a decent job in your life, have you? Content to toy-boy to some rich old woman, serving her until she died, and probably shocked to the core when you learned she never bothered to include you in her will. Such a pity,' she added, her voice dripping with sarcasm. 'Still, it brought you here, to us. To me. To do whatever I say. And love it.'

Bonnie saw Rafael bristle at Paige's taunts, his fists tighten at his sides. But Paige just grinned, as his penis rose to full thickness in her grip. 'You see?' Paige continued. 'Put aside your male ego; it means nothing to me.'

She moved on to Zoe, who could barely contain her trembling. Paige puckered her lips in mock sympathy, stroking the girl's face as if calming an agitated mare. 'Poor dear, why so nervous?' Paige's hand descended to Zoe's left breast, fingers running around the hardened nipple. 'Didn't the clubbers call you Daredevil, willing and wanting to push the envelope of propriety? You streaked in public, participated in a boat orgy on the Thames, performed oral sex on the lead singer of a rock band – in the middle of one of their concerts.' Paige's fingers trailed further down as she spoke, stopping and cupping Zoe's swollen pubic mound. 'And you're nervous before me? Perhaps I should be flattered. Or maybe it's just the company you've been keeping lately, dragging your standards down.'

Which brought her to Bonnie. At first her hands followed the same trail as they had on Zoe, though Paige's expression had turned from cruel amusement to undisguised dislike. 'And you. Maybe you think you're different from these two, but you're not. They came here of their own free will, but you've repeatedly chosen to stay, of your own free will. I've made you pay for that mistake, and will continue to do so.' The stark honesty of her threat was chilling. Her fingers took Bonnie's left nipple between them, squeezing, first gently, almost lovingly, before gradually building up the pressure, until Bonnie winced with the pain and fought to suppress the need to cry out or pull away.

'Kane seems to have abandoned your training,' Paige noted, clearly relishing the look on Bonnie's face. 'Almost as if he wanted to sabotage his own protegee's progress. And I normally wouldn't lift a finger to assist him, but this is a matter of personal pride to me.' She released Bonnie's nipple, then nodded towards Zoe and Rafael. 'You two, confine her to the chains.'

They instantly obeyed again. Bonnie did not struggle or resist, determined despite, or perhaps because of the pain Paige had just inflicted, that from this point on she would remain stoic. Her friends said nothing, wouldn't even look into her eyes, as they fastened the thick steel cuffs around her ankles and wrists. Bonnie shuddered at their brutal coldness, as she did at the feel of the metal floor plate beneath her feet. When she was secured her arms were drawn up to the ceiling as Paige worked the pulley, securing it only when Bonnie was stretched up, on the balls of her feet.

Bonnie twisted at the sounds behind her, desperate to know just what else was in store for her, but it was only Paige undressing. 'Don't be so impatient, my dear,' she smirked, 'you'll get a good look at me soon enough.'

Bonnie turned away and felt Zoe touch her stomach; a simple gesture of support that meant a great deal to the trussed girl.

And it didn't go unnoticed. 'We'll have none of that, Zoe,' said Paige. 'She's only to be touched by me.'

The hand withdrew as Paige returned into Bonnie's view, as naked as the rest of them. More so, in fact, as she wore no collar. But there was no mistaking who was in charge.

Her lithe frame was accentuated by her lack of clothes, though her ample breasts, beginning to show signs of losing the war of attrition with gravity, foiled any plans for a career in the ballet. Her skin was the colour of polished oyster, and made her tattoos ever more distinctive. She had a thorny rose on her right thigh, a galloping black steed on her shoulder, a butterfly perched on the nipple of her right breast, and an eagle below her navel, wings outstretched towards her hips, its talons curling into the trimmed nest of her blonde pubic hair.

Bonnie couldn't help but stare. Paige moved closer, until their nipples almost touched. The rich smell of tobacco and wine made an odd, but not unappealing, assault on Bonnie's senses. 'Like what you see?' Paige whispered huskily. 'I've had many worshippers.' She glanced at Zoe and Rafael. 'I shall have two more tonight. And you... you will follow.'

The sheer arrogance of the woman, matched only by her half-brother Kane, goaded Bonnie into clenching her jaw and her fists, refusing to play along.

Paige laughed and reached out, her touch electric against Bonnie's skin. 'Your eyes say no,' she teased, her fingers descending between Bonnie's legs, nestling in her pubic bush, and her varnished fingertips grazed the lips of Bonnie's sex, 'but your body can't lie to me.' She dipped into Bonnie's vagina, finding it wet and welcoming. Bonnie whimpered, then groaned as those fingers slid all-too-easily into her. The effect was spectacular, making Bonnie quiver.

Paige moved even closer, until her breasts moulded against Bonnie's. Bonnie tried to push back, to feel the pressure increase on her aching nipples, but she barely had enough leverage to keep steady. She could feel the heat from Paige's mouth as the woman whispered, 'The fifth slave's law: *A slave can only achieve true satisfaction when she has learned not just to obey, but to want to obey, not just to accept punishment, but to desire it.*

'That's what Kane referred to earlier. Maybe he thought he could embarrass me into abandoning my plans for you, so he could come along and succeed where I would have failed. But I will not fail. You'll want to touch yourself, but you can't. You'll want to close your eyes, but you won't. Before long I'll have you begging to lick my feet.'

The words sent an uncontrollable pulse to Bonnie's vulva, but despite the pleasure of it, Bonnie gasped and sighed, 'N-never.'

Paige sniggered. 'Never say never, my dear. I'd bet a box of Havana's finest that you won't last ten minutes.'

She withdrew her fingers, bringing them to her mouth to smell and taste Bonnie's dew, before reaching out towards Zoe and Rafael and grabbing their collars. 'And you two: don't even think to deny you find the idea of worshipping my body in front of this wretch appealing. Rafael can't hide his reaction, and your eyes give you away too, Zoe. You may be friends together, but your urge to serve me is undeniable.'

Bonnie watched helplessly as Paige drew the two hares to her bed, and the threesome climbed onto the black silk sheets. Paige closed her eyes and stretched out, languishing as they began touching her and stroking her. Zoe moved up and kissed her, and Bonnie could see her lips peeling apart and imagined her friend's tongue slipping into Paige's mouth. She watched Paige open her eyes, her tongue probably dancing vibrantly with Zoe's, as Rafael ran confident hands over Paige's gently writhing body.

The sheer erotic charge in the room made Bonnie quiver, and her arms tingled uncomfortably above her head. Her mouth was dry, and she was coated by a delicate sheen of perspiration.

Paige rolled and guided Zoe beneath her, trailing kisses over her firm breasts, across her stomach to the pink folds of her moist labia, parting their succulence with her fingertips and drinking in the released perfume. She paused, and then pierced Zoe with two straightened fingers. She paused again, gauging Zoe's reaction, and then her tongue joined her two pumping digits, lapping at the nectar and teasing the engorged clitoris. She was clearly no novice to the pleasures of the female flesh. Zoe moaned and arched her back, her breasts rising invitingly, and Paige glanced at Bonnie; silently taunting and challenging her bound slave.

Bonnie squirmed impotently in her metal bonds, eddies of pleasure churning upwards in greater intensity as she rubbed her thighs together, feeling them moisten with her juices. She could barely control the dark sensuality that had risen from within since arriving at Iniscay, and now was no exception. She could imagine herself being touched, as Zoe was being touched; giving pleasure and receiving it. If she concentrated hard enough she could almost feel the touch of soft flesh upon her own, caressing, demanding. It seemed so real, and was so unfair.

Rafael did not remain inactive among the threesome, moving behind Paige's crouched body, reaching between her parted thighs and delving deep inside her with expert fingers. Her mouth still planted on Zoe's vulva, Paige groaned aloud, bucking against his rapid thrusts.

Bonnie twisted, earnestly rubbing her thighs together, her pussy pulsing with eager passion. The frustration was worse than being chained to the post before Martin. She wanted to close her eyes, her ears, her mind to it all, but tortured herself with the knowledge that even if she could shut down her senses, she wouldn't. Paige had been right, damn her.

Paige lay on her back, her head hanging over the foot of the bed and her hair sweeping the carpet as she stared at Bonnie, while two pairs of hands and lips worshipped her. Rafael worked his way to her sex again, drinking her copious juices, as Zoe worked on her upstanding nipples.

Bonnie was on fire as she watched Rafael mount Paige, pumping into the woman like a rutting stag. And still Paige stared at Bonnie, refusing to release her, giving no quarter in the battle of wills. Bonnie was consumed, her mind and body spiralling into an undeniable climax, matching the lovers on the bed. She watched Rafael, his shaft driving in and out, his balls slapping against his mistress.

And that was enough for Bonnie. The orgasm swamped her and she cried out, losing all self-control as the climax washed over her in unrelenting waves, and her head lolled forward, her chin on her chest.

The chains clinked as they slackened and Bonnie was vaguely aware of the tension on her arms lessening. She collapsed to her knees, as much from surprise and exhaustion as from the aftereffects of her climax, the strength and will long since drained from her like water from a sponge. Someone – she opened her eyes again to see it was Paige – stood before her, still naked, having left her two lovers watching from the bed. The aroma of Paige's sex, mingled with the scents of Zoe and Rafael, was rich and heady.

Bonnie, her wrists and ankles still chained, looked up into a triumphant smile, and listened vaguely to the monotone voice or her tormentor. 'Well, Bonnie? Did you appreciate your punishment?'

Tears meandering down her cheeks, Bonnie nodded weakly. 'Y-yes... mistress.'

There was an undeniable look of triumph in those hazel eyes above Bonnie, as Paige took a handful of her slave's hair. 'So, what should you say?'

'Thu-thank you, mistress,' she stammered, between gentle sobs.

Paige pretended not to hear, clearly delighted by the first response, nevertheless. 'What was that?' she goaded, humiliating Bonnie to the utmost. 'What did you say, you snivelling little creature?'

Bonnie was stunned by the sincerity, not only in her words but in her heart, as she repeated clearly, 'Thank you, mistress.'

Paige's smile spread into an ecstatic grin. 'And what should you do to thank me properly – conclusively?'

Bonnie hadn't forgotten. It was now inevitable that this woman would command her totally. She lowered her face and began kissing Paige's feet in homage.

It was later, in a more temperate frame of mind, that Bonnie's pride began to torture her for crumbling before Paige. Had Paige beaten her to defeat it would have been different. But the woman hadn't even touched her, and still Bonnie fell under her spell, convinced now that the Castlewell allure was not limited to the men.

It was a further degradation to see Zoe and Rafael. What must they think of her now, having witnessed her descent into total submission to that bitch?

She avoided them for the rest of the evening and most of the next morning, until Zoe confronted her whilst dusting in the library.

'Bonnie, I must talk with you,' she said.

Bonnie never looked away from her task, trying to ignore the girl. 'I'm really very busy, Miss Zoe.'

Zoe moved close to her. 'Bonnie, I just wanted to apologise.'

'Apologise?' Bonnie was surprised. 'Why should you do that?'

'If Rafael was here he'd be apologising, too,' Zoe explained. 'We should have stood up to her. I was afraid; afraid of being disqualified from the hunt. But it wasn't just that. I... I wanted to see you chained. I wanted to worship Paige in front of you, to tease you like that.' She looked away, blushing. 'I'm ashamed of myself.'

Bonnie's head span at the unexpected confession. And there she was, ashamed of her own behaviour! It was such a sweet gesture on Zoe's part, that Bonnie dropped the duster and wrapped an arm around Zoe, pulling her close and hugging her tightly. 'Don't worry about it,' she said, 'we're all slaves here, one way or another.'

Zoe stroked Bonnie's hair and looked at her affectionately. 'So, what do you think will happen now, with Kane and Paige and yourself?' she asked.

Bonnie pondered the question for a while. 'Well,' she eventually said, 'Paige will think she's broken my spirit and that any further intimidation on her part will send me packing – assuming she doesn't claim me as a gift for her father. I don't know about Kane; he seems to be avoiding being close to me. Sometimes he even takes sides with Paige, like he did at the dinner table the other night. Maybe he wants me to go, too.' Her brow furrowed with thought. 'After the beating the night before he told me that being a master has its restraints, too. He seemed almost flustered...' she lowered her eyes, feeling silly for the opinion she was about to voice. 'I... I think he's attracted to me... and not just as a slave.'

'I know how he feels,' Zoe confessed quietly, her warm breath ruffling Bonnie's fringe.

Bonnie smiled, melting before the sexy beauty of her new friend. 'I have to somehow gain an advantage over them both,' she said, trying to concentrate on the matter at hand. 'The hunt is one important key. And Martin's the other.'

'Martin? Are you sure?'

Bonnie nodded. 'I am.'

'Well then,' Zoe smiled, with a conspiratorial glint in her eye. 'Work your immense charms on him.'

Bonnie thought about Martin's confession to her, and shook her head. 'It's not that simple... but there may be a way...' She glanced at Zoe, a plan unfolding in her mind. 'If you and Rafael will help me.'

'Anything, anytime, anywhere,' Zoe said confidently.

Just then the library door burst open and Janine stomped in. 'There you are, you lazy cow!' She held up a damp, dirty dishcloth; a prosecutor presenting damning evidence to the jury. 'You left this hanging on the kitchen sink, instead of depositing it in the laundry bin!'

Bonnie sighed wearily. 'You know I didn't do that,' she said, although she knew there was absolutely no point in arguing; they would punish her anyway.

Janine stiffened at the audacity of the girl, and flung the dishcloth at her. 'How dare you accuse me of lying,' she snarled menacingly. 'How dare you!'

'Now, there's no need for—'

Janine stabbed a finger in Zoe's direction. 'And I advise you not to interfere with Manor business!' She reached out and grabbed Bonnie by the wrist. 'Come on you trollop, I'll punish you in the kitchen so we won't upset your girlfriend—!'

That did it. Savage anger welled within Bonnie; anger from her continuing humiliation at the hands of Kane and Paige, and from Janine's repeated and unfair harassment. It rose and galvanised her body, and snatching free from Janine's grip, she swung a fist through the air. From Janine's expression, she only registered the approach of the tightly clenched missile at the very last moment. The blow caught her on the side of the head and she crumpled to the floor, her howl of surprise and pain echoing around the library.

Bonnie stood there, her breasts heaving as she breathed heavily, her knuckles smarting, feeling as astonished as Zoe looked. Then Janine was up again, fighting back like a spitting cat and sending them both to the floor, shouting and biting and pulling each other's hair, oblivious to Zoe's attempts to break them apart.

It took a seldom heard though nonetheless compelling voice to stop the fighting. 'That's enough!'

Bonnie and Janine looked up from behind their dishevelled hair at the figure of Victor Castlewell, standing in the doorway, a leather-bound book under one arm. Dressed in black, eyes ablaze but unreadable, he could have been some stern minister about to deliver a sermon to his God-fearing flock. Without taking his eyes off the two girls on the floor, he set the book on a nearby side-table and clutched his hands behind his back.

'When I was a soldier in the Italian Army,' he began, once certain he had the full attention of the disorderly threesome, 'I grappled with a fellow sergeant over a local woman. An officer who encountered us demanded an explanation. The sergeant and I forwent our differences long enough to both claim it was simply an exercise in unarmed combat. I tell you this because, as with that officer long ago, any similar explanation for your behaviour now will be equally discounted as fanciful.' He smirked, the most expressive look Bonnie had ever seen on his face, and his story the most words she had ever heard him compile at one time.

Janine immediately pushed Bonnie away and managed to scramble to her feet. 'Master,' she blurted, her shoulders rising and falling violently as she struggled to control her anger, 'this slave attacked me, without provocation!'

'That's not true, Lord Victor,' Zoe insisted, with surprising poise. 'Janine insulted me, and Bonnie was doing nothing more than defending me.'

'Lying bitch!' spat Janine.

'I said, that's enough,' Victor repeated with calm authority, and the squabbling females fell silent as if someone had thrown a switch.

The door opened again and Kane entered. 'What's all this, father?' he asked. 'What's happening?'

'Nothing more than a difference of opinion, it would seem,' said Victor, his inscrutable eyes never leaving Bonnie.

'I think I'd better deal with this,' Kane said, stepping forward determinedly. But Victor held up a hand before his son, stopping him in his tracks without looking at him.

'No,' he said firmly, 'they'll deal with it… in the cage.'

Kane frowned. Janine breathed sharply. And Bonnie glanced at Zoe, seeing a similar lack of comprehension as her own in her friend's expression.

It was quite literally a metal cage, a little higher than a tall man, and roughly three metres square.

It was behind the stables, and most of the household had gathered there to witness what promised to be an extremely entertaining contest. Bonnie and Janine stood naked, eyeing each other with clear hatred while Tim prepared a long leather strap with a loop at each end.

Kane stood on a small dais grandly announcing the few rules of combat, for the benefit of Bonnie and those who had not yet witnessed such a contest on Iniscay.

'You enter the cage together, tied at the wrist,' he bellowed. 'No permanent damage is to be inflicted by either of you, but otherwise, the fight continues until one of you relents.'

'And what happens between the two of you in the cage, stays in the cage,' Victor added. 'I would be extremely disappointed if this needs to be settled again at a later date.'

Zoe and Rafael were with Bonnie, massaging her back and shoulders to loosen the muscles. Zoe kissed her on the cheek, and then Kane approached and attached one of the leather loops around her left wrist, as he had just done to Janine. They were only about a metre apart now, and would stay that way until the fight's end. Janine swore under her breath at Bonnie, but Bonnie refused to be goaded, and took the opportunity to assess her opponent for one last time. The cage door opened with a tired creak and a clang, and then Janine tugged on the lead, and they step inside.

'The fight commences when the door closes,' Kane declared melodramatically, unable to restrain his ardour. 'And may the worst girl win!'

Janine turned on Bonnie and slammed her into the cage barely before the door was closed.

The spectators moved to completely surround the attraction, shouting encouragement and advise, some supporting Janine, but most rooting for Bonnie, having seen her on the receiving end for much of the past week.

Bonnie kept her free fist raised, while her bound hand

twisted to grasp the strap that connected her to her opponent, determined not to let the little hellcat take advantage again; she may have fought in the cage before, but never with Bonnie!

Their heels and toes dug into the dry dirt beneath, sending up clouds of dust. Bonnie's mouth and nose filled with it. She moved forward and took a swing at the dodging girl ahead of her, bold and hard. And, unfortunately, telegraphed from a mile away. Janine easily dodged the swipe. She, on the other hand, wound up and slammed Bonnie full in the face, knocking her to the ground and nearly falling herself due to the wrench on the strap.

Such was the speed and severity of the blow that the spectators fell into silence, as if unsure of what they'd just seen. Stunned and shaken, Bonnie quickly checked her teeth with her tongue, and was relieved to find nothing broken or missing... just extremely sore. Above her, Janine was grinning, silently motioning for her to rise and take another blow.

But Bonnie kicked hard at Janine's legs, landing a lucky blow on her knee. Janine fell too, to the returning cheers of the spectators, and Bonnie moved to sit on her and pin her down. But Janine recovered enough to struggle, their efforts somehow bringing them back to their feet again.

They circled each other, each keeping a tight pull on the strap, never daring to look away, asking for no quarter, and receiving none. For Bonnie, who had never been in a real fight before, it was both a terrifying and exhilarating ordeal. She'd never felt so alive or so alert. And despite Janine's experience in such conflicts, Bonnie sensed that she had the greater strength, and that would eventually be the deciding factor.

And so it proved as they finally came together, breast to breast, gripping each other, seeking some advantage, some mistake the other might make that could be exploited. Bonnie glared into Janine's eyes, reflecting the hatred she now felt. Then Janine spat in Bonnie's face, trying to shock or distract Bonnie enough for her to seize control. But it didn't work. In fact, it incited Bonnie – into feinting to one side. Suddenly no longer pushing with all her might against her opponent, Janine tumbled forward. Bonnie sidestepped neatly and kicked her in the rump as she stumbled facedown into the dirt again.

Bonnie wasted no time, falling onto Janine's lower back and twisting the girl's free arm behind her until she howled. Teeth clenched, eyes wide, Bonnie snarled, 'That's it, bitch! Give in!'

'Fuck you!'

Janine struggled, but Bonnie pressed her advantage, using just enough force to make Janine cry out again. 'Well?' she panted. 'What now?'

The crowd fell silent as Janine gasped, collected her breath, then nodded weakly.

'It is done,' Kane declared.

The onlookers mumbled their approval, but Bonnie barely heard them, more intent was she in removing the strap from Janine's wrist, and then her own. Then she rose and used the leather strap to beat the girl's vulnerable buttocks, again and again, releasing what little angry energy remained within her, and relishing every second of it. Only when she tired did she drop the strap onto the ground beside the conscious but still-prostrate figure of her former opponent. And Bonnie knew, with a cathartic rush of certainty, that Janine would never trouble her again.

The door was opened, and Bonnie hobbled out to the congratulations of her supporters. She looked at Victor, Kane, and Paige, standing together, and waited, heedless of her nudity, until the sounds of the people around her evaporated. 'Now, if you'll excuse me, masters and mistress,' she said, with as much dignity as she could muster, 'I still have much work to do today.'

And then, collecting her clothes and departing with Zoe and Rafael, she never heard Victor murmur, 'She's quite a specimen. I shall enjoy taking her from you, Kane.'

Paige huffed and stormed back to the house without comment. Victor smirked, fully aware of the rivalry between the siblings; her reaction was completely expected. Less expected was Kane's, who also stomped away in a silent tantrum. It took a moment for Victor to divine the reason, but when he did, his smirk grew into a broad smile.

Chapter Ten

Bonnie felt more trepidation now than she had before entering the cage with Janine. It was evening, long after her duties had been fulfilled, and not long after spending time with Rafael and Zoe, preparing herself for what was about to follow. If she'd miscalculated and he reacted the wrong way, she knew she would be less fearful than regretful, but that it would, in its own way, hurt as much as any physical punishment.

Music could be heard from the games room, but the second floor was quiet and the corridors, mercifully, empty. She stopped outside his door and looked down at herself, certain she must appear ridiculous. Still, nothing ventured... she tapped tentatively on the door.

There was an anxious pause, and just as she considered aborting the ridiculous scheme, a familiar voice called and bade her enter.

Summoning her courage, she slipped into the room and quickly closed the door behind her, unable to turn back now. She was immediately struck by the living room section of Martin Castlewell's suite, which reminded her so much of her office in her old life. There were bookcases crammed with a personal library on all subjects, magazine clippings stacked haphazardly on free spaces, one wall covered with flow charts and diagrams, and a table cluttered with electronic parts and scattered tools. It was almost purely functional, with no regard for social calls, and seemingly chaotic, but in fact possessing an organisation identifiable by the occupant alone.

Martin sat in front of one of two monitors on a computer table, tapping away at the keyboard. 'Yes, who is it?' he said, without looking up.

Bonnie opened her mouth to speak, then caught her reflection in a full-length mirror. She was dressed in a black T-shirt and jeans, donated by Rafael, her breasts flattened by wrappings of cloth so as to be no longer prominent, her hair tucked beneath a baseball cap, and her face free of make-up. The oversized clothes were baggy, giving her a youthful look. Overall it was an arresting illusion, at least at first glance, and she hoped it would suffice. She cleared her throat, holding onto the handle of the leash now attached to her slave collar, the cold links of the chain tickling her bare forearm. Then she answered uncertainly. 'It's Bennie, sir. The new assistant groundskeeper.'

Martin looked up, amazement freezing his expression. 'Bonnie?' he gasped incredulously. 'Is that you?'

She stepped forward. 'No sir, not Bonnie, it's Bennie. I've just arrived on the island, and they sent me to see you.'

Martin rose, his work forgotten as he continued to stare. 'Bonnie, what the hell are you doing?'

She continued to feign innocence, finding the role easier to play than anticipated. 'I don't know what you're talking about, sir. As I said, I've just arrived here, and I've been told you'll be teaching me the ropes.'

'I don't believe this,' Martin said, shaking his head. 'I just don't believe it.'

'Please, sir,' Bonnie said, reaching out to touch his arm. 'I need you to guide me. I'll do whatever you want.'

A little perspiration broke out on Martin's forehead. 'Whatever...' he stopped and cleared his throat a little, 'whatever I want?'

She nodded, pouting, and handed him the free end of the leash. 'Just tell me what I must do, sir.' She couldn't quite read what was in his eyes, but it seemed positive. And so she held her breath, sensing the moment was right, and slowly lowered her hand to the front of his trousers. She watched his face, trying to gauge his reactions and mood, not wanting to make any mistakes now, and sighed quietly with relief as her palm encountered the warm and prominent outline of an erection within the taut material. She silently congratulated herself for the ingenuity of her seduction plan.

Martin shuddered and pulled on the leash, drawing her close into a clumsy embrace, their lips grinding and tongues entwining. Bonnie was taken aback by his rough intensity, and only when he thrust a hand down between her legs and found a bulge there equal to his own, did he pull back, his eyes wide as he stared down. 'What the...'

Bonnie shuffled back a little, surprised at how turned on she was by this bizarre encounter, and unzipped and opened her jeans. She freed the large plastic cock she wore strapped to her hips inside the jeans; another donation from Zoe. Looking up into Martin's eyes she gripped the pink shaft and massaged it idly, suggestively. 'Surprised?' she asked, innocently.

'No,' he whispered. 'Envious.'

Then he was upon her again, kissing her passionately, her rigid cock digging into his own crotch. The throbbing between her thighs, no longer to be regarded

169

as nerves, had grown more insistent; this role-playing had sparked a new excitement within her, sending her sex into a fluttering, pulsing state of desire. Squirming from his avid grasp she sank to her knees and reached out to unzip his tented trousers. Once they were gaping she rummaged inside and tugged forth his erection. His shaft bobbed into view, long and thick with a pronounced ridge around the helmet. She gently held it by the base as she had done her own, looked up with sparkling eyes that conveyed anticipation, and cooed breathlessly, 'You have nothing to be envious about, sir.'

He closed his eyes and groaned softly as she whispered, 'Bennie would like to suck your meaty cock, sir,' and then took his bursting erection into her mouth without awaiting a response. He tasted salty on her tongue, and she could feel him stiffen further inside her as his balls worked free and bobbed against her chin while she rocked slowly back and forth. She licked along the veined underside, enjoying the moans she induced from him, as she relished the swell of her breasts against their constricting strapping and the gathering dew as the base of her own cock rubbed rhythmically against her erect clitoris.

'No,' he suddenly gasped, his breath quickening. 'Not like this.'

Though disappointed, wanting to accept the poor man's seed into her mouth, Bonnie allowed his cock to plop wetly from between her lips. She wiped the back of her hand across her mouth and tasted his pre-come, then looked up, a picture of wide-eyed innocence again. 'I've never done anything like this to another man, sir,' she said quietly. 'I hope I please you.'

Martin just looked down at her, apparently frozen to the spot, his erection pulsing before her face. So she stood up, took him by the hand, and led him through to his adjoining bedroom. Their rigid penises swayed in unison as they walked together in silence.

When she reached the bed Bonnie turned and kissed him, gently milking his cock in her fist. With her free hand she unfastened his trousers and allowed them to drop to his ankles, and then levered off her trainers and dropped her jeans. She stepped out of them and urged the dumbfounded Martin onto the bed, and as he knelt on all fours she eased off his shoes, untangled his trousers from his ankles, and then slid his underpants down and off. He was breathing heavily, but did nothing to object or resist. Bonnie found the small tube of hand-cream hidden in the pocket of her discarded jeans and coated the false cock sprouting from her groin, the unbelievable excitement of the encounter making the breath catch in her lungs. Then she heard Martin groan as her weight joined his on the mattress, and she settled between his parted knees. She felt nervous, not really knowing what to do, but she took a deep breath, held the plastic cock and pressed the tip between his buttocks and against his puckered entrance, and slowly leaned forward.

Martin's back arched and his head lifted as she sank into him until her pubic down buffeted gently against his bottom, and Bonnie knew she was fully embedded inside him. 'Are you okay, sir?' she whispered breathlessly, but all he could do was grunt and nod his head limply in reply. 'Do you want me to move?' she asked again, genuinely unsure of what to do, and not wanting to hurt him. Martin nodded again and shuddered. Bonnie withdrew until just the bulbous tip was lodged in his rectum, and then pushed forward again, her confidence building. Then she reached beneath him, one hand cupping his dangling balls and the other curled around his prick. It throbbed in her tight fist, and as she set about a gently sawing rhythm in and out of his backside, Martin groaned loudly and she heard his spunk thrum down onto the duvet beneath his bucking hips. She squeezed his helmet affectionately and felt more of his warm seed ooze between her fingers as she massaged it from his balls. Bonnie kissed his shoulder and they slumped forward together onto the soft comfort of the bed.

They remained like that for a while, relaxing in each other's arms, saying nothing. And then Bonnie felt a stirring in her hand, and slowly, very slowly, Martin's dormant and sticky penis reawakened and grew to its former proud state.

'I'd like to do the same to you now,' he whispered through the darkness. 'If you're willing, of course.'

Bonnie didn't know what to say, but she didn't want to let him down, and the idea of doing something so wicked secretly thrilled her. 'I—'

'It's okay,' Martin said prematurely, 'I understand.'

'Let me finish,' whispered Bonnie. 'I was going to say, I'd like to try it with you... if you're gentle with me.'

Martin rose and she let him position her as she had done him. He managed to find the tube of cream and prepared himself, and then shuffled between the beautiful girl's thighs, asked her if she was ready, and then penetrated her bottom with one lunge.

It hurt her, but the pleasure gradually eclipsed the

discomfort until she was revelling in the delicious sensations. She buried her face in the bedcovers as she cried out, the climax taking hold of her with surprising ferocity.

Martin came too, and she used her tight rear passage to drain him of every last drop. Then he collapsed on her. Bonnie supported him for a moment, until he withdrew, and they nestled together like spoons. His arm lay over her, his softening cock nudged between her cheeks, their come mingling and seeping quietly from her channel.

'Why do you stay here, Martin?' she asked quietly. 'You're far too nice for such a place.'

He found her tightly encased breasts. 'This was a nice touch,' he sighed dreamily, ignoring her question.

She tilted her face towards him persistently. 'Well? You've brains and talent—' She felt his body tense as he interrupted.

'So all I need now is courage to leave the island and go out into the big wide world. Unless...'

'Yes?' she encouraged.

'Unless,' he repeated, in the same speculative tone, 'unless, of course, you came with me. You have courage enough for both of us.'

Bonnie stared into the dark, before replying. 'I can't,' she said. 'My destiny is here in some fashion. I can sense it, as I've never sensed anything before.'

'But you're abused here. You're treated as a slave.'

'It's my own choice, Martin,' she insisted. 'I have a role to play here, maybe in the house, maybe even in the hunt—'

'Forget the hunt, Bonnie,' he interrupted again. 'You couldn't win it. None of the hares could.'

Bonnie didn't like what she was hearing. 'Why not?' she probed. There was a pregnant pause, and she could sense his internal struggle.

'Don't ask me, please Bonnie.'

She wanted to delve further, but decided against it and settled down again. 'Let's just go to sleep,' she whispered.

Martin agreed, soon falling into a deep slumber. But after a time Bonnie gently eased herself from him, picked up her clothes and shoes, and left the bedroom. Once in the living room she removed the suddenly ridiculous-looking dildo, slipped back into her clothes, and then moved to the computers, which continued to glow and hum quietly through the darkness of the room.

She made a cursory examination, and couldn't believe what she saw; they were undoubtedly password protected, but her unexpected entrance earlier had caused him to forget to shut them down. She had access!

Skills she hadn't used in weeks resurfaced, her mind scanning menus and submenus, seeking answers to so many questions.

Soon she learned that one terminal gave her access to the outside world, through modems and televisual conference comlinks. It seemed Victor Castlewell used this to do his legitimate business. But the second monitor appeared to be part of a separate, hardened mainframe, with no access to it except from here, and perhaps one other place. That indicated a closed system, and behind it a great anxiety about anyone finding out its secrets.

This, too, was open to Bonnie. And as she began accessing its secrets, she finally understood what Martin had meant; whatever the hunt entailed and whoever was involved, none of the hares had a chance of winning.

Chapter Eleven

'I think I'm a present for Victor Castlewell, once I've been prepared. I'm... I'm still trying to decide why I remain.'

Martin sat before the scanning monitor, replaying the recorded incident of Bonnie in the gym's showers with Zoe and Rafael, before Kane's arrival. They'd thought to turn on all the showers around them, so the noise and steam would affect anyone covertly watching and listening.

Unless those watching and listening had the right equipment to filter out the unwanted distractions, leaving only the naked bodies, and naked voices.

Martin reached for his mug of cappuccino, graciously provided by Delilah, who in all her years of service on the island – and before, when she was Victor's private cook in the outside world – had always been there for his needs. He sipped cautiously, drinking in not only the taste but the heat; though the house was kept at a constantly comfortable temperature by the computer, it always seemed colder at dawn.

He smacked his lips; how such simple pleasures can mean so much, he thought. Then he reran the tape, increasing the fine-tuning on the sound and visuals. Bonnie's naked form clarified, grew closer to the truth he held not only on canvas, but in his own mind. So many of the fools who willingly ventured into this bizarre world of his father's design were deadheads who deserved everything they received.

But not Bonnie.

The beauty of her mind was a match for her body. He reached out to the screen, as if to stroke the curve of her breasts. Yes, unbelievably, Martin now understood what Kane, and Paige, and the others, saw in this one.

He watched Zoe glance at Rafael, before turning back to Bonnie. *'Have you ever been involved in the S&M scene, Bonnie?'*

His beautiful angel paused, before answering, *'Not before I came here.'*

Martin grimaced, as if something was wrong with his coffee. With statements like hers, and her subsequent reactions, he could understand how his siblings might doubt Bonnie's story. If she was new to the Scene, then she'd taken to it more swiftly than a duck to water. She could easily be some sort of government or corporate spy, or a journalist. The possibility remained open, as a professional in either job would surely have been willing to go as far as Bonnie had in the pursuit of evidence, a story, or material for blackmailing the Castlewells. If so, could he track down who had sent her?

On the screen Bonnie was kneeling, following Kane's off-screen directing, going down on Zoe. Beneath his dressing gown, Martin's penis stirred to life. He recalled her initial meeting with his family, when she was first being prepared in the Playroom. Paige had remarked how unlikely it was that a girl such as Bonnie could find herself in a place like this. Secretly, Martin had agreed; he'd learned long ago that when something appeared to be too good to be true, it usually was. On the other hand, Kane had been right, too; sometimes fortune did smile, even on the hopelessly decadent and unworthy. On another hand, however…

He shook his head and chuckled into his coffee. He sometimes felt as if father had selectively bred children by his three mistresses; Kane to play the cool aristocrat and charm the women, Paige to play the hot-tempered hellion that kept Kane in check, and Martin to do the drudge work. Not that he minded much. Let them play their little games; he had other things to occupy him.

The office door swung open and Kane, dressed in a black and red kimono, entered. He stopped before the desk and folded his arms across his chest. 'This had better be worth waking me—'

Martin cut him off, striking a few controls. 'You were the one that wanted to be alerted if Bonnie was up to anything unusual. "Day or night", was, I believe, the phrase you used. I ordered the computer to wake me if it detected Bonnie leaving the house… and it has.'

Kane turned to face the bank of nine television monitors on the wall beside the door, just as it opened again and Paige joined them, yawning in an aquamarine dressing gown. 'This had better be worth waking me up for, Martin,' she complained blearily.

He smiled, wondering if they'd taken lessons in arrogance from the same instructor, and watching as they glared at each other. Eventually they called a silent truce, and both turned to the bank of monitors. 'So,' Kane broke the uneasy silence, 'what's she up to?'

Martin sat up straight and keyed in a pre-programmed sequence, showing recordings just taken from external cameras at different angles: the south-eastern trail towards the cove, with Bonnie in her grey jogging outfit and trainers, running along with two others.

Paige was watching closely. 'Are they—?'

'Zoe and Rafael,' Kane answered absently. 'The two hares she seems to have made allies of.'

'Mmmm,' pondered Paige. 'Janine said she was talking alone with Zoe in the library yesterday. That's what caused the showdown in the cage.'

'Yep,' Martin concurred, pretending to examine some notes. 'The scans indicate that she's spent more time alone with them than anyone else.'

Kane nodded at the lower right screen, which was still playing the recorded scene in the shower. 'Did you manage to clear that up?' he asked. 'Did you hear what they were talking about before I surprised them?'

'No,' Martin lied, more easily than he would have imagined.

Kane looked back at the live images. 'Are they escaping? Meeting some boat, perhaps?'

'Actually,' Martin said, pausing to yawn, 'they're jogging. I heard them say so several times.'

Kane turned on Martin in disbelief; a disbelief matched and mirrored by Paige. 'And you woke me up just for this?' he snapped incredulously. 'To watch them jogging?'

Martin rose to his feet, setting his mug aside, appearing to be the very font of innocence. 'I don't recall you – either of you – specifying anything unusual except for jogging. It's hardly my fault you give such vague orders.'

Paige bared her teeth. 'Prick,' she hissed, before storming out of the office with a whirl of her dressing gown.

Martin looked at Kane, who had turned back to the screens. 'I want a copy of everything she's done, every room she's been in, audio and video, since her arrival.'

'Not possible, Kane, and you know that. Our own suites don't have any hidden cameras and microphones. It's just the hares' rooms and the common rooms—'

'Then get me what you can,' he interrupted firmly, his eyes still fixed upon the images. 'And soon. The hunters arrive this afternoon.'

Martin was about to tell Kane he already knew that, but decided to refrain from doing so, gazing not at the screens but at his half-brother. He knew Kane wasn't concerned about security, that he didn't want the recordings for business. For a moment Martin shared an empathy with him he had never known before. It was a remarkable experience, for the split second it lasted. 'Will she be a part of the hunt?' he asked.

'If he wants her, he'll include her,' Kane said enigmatically. 'And he'll ensure she's captured for his own pleasures, and not for the other hunters.'

Martin looked beneath the surface of Kane's words and decided to pry a little deeper. 'And have you prepared her for what lies ahead?'

'She's just about ready.' Kane tensed a little. 'Do you have any other questions, brother?'

Martin's expression hardened and he leaned forward, his hands on the desk, his stare challenging. 'Yes, I have. Why are we such grovelling little wimps? You, me, and Paige. Why do we give so much of ourselves to that man – our lives, our time, our devotion – to get so little in return? Tell me, Kane… why?'

Martin was surprised to see his words had got to Kane. Their eyes met – really met – just for that instant, before Kane turned away with a mortified blush creeping into his cheeks. Martin, without ever wanting to cut him any slack whatsoever before, now averted his stare, pretending not to notice. But he listened as Kane replied. 'I know why Paige and I do it. Only you know why you do it.'

Martin watched him leave without another word. He sat down again after a time, lifting his mug to find his drink had chilled. For want of anything better to do he started work on Kane's request, calling up all visual and audio records of Bonnie since she'd arrived. It was easy enough, because the computer kept constant track of her through the transponder in her collar, and could cross-reference that with the secret recordings it automatically made of everyone, with special high-definition documentation made if the computer recognised certain key words and phrases involving possible sexual activity.

What Kane and Paige didn't know was that their suites were monitored, as per father's wishes. Martin had at his disposal recordings of times Bonnie spent in their respective suites, as well as past liaisons with the other staff, and the hares. Of course, Martin would not include those sessions in the disc he'd prepare for Kane. Oh no, those were for father's private collection. Father had shown interest in Bonnie lately, too. Wheels within wheels.

Martin refused to allow his own rooms to be monitored, and as he was the only one on the island able to operate this equipment, even father couldn't refuse him. And he never passed on to father any knowledge of Paige's conspiracy with Janine to intimidate Bonnie into leaving the island, half-hoping that Bonnie would do the sensible thing, and get away. Nor would he reveal Bonnie's conspiracies with Zoe and Rafael. And of course, father and Kane would never learn of Martin's own wonderful times with her.

He turned in his chair and faced the window, where the sun was turning the dawn sky a patchwork of pastel pinks and blues. He always tried to convince himself he was separate from all that passed on Iniscay, something above his family and their intrigues and vices. But Bonnie's words rang loudly in his mind: *'Why do you stay here, Martin?'*

At one time Martin had answers for why he remained: fear, and loyalty.

But now, only the question remained.

When Bonnie had seen the wall map of the island in Martin's office, it immediately struck her how it was shaped like nothing more than a bird, a bird with the manor and the surrounding gardens at its heart.

'A bird of prey,' Isobelle had clarified for her, as she helped her clean up. 'According to Lord Victor. A kestrel, diving to attack its prey, its wings folding back towards its body. He'll entertain no other comparison.'

Knowing the man's predilections for hunting, and the life he espoused here, it was not surprising. The image stuck with Bonnie. Seen in context with the mainland, it seemed to be escaping from it towards freer climes, as the Castlewells had escaped from the outside world and its constricting mores. Only when she had begun her dawn run with Zoe and Rafael was she able to fully appreciate the beauty and splendour of her new home.

They'd started in the cove where MacTaggart had first deposited her. From here the mainland was in view, the village a white smudge, the dawn light bent around the slopes, filling valleys with slate and emerald shadow.

Her initial look at the map had convinced Bonnie that

Iniscay wasn't as big as she first imagined, but her first run dispelled any such conviction. They jogged eastward, scattering colonies of nesting or foraging birds. They protested, none more loudly than the gannets, who despite their cute appearance sounded like shrill harpies. Occasionally Bonnie would glance back, expecting to be followed, but seeing only their own footprints behind them.

As they neared the eastern tip the island grew stark, with sand dunes bound by soft marram grass, and further inland, greensward, rich with lime from the shell sand, supporting carpets of wildflowers.

Changes could be seen once the runners left the eastern point and proceeded northwards. The island's trees, which in the landward side almost reached the water, here were farther back, fronted by patches of peat bog, and dotted with gnarled grey rocks and lochans of brown, bitter-looking water, the air full of bog myrtle and young fern.

'You'll find some of the oldest ruins on the island there,' Isobelle had told her. 'Or at least a few stones. Outposts and shepherds' cottages, now all at the bottom of the bogs. Why they always built there and not further inwards...' She had shrugged, uncomprehending.

But Bonnie knew. The incessant prevailing winds struck the runners with bullets of sea-spray, and Atlantic rollers crashed against rocks with massive impacts. Watching this interplay divined a schoolgirl memory, a quote from a forgotten poet: *The Sea has no King*.

To live here, to look out into the Atlantic, to believe it was truly at the edge of the world, was to be both seeker and participant in some primeval mystery; and if one watched at the right time, a hint of that mystery might be revealed.

Such was the impassable nature of the island's head that they had to divert onto a trail that would lead them through the south-west woods back to the manor.

The run took Bonnie beyond any prior physical activity, so much so that she thought it might carry her to the edge of exhaustion and make her unable to complete her duties for the rest of the day. Fatigue had arrived, and was promptly surpassed, replaced by exhilaration. She'd felt the tiredness drop away and a fresh new energy enter her limbs. It was as if running in this place of stark simplicity, where all worldly connections had seemingly been severed, had somehow burned away her own links, leaving behind only her true self – or perhaps imparting to her secrets of being at one with her home.

Around them now the slim black boles of smooth-barked trees reared up, almost completely shutting the sky out with their thick crowns of whispering leaves, reaching up like supplicants to the sun god. Yet light persisted, dripping down to the leaf-carpeted earth below. Through it all Bonnie was struck by how the struggle for power and survival was edified here, and not just by the human inhabitants. Gulls and other birds dived to the rocks to forage for unguarded eggs and chicks. The plants grappled for light and moisture. And there was the eternal battle of sea against rocks, their conflicts too slow for human comprehension, but no less relentless and unyielding.

They were a reminder of why she chose to run this morning, and a reminder that thoroughly spoiled her sense of exhilaration. She began slowing down, allowing Zoe and Rafael to continue for several metres before calling out breathlessly, 'Wait... give me a minute!'

The couple slowed and stopped, and walked back to where she stooped with hands on knees, breathing deeply. Zoe, dressed like Rafael in sweat-stained T-shirt and shorts, placed a sympathetic hand on Bonnie's arched back. 'Tough going, isn't it?' she panted.

Bonnie nodded wordlessly, mopping her face with the sleeve of her jogging top. She glanced about, as if only interested in the sylvan beauty around her. A cool dry breeze was blowing in from the sea, sculpted and filtered by the trees from a rough slap into a gentle stroke, disturbing branches and wafting the smell of fresh wood and earth and salt into their faces.

Bonnie straightened up, grinned sheepishly at Zoe and Rafael, leaning against each other as if for support, and raised an inquiring finger. 'Would you excuse me a moment? Nature calls.' She ventured into the woods without waiting for an answer. Off the trail, fallen leaves and branches that rustled with each step carpeted the earth.

Bonnie ignored them, her mind on other things. One of the units should be close by... There! She knelt, unwilling to touch it, content to silently examine it. Yes, as she suspected, it was environmentally secure, almost completely camouflaged, with an independent power source, and co-ordinates stamped on the side that corresponded with markings for this location on grid maps Martin held in his secured computer. After a moment she found the other one nearby. They were parallel independent systems working in tandem to reduce false signals and compensate for a malfunction in one. Had she the time and opportunity earlier she probably would have found more along the trail.

Her admiration at the scale and detail of the operation was eclipsed by her rage at its implications, not just for her but for the others.

Unless she nursed her fledgling plans into maturity.

Zoe's voice carried to her ears, like the cry of one of the native birds. 'Bon-nie! What's wrong, run out of paper?'

Bonnie smiled despite herself and rose, wiping dirt from the knees of her jogging bottoms and making her way back to the trail. It pained her to have to remain secretive, but she believed it to be for the best – for now.

She emerged from the woods, pretending to adjust the waistband of her bottoms. 'Sorry to keep you waiting,' she said.

Rafael grinned at her, resting a playful elbow on Zoe's shoulder. 'Hope you washed your hands, slave girl.'

Bonnie stuck her tongue out at him, then glanced down the trail, then back again, recalling where they were on the map. 'I'm about to,' she said. 'Want a real race?' She took off before they could react, but she heard them quickly catch up. They drew closer, then alongside her. She knew they were in better condition than she was and could pass her easily, if they knew their final destination. But only Bonnie knew.

She took them to the island's southern pond, fed by a stream that Bonnie had once knelt at to drink from, that first day just after Kane had caught her, and where Bonnie had been bogged down in the mud with Paige's cart.

She cast aside such melancholic thoughts in favour of a burst of delight, as she ran to the edge of the pond and straight in, splashing all the way to the centre, where she knew – from the maps – it was waist deep and safe to swim in. And Bonnie did just that, oblivious to the chill of the water and the calls of her friends, certain she was mad. She grinned to herself, performing a lazy backstroke towards nothing in particular. And her grin widened as she heard her friends also splashing with yelps of shock and joy into the cold water.

Bonnie gazed up at the rich blue cloudless sky.

'I think she's been at the loopy juice,' Rafael laughed.

'I think you could be right,' Zoe agreed. 'She's completely gone.'

Bonnie listened to them but said nothing, simply enjoying the refreshing water, but wishing she'd stopped long enough to remove her clothes and keep them dry. That wish increased when she eventually emerged from the water and flopped ungracefully onto the bank. She was suddenly cold, and the chilly breeze clung to her. She took her clothes off and cast them aside, hoping she would dry and warm up quicker without them. Rafael and Zoe waded out too, the water dripping from them.

'So, here you are.'

The three of them looked around in surprise at the sound of the unexpected voice. It was Kane, sitting astride Shohan, suddenly there, like a phantom.

'You two,' he said, nodding at Rafael and Zoe, 'pick up your clothes and get back to the manor. The hunt is tomorrow, as you know, but you're to be prepared in an hour's time.'

Bonnie watched as they quickly grabbed their things and scurried away through the undergrowth.

Once their retreat could no longer be heard Kane

dismounted and took a leather lead from the saddle. He walked to where Bonnie crouched on the bank of the pond, squatted down and tied her wrists behind her back. 'My father bought this island twenty years ago,' he said, 'when I was sixteen. He spent a year having it refurbished. My mother had long since left. She returned to Osaka with father's generous pay-off. Paige and Martin were still in boarding school, and their mothers hadn't been paid off, at that time, so they remained in our old house in Berkshire. And of course there were father's slaves. On your knees.'

Bonnie obeyed without a hint of mutiny, wondering why Kane felt it necessary to confide in her.

'There was one slave,' he continued, as though not really aware of what he was saying. 'Daria. She was a tall and gorgeous American brunette with a voluptuous hourglass figure. I was in love with her, but she always turned her nose up at me, insulted me, even in front of father. And he did nothing about it. I hated him for his lack of support.

'Then, on my seventeenth birthday, father called me to his bedroom. I expected to receive a substantial cheque, as I did every year. Instead I found him sitting in his favourite chair, drinking brandy, while Daria lay in the centre of the room, naked, bound as I'm binding you now. Lie on your stomach.'

Bonnie did so, her breasts moulding against the earth. 'He poured me a brandy, told me to pull up a chair, and proceeded to tell me about the slave laws. How a slave must obey, how they exist only to satisfy a master's needs, how they are nothing without a master, how punishment is in fact a blessing, and how a slave can only achieve true satisfaction through utter devotion.'

He rolled Bonnie onto her back, and she winced at the discomfort of having her arms pinned beneath her. She looked up and watched as he undressed.

'Father said Daria was my seventeenth birthday present, and I could do whatever I pleased with her. I finished my brandy, rose, and examined her. Those eyes, once haughty and superior, now radiated fear, uncertainty... but also desire. She'd teased me about being a virgin; little did she realise she'd help me deal with that.'

Kane was naked. His penis was fully erect, the tip glistening. Without further ado he knelt before her and hauled her legs apart. He shuffled closer, leaned over her, and with little ceremony he stabbed with his hips and was inside her.

Bonnie sighed and arched her back. Despite Kane's slightly sinister demeanour she couldn't ignore the pleasure his rigid cock was giving her. She had not wanted to reveal to him how aroused she had become, how receptive and willing she was to the ordeal. But, with the ease at which he had penetrated her made possible only by the amount of lubrication she had produced, it was inescapable. She relaxed a little and let the muscles of her vagina squeeze around his probing shaft.

'He left me alone with Daria, inviting me to join him for more drinks that evening,' continued Kane, his buttocks clenching as he slowly ground into the bound girl beneath him. 'That day I truly learned how to indulge myself and tried everything I had only ever read about. Before long I'd brought Daria to her knees, figuratively and literally. And when I finally joined father for drinks I proposed adding a sixth law, one to which he readily agreed.'

Kane put his lips close to Bonnie's ear, as if to ensure he had her full attention. 'Do you want to know what it was? *Slaves never win*,' he smirked. 'That was it. Simple, but striking. And undeniable. *Slaves never win*. Remember that, my dear little slave, if you remember nothing else. Do you hear me, sweet Bonnie?'

She never answered, focusing instead on the fire he was stoking relentlessly with every thrust. She worked to tighten her channel around him like a vice as he almost completely withdrew, and then plunged aggressively into her. His sweat mingled with hers, the grunts of his arousal complementing the musk of her own, until she joined him in mouthing her pleasures to the silently watching woodland. In the hushed quiet that settled over the scene his swaying balls slapped audibly against the cushion of her flesh.

Her pussy convulsed around him as her orgasm overcame her, precipitating his. And when his arrived he lost control, collapsing over her as she drained him of every last drop of seed. And Bonnie knew what he'd lost when he came, what that look of surrender in his eyes had meant.

And just in case he still hadn't worked it out, she whispered, 'I won.'

Chapter Twelve

After untying her wrists, Kane tersely ordered her to go back and clean herself up in the stables before entering the house. Then he dressed and rode off. She watched him leave, unsure of what she should have been feeling at that moment.

So she walked back to the house, stopping only once more to check on another of the installations the Castlewells had hidden, her mind racing ahead.

She entered the stables. 'Tim? Are you there?' she called.

There was no answer. She ventured further inside, reaching up to stroke the faces of the horses in their stalls, feeling their warm breath on her hand. She continued on until she reached the anteroom where she'd first seen Tim working. It was empty, but a door that had been closed before was now open, and she indulged her curiosity by gingerly peering through.

It was a workshop of sorts. Battered wooden benches lined the walls, beneath racks of tools and cabinets with tiny drawers. Ropes, pipes and cables hung from the rafters like snakes, and there was a warm, dry scent of sawdust in the air. In one corner was a deep porcelain sink with twin taps.

Beside it was a large metal tub. She approached and saw a well-worn tablet of pink soap sitting at the bottom with a washcloth. Perhaps this was where Tim performed his own ablutions.

There was a coil of black rubber hose beneath the sink, and Bonnie guessed it was for filling the tub. She tested each tap, found one to have surprisingly hot water, attached the hose to it, and watched the water swirl around the bottom of the tub.

'Miss?'

Bonnie spun round, but it was only Tim. He was carrying a tool-box, which he set down on the nearest bench with a clanging thud, and stared at her.

Bonnie felt like she'd intruded on his private little world, and sheepishly she shrugged and explained, 'I was told to come in and wash off. I called for you first.'

'It's all right.' He wore a baggy shirt that nevertheless set off his masculine frame, and his thigh muscles strained against the restrictive confines of his dirty jeans. Without further ado he tugged his shirt up and over his head, revealing his bare chest. He dropped the grimy material beside the tool-box and approached, taking the hose from her and feeding more of it into the tub, until the mouth was beneath the level of the steadily-rising water, and would remain there unaided.

Then he turned to Bonnie. She could smell his sweat. It was the sweat of a man who seemed to do more work before dawn than most so-called men did in a whole day. Her breathing quickened, and she felt hot, though she knew it wasn't due to the rising heat from the tub beside her. She looked up into his eyes, and feeling flustered and unsure of what to do or say, she blurted stupidly, 'I – I'm sorry I've not come to see you again sooner—'

'It's all right,' he assured her again. His voice was as deep as ever, a leathery voice that could hug her and keep her safe – or bound and at his mercy. Without asking permission he removed her wet jogging top, leaving her in just sports bra, bottoms, and collar.

'Yes,' she whispered breathlessly, 'I guess it is.' She reached back and undid the clasp of her bra, letting the straps slide down her arms, and letting him remove it completely. She studied his face, seeking a change of expression, some chink in his armour. But that was wrong; she was thinking too much of Kane. Tim was as open as the greensward. He had no reason to hide anything – including that bulge in the crotch of his jeans.

Bonnie clutched the edge of the sink as Tim knelt and removed her wet trainers. She stared down at his broad chest and shoulders. Then he reached up and took the elasticated waistband of her wet jogging bottoms, and the knickers beneath, and drew them down together. Her breath caught in her throat and she shuddered as a calloused hand delved between her thighs. Her sex boiled, despite its earlier appeasement, and its heat permeated her body.

Tim turned off the tap and removed the hose, and then held her hand as she stepped into the steaming water, as if she were a lady being helped into a carriage on the way to the opera. It was a tender moment that struck her. She sighed pleasurably at the caress of the silky water on her skin, and was eager to immerse the rest of her body into it and allow its warmth to relax her chilled muscles.

'Kneel,' Tim instructed.

She obeyed willingly. The water lapped gently around her hips, enveloping her bottom and sex in a warm blanket that matched the heat and moisture she felt within.

She gripped the sides of the tub, feeling slightly heady, as Tim took the soap and rubbed it thoroughly into the washcloth, pink-white lather tumbling like snowflakes from his hand.

Then he began to soap her body, first her back, then shoulders, then her neck beneath the collar, then her arms. It was a deeply sensual experience, feeling the gentle power behind his touch, and the gentle caress of the soap and water as they trickled from his hand and trailed like fingers down her serene yet stimulated torso. She closed her eyes and sighed, leaning back slightly as his hands moved to her breasts, lifting and kneading each in turn, his touch carrying her further into heaven. Her hands joined his, rolling her breasts upward as if in offering to him. Which of course was the case. She offered him everything she had – everything she was.

His attention drifted to her belly, then beneath the waterline and between her thighs. She parted them as much as she could within the confines of the bath, and Tim ventured further, his hand dipping further beneath the surface of the water to massage her yearning sex lips, his fingers pressing into the washcloth to gently prise her open. Sexual desire flooded through her body and she purred like a kitten.

'Lean forward,' he whispered, 'and close your eyes.'

Bonnie obeyed, her arms sinking into the water as her palms flattened against the base of the tub, her bottom out of the water and dripping with suds. She imagined what it must look like to Tim. Perhaps that was why he paused in his ministrations, to admire her figure. Perhaps he might even join her, as unlikely as it was; the tub seemed barely large enough to hold him.

Then he continued soaping her back, fingers running

lightly over her spine to her buttocks, moving to one cheek, then the other, using potent sweeps around her flesh, squeezing the cloth to let water seep down the deep crevice and through to the cleft between her thighs.

Hands parted her cheeks, revealing the puckered hole of her smallest orifice. A determined finger probed, and she moaned. Whatever he wanted of her, she would comply.

The finger remained there, gradually working its way inside. The effect on Bonnie was unbelievable, her muscles gripping the intruder, refusing release. She savoured the exquisite rush possessing her, her back arching and her head jerking up.

Then his other hand was at the plump folds of flesh that hugged the entrance to her sex, his fingers meeting the eager clitoris and swimming through the dew collecting there.

Bonnie began to back onto these wonderful fingers, feeling her orgasm approaching quickly and easily. Her body tightened, and she almost crumpled into the water as the initial waves struck her. She gripped the tub's sides until she thought her fingers would pierce the metal. Her heart pounded in her chest as Tim continued to work his magic on her. But, through a haze of ecstasy, she knew the fingers strumming such sweet music on her erect bud and pushing into her vagina felt different… more delicate…

And then, to her chagrin and horror, she heard laughter close to her ear… familiar female laughter. She didn't even have to open her eyes to know it was Paige. The laughter died and the fingers slipped away, leaving her feeling empty and incomplete, despite the sweet pulses of her subsiding orgasm.

Paige straightened up and snapped her fingers. Tim was immediately by her side like an obedient puppy, his head bowed as though he wanted petting. 'Good boy, Tim,' she said, as she took the towel he held for her.

Disappointment swamped Bonnie as she stared up at him, slowly comprehending what was going on. He, however, refused to meet her accusing stare. 'Oh, don't blame him, my dear,' Paige said, her voice full of amusement as she casually discarded the towel on the dusty floor. 'He was merely obeying orders to put you at ease. And he's very good at obeying orders, aren't you, Tim?'

Tim shuffled his feet. 'Whatever you say... Mistress Paige.'

'Whatever I say,' she chuckled thoughtfully, clearly savouring the words. 'How sweet. Words to live by.' She nodded towards the door. 'Now, get back to your work.'

'Aye, mistress.' He strode out quickly, though not quickly enough to avoid Paige's departing slap on his muscled buttocks. There was a loud slam of the outside door, and Paige whistled with mock fear. 'My,' she said theatrically, 'he is an angry farm boy. And there's me thinking the illiterate cretin's a rock, unmoved by anyone or anything.' Her gaze burned into Bonnie. 'You seem to have a disruptive influence on us all, dear little Bonnie.'

Bonnie tried to cover her slippery breasts with her arms. 'Why did you—?'

'Why did I touch you like I did?' Paige shrugged, retrieving a silver case from a pocket of the long coat she wore, and lighting a cigar. 'Maybe to watch that moment of revelation on your face, when you realised it wasn't darling Tim.' She shrugged again. 'Or maybe I've fallen in love with you.'

Bonnie could not believe what she was hearing. 'But—'

Paige's expression suddenly hardened. 'Now stand up,' she snapped. 'And put your hands behind your head.'

Knowing better than to question by now, Bonnie obeyed, feeling the air cold against her wet skin.

Paige drew deeply on her cigar, deliberately letting her eyes roam over Bonnie's charming nudity. 'Before I continue,' she eventually said, 'I must ask you about the other night, in my bedroom. How did it feel, being dragged down to levels of hitherto unimagined humiliation, but enjoying it?'

Bonnie breathed in deeply. The evening had been remarkable; watching Paige with Zoe and Rafael, being confined and unable to participate or even touch herself, but nevertheless achieving orgasm. It had been sincere appreciation that made Bonnie kneel before Paige afterwards and grovel. On reflection, she lost all shame during the incident. 'It... it was marvellous,' she whispered, her shame with her once again.

Paige smiled and licked her lips. 'It was, wasn't it? To bring you to your knees like I did.' She tapped a little ash from the cigar. 'And were you truly grateful?'

Bonnie nodded. 'Yes, mistress... I was.'

Paige nodded, clearly not surprised by the answer. 'Good.' She took another deep drag and allowed the smoke to drift slowly from her open mouth. 'Now then, I'm here to inform you that my earlier offer is rescinded. You're here to stay.'

The finality of the unexpected announcement stabbed Bonnie like an icy knife, and she instantly wished she'd taken that avenue of escape before it had been closed. 'May…' she said timidly, suddenly feeling extremely alone, 'may a slave ask why?'

Paige snorted. 'It's because of a look I saw in Kane's eyes; you make him reckless. I'm sure by now you've learned or guessed your ultimate fate: to be the plaything for our father. And yes, I feared Kane making a present of you would elevate him in father's eyes. But now I see something new in Kane. An obsession. And because of it he'll never last long enough to enjoy the fruits of any additional favours father might grant him. He'll fuck up along the way, and I'll be here to take his place. Whatever the outcome, of course, you'll remain as you are… a slave.' She stepped forward and allowed the smoke to drift into Bonnie's face, and then dropped the cigar into the water, where it sizzled and fizzed and turned a nasty black colour. 'And in case you're unaware of the sixth slave law, it states: *Slaves never*—'

'*Win*,' Bonnie finished, holding and returning Paige's cold grey stare. 'Kane already told me.'

Paige suddenly looked uncomfortable before Bonnie's unexpected stance of defiance. 'W-what the hell is wrong with you?' she mumbled, her tongue suddenly too big for her mouth.

Strangely, and curiously, Bonnie could feel the tide changing, and the power struggle shifting slightly. 'You,' she said, her confidence slowly increasing. 'You try so hard to be like your older brother. You're desperate for confirmation that you humbled me as well as Kane would have done. You play with his toys to show off for your daddy. But in the end, you come across as a

197

mere imitation of Kane… and a poor one at that.' She held her breath, barely able to believe what she'd just said, and wishing she hadn't.

Paige visibly shook, boiling with anger searching for release. Her hands balled into fists, and then she darted around Bonnie, the focal point of her rage, and snatched the rubber hose from where Tim had left it. Before her target could properly protect herself Paige raised her arm to strike. Bonnie closed her eyes and remained passive, resigned to the assault.

But nothing happened, and Bonnie held her breath until she heard the hose hit the floor and Paige curse and storm away.

The hares were gone, vanished, with no explanation from anyone. Not even Janine who, from her skittish behaviour around Bonnie since their fight in the cage, seemed to have had the wind taken out of her sails. Or maybe, with Paige's offer of helping Bonnie leave now withdrawn, there was no need to continue to harass Bonnie into considering the option? Still, Bonnie suspected where the hares had been taken.

At midday she was summoned to Victor Castlewell's suite in the attic.

Unlike the rooms in the rest of the attic that she'd been in, these were still open to the roof rafters, their great oak beams climbing from the walls to steeple at the summit. It was as though she was in an old church.

A huge fireplace tried to dominate the living room, with some measure of success. Logs crackled and spat, and threw out a reassuring warmth. But that dominance was somewhat diluted by the trophies; animal heads that hung on the walls, all staring down accusingly at her with black glass eyes.

'Quite a sight, aren't they?' The question came from a chair facing the fire. Victor Castlewell rose, turned, and faced Bonnie. He was wearing a rich cerise dressing gown, with a matching cravat. 'What do you think of them?' he asked, amusement in his eyes. 'Be honest, please.'

'I… I'm not sure what to think, sir.'

'You disapprove,' he ventured, smiling. 'So many of your generation do. They would see me as a murderer. But it was different in my day. I didn't go out with automatic weapons and radar and an army of bearers. It was one-on-one, and all I had was my gun.' He reached up and pulled open his dressing gown, enough to reveal a trio of dark parallel scars extending from his right collarbone across his pectoral. He smiled at Bonnie's reaction. 'The tiger who did this thirty years ago certainly preferred those odds to what he'd experience today with the poachers.'

He closed his gown and turned, and made a slow orbit around the room, staring at each of his trophies. Bonnie followed, suspecting she was expected to.

'I could have the scar removed,' he went on, 'but I prefer to be reminded of my past, that I did not always live like this. I was born Vittorio Castligione, a poor boy of Milan. But unlike my contemporaries, content to waste their lives in the drudgery of menial work, I hungered for more. So with a hunter's instinct I sought out my targets, educated myself, and focused my efforts. Businesses, investments and wealthy lonely women were soon in my grasp. And with growing wealth came the opportunity to go on safari, to do something I'd wanted to do since seeing one in the newsreels of the

Saturday afternoon cinema.' He patted his chest. 'This was the result of my first safari.'

He turned and held out his arms expansively. 'And all of these trophies are the result of a lifetime of doing in the wilderness what I've always done in the boardroom and the bedroom; stalking my prey on equal terms, taking it for my own, and defeating it. It added a spice to my life; the challenge of pursuing a fellow animal.' He inhaled deeply, as if the memories could conjure up the hot air of the Serengeti or Burma. 'But my business and personal conquests were but shadows of the excitement I felt in stalking my prey on the true hunting grounds.' He sighed, as if the memories were fading. 'Alas it became a dying art, as the great beasts dwindled in numbers. Now they are pitifully few, and confined to tiny preserves. And rightly, too,' he added, with genuine sincerity. 'They deserve it.'

'So you gave up hunting animals,' Bonnie dared suggest, 'and started hunting humans?'

He grinned at her, like a parent correcting a child's misapprehension of adult matters. 'Not to kill, of course. I may be eccentric in the extreme, but I am not completely insane. But yes, every year for the last twenty me and others like me have hunted a select group of young volunteers on this island. Volunteers found through Martin's computer work, and the fieldwork of Kane and Paige. They're given hints as to what awaits them here, but are not rewarded with the full story until the day before the hunt, as the hares were this morning. They understand the risks and the rewards, and accept them. For those hares who remain uncaught—'

'A lifetime of fortune,' Bonnie finished for him. 'May I ask what that entails, exactly?'

He made a noise of assent, and then directed her to a red curtain which was draped across one corner of the room. Directly beneath the curtain could be seen the base of what looked like a white marble pedestal. 'Excuse the dramatics,' he said, 'but it impresses the hares when they first see it.' He reached out and drew the curtain back.

Bonnie's eyes widened. It was a pedestal, waist-high, and perched on top of it was a small statue of a proud woman in a short but flowing gown, wielding a bow and poised to deliver an arrow at some unseen target. The statue's polished surface gleamed in the firelight, and Bonnie had no doubt that it was solid gold.

Victor patted the back of the statue reverently. 'This is Diana, Roman goddess of the hunt. To the winners, a lifetime of fortune means a statue like this for each of them, or its cash equivalent. Which in present terms is equivalent to five hundred thousand pounds.'

Bonnie drew in a sharp, deep breath. Five hundred thousand? If that was at stake, no wonder so many would risk the hunt. But on the other hand... 'What... what of those who get caught?' she asked tentatively. 'What is—?'

'A lifetime of servitude?' Victor waved to a door in the far wall. 'Would you follow me, please?'

They moved into what appeared to be his office, judging from the huge mahogany desk with the monitors for conferencing. But Bonnie's attention was drawn to the pictures on the wall, hung from floor to ceiling. Paintings, etchings, charcoal drawings, some old, some young, of many sizes. But all of women: naked and half-naked, supine, kneeling, sitting or standing, of all shapes, sizes and colours. And all in some form of submission, whether by chains, ropes, belts, or simply desire.

Victor looked at them with pride in his eyes. 'Martin is as exceptional an artist with the brush as he is with the keyboard, though one can see improvements to his style as you look back at his earlier works.' He pointed to those nearest the desk, then slowly to the rest. 'All souvenirs of my past personal conquests. My trophies.'

Bonnie tried counting them, giving up after thirty. 'Where's mine? The one Martin did of me this week?'

She watched Victor saunter to an object covered by a grey dropcloth, and sweep it dramatically aside to reveal the canvassed drawing of her. Martin had embellished it further after she'd posed for him, adding background and shading. Victor was right; his son was good. 'Why is it not hanging up?' she asked, secretly feeling inexplicably disappointed.

'Why, my dear,' he responded confidently, 'I haven't caught you… yet.'

His words chilled her, as did realisation as she scanned the wall of nameless women. 'And that's the fate of those who lose? To serve you for the rest of their lives?'

'To serve those hunters who catch them,' Victor corrected. 'For the rest of their lives, or until their master or mistress tires of them and frees them, or trades them to another master or mistress.'

'Is that what happened to all these?' She indicated her predecessors. 'How long did they last with you?'

He shrugged. 'That depended upon their spirit, their initiative, and their drive. I sense you possess all of these traits in great quantity. I've watched recordings of your performances with my children. I saw your fire in the cage. You could make superior game for tomorrow's hunt.' He took a step forward. 'Well? Will you join the hunt? Or should I just take you now?' The way he said the last made it clear he preferred the former choice.

Bonnie glanced in the direction of the trophy room. 'When was the last time a hare won the hunt?'

Victor didn't need to search for an answer. 'Oh, not for some long time now.'

Bonnie wasn't surprised about that. She quickly estimating how many hidden sensors and cameras and microphones were needed to properly blanket the island and make every hare a sitting target.

'But perhaps you'll be the exception,' he patronised, clearly finding the notion of that outcome highly amusing.

'May I think about it?' she asked, beginning to believe that she actually could upset the odds, and finding the prospect surprisingly exciting.

Victor's smile took on a steely edge. 'You may, but don't take long; the guest hunters will be here soon.'

It looked like the same helicopter that had brought supplies earlier in the week. This time, however, it deposited three individuals and various items of luggage.

Bonnie and Isobelle, washing the lunch dishes, watched from the window as the three newcomers were greeted by Kane and Victor, and helped with their bags by Tim and Janine.

'No one new this season,' Isobelle noted, dividing her attention between the dishes and the view from the window.

'You know them?'

She nodded. 'The one on the left's Ibram Al-Nasseid, a shipping industrialist. They say he keeps an actual harem back home.'

Bonnie studied him, a broad barrel of a man with a ruthless stare that made her skin crawl. 'And what about the others?' she asked, trying to drag her attention away from him.

Isobelle pointed a sudsy finger at the man beside Al-Nasseid; a tall thin specimen with worldly lines on his face and strands of white in his iron-grey beard. Dressed in deceptively simple black, striding proudly, he looked to be a contemporary of Victor Castlewell's. 'Colonel Nikolai Krylov, retired. Russian, obviously. A businessman with shady dealings everywhere. Not a bad set up if you like eight month winters and bootleg designer clothes.'

Bonnie absorbed this, her eyes fixing on the third figure, a woman with ebony skin, muscular-looking yet maintaining elegance in her poise. She had prominent cheekbones, full lips and large breasts. She moved at a quicker pace than the others, as if eager for the sport to begin. 'And her?' she asked.

Isobelle sniffed, clearly trying unsuccessfully to hide her unease behind disdain. 'Doctor Ursula Yates. American. Runs a health farm in Nevada; at least, that's what she calls it.'

Bonnie regarded them all. 'I wonder which one would be the best to be captured by?'

Isobelle shrugged. 'Don't ask me. If I wanted to worry about such choices I'd have accepted the offer of joining the hunt five years ago.' Her face grew severe. 'Of course, knowing what I know now, I made the right choice.' She spoke freely, guessing perhaps that Bonnie had also refused the hunt, and would understand her insinuation.

Bonnie did understand. But she also knew that she would accept the offer of the hunt – if she could get to Martin's computer first, and then to Tim.

'I can't believe you're going through with it.'

'Martin,' Bonnie protested, 'try to understand—' but he rose sharply from behind his desk and made for the door. Bonnie could have let him go, but followed, catching him by the arm and making him stop and face her. 'Martin, it's my choice. I know exactly what I'm doing. You have to believe that.'

'You're worse than the rest of them,' he accused unfairly. 'You understand you have no chance of winning, but you're caught up in all this stupid fantasy.' Suddenly he stared at her as if for the first time. He looked haggard, worn. 'You're doomed,' he said sadly. 'Can't you see that for yourself?'

Bonnie wanted to tell him, wanted to explain everything. But she didn't dare, not while her plan had a chance of succeeding without his help. As much as she thought she understood him, she couldn't take a chance of confiding in him now and risking his father suspecting him of collusion should it all go wrong. Instead, she reached up and cupped his face. 'If I'm doomed, doesn't the condemned get a last request?'

He didn't want to succumb, but slowly he nodded. Pressing against him, she could feel his erection through his trousers, and drew him further into a kiss, finding his tongue. When he finally responded the rush of pleasure through her body was almost too much. Still kissing her, he reached up between them, squeezing and stroking her aching breasts until they popped out from her corset. She moaned, wanting more.

As if he could read her thoughts, one hand crept down to stroke her stockinged thighs, stopping at her knickers, before trailing round to cup and squeeze her fleshy bottom as he had done with her breasts. He still wasn't urgent enough for her, though, so she squirmed out of her knickers and kicked them away. Taking her lead, he cupped her bare bottom and his stiffening cock buffeted against her flat tummy, demanding attention.

So she offered it, undoing his trousers and tugging them down before reaching for his naked erection, now standing proudly. They kissed again as she drew his foreskin back and forth, unable and unwilling to fight the exquisite sensations stirring her insides.

'Come on... come on...' she found herself urging hungrily, and then Martin lifted and impaled her on his rearing column of erect flesh, and she sighed ecstatically.

Despite the mutual urgency, once joined there grew a remarkable complementary rhythm; a harmony to their duet usually reserved for lovers who had coupled for years. The outside world was set aside as they drove at each other with a graceful affection, Bonnie's dizzying climaxes bursting one after the other, splintering her breath into ragged moans. She cherished every moment, until inevitably his willpower waned and he succumbed to that release of pleasure, tensing as he climaxed within her, digging his fingers into her buttocks.

Afterwards she persuaded him into his bedroom, offering a body massage that eventually relaxed him into a deep sleep.

Then she returned to his computers. They were still

open; a bad habit of his, no doubt picked up because he was the only one on the island with any interest in the operation. She began quickly accessing his codes, stopping to crack her knuckles, feeling rusty. But she regained her skills directly. The sequences she saw reminded her of a safari park security system she'd debugged a few years before. But it wouldn't be easy; Martin had had years to perfect the system, and would probably notice new anomalous commands if she took the obvious paths. But she didn't. So she continued, mentally crossing her fingers.

Chapter Thirteen

The rest of the day went smoothly, and bled into evening. The guests paid scant attention to Bonnie and the rest of the staff as they ate and drank and conversed with the Castlewells – minus Martin, as usual.

At one point Bonnie managed to slip out to see Tim, and returned prepared to inform Victor Castlewell that she was ready to accept his challenge. Then, while serving drinks to the group as they played poker in the games room, she was mentioned openly by Krylov, who reached out and boldly cupped her right buttock. The cold mauling made her cringe and want to slap his sleazy face, but she bit her lip and suppressed the urge.

'A fine new specimen you have here, Victor,' he said, his voice heavily accented.

Victor raised his glass in acknowledgement of the compliment. 'Bonnie is one of Kane's protegees, my friend. I've been given good reports about her.'

Paige threw down a card and lit a cigar. 'Don't believe everything you hear, father dear. I've had to beat her frequently for sloppy housework.'

Krylov squeezed again, then slapped her bottom as he laughed. 'That's not necessarily a bad thing, eh?'

Dr Yates stared at Bonnie openly, rapaciously. 'Pity she's not in the hunt,' she said, almost to herself.

'She could be,' Victor corrected. 'Well, Bonnie, have you made a decision?'

Bonnie lowered her eyes as she turned to him,

plucking up the courage to take the plunge, knowing there would be no going back. 'Actually, master, I *would* like to join the hunt.'

Kane nearly spilled his whiskey as he petulantly slammed his crystal glass on the table. 'Are we here to play cards, or to talk about meat?'

'Temper, temper, son,' Victor soothed mockingly.

'Good looking meat, though,' Krylov noted quietly, watching Bonnie suggestively from between bushy eyebrows and the sparkling rim of his glass as he took a sip of vodka.

Despite her revulsion, Bonnie smiled at him and pouted a little. But the smile faded as her gaze trailed to Al-Nasseid, and the cruel glint in his eyes that spoke silent volumes.

'You'll prefer the other hares,' Paige assured them, her brash voice interrupting the disturbing silence that hung between Bonnie and Al-Nasseid. 'I've had this one. She's not meat, she's meringue; pleasing to the eye, but crumbles easily at the merest touch.' She roared loudly at her own clever quip, and Krylov and Yates joined her in polite laughter.

Bonnie clenched her fists with fury, unseen by the others. Arrogant bastards! Oh, how she was determined to prove them all wrong, and make Paige eat her bitchy remarks. As much as she was repulsed by the idea of seeing through this part of the plan she'd formulated earlier, she knew it had to be done. She simply had to win their confidence, and lull them into a false sense of security.

Bonnie took a long, deep breath.

'Ladies and gentlemen,' she said, fighting to quell the wavering in her voice. 'Is there anything special I can do for any of you?'

The conversation around the table stopped and all eyes fixed upon her, making her feel vulnerable beneath their scrutiny.

'Well now,' Victor Castlewell eventually said, nodding to his offspring, 'I think it's time we left our guests to relax after their long journey.'

'But—' Kane started to object, suddenly losing interest in the cards, but was silenced by his father's raised hand. Victor nodded an unspoken order to the two, and with petulant frustration etched on their faces they stood and skulked out of the room in his wake.

Once the door was firmly closed behind them Bonnie approached, with trembling legs, the three remaining at the table. She edged between Krylov and Yates, not too keen to get close to Al-Nasseid. 'Oh, have I disturbed your little game?' she asked in mock innocence. 'I'm *really* sorry.' She seductively moistened her lips with the tip of her tongue, trying to portray her best baby-doll act for the titillation of these three lechers. 'I suppose I'll have to make it up to you – or at least, to the winner.' She looked at the table, where cards lay discarded and coloured plastic chips were in varying piles before each player. 'So, who has the most?' she purred suggestively. Al-Nasseid still worried her, and she didn't fancy having to seduce another woman in front of an audience, so she focused on Krylov – unattractive though he was. She stared at his winnings, then blatantly down at his tented groin. 'Well,' she whispered sexily, 'it seems you have the biggest stack.'

He put his drink down, shifted his chair round slightly from the table, and leered at her. 'That sounds about right, *devushka*.' He patted his knee, inviting her to sit on his lap.

But Bonnie wanted to get the ordeal over with as quickly as possible, so she knelt down, guided his knees apart, shuffled between his thighs, and stared at the swelling lump inside his trousers. She froze for a moment, and then, forcing herself to continue, she hesitantly reached to touch it. 'I'm... I'm not sure I'm ready—'

'Yes, you are,' he assured her, enjoying her reluctance, not realising it was genuine. 'And yes, you will continue.' As if to convince her further, he grasped a handful of her hair and pulled her a little closer.

Bonnie could feel the warmth of him beneath her hands as she fumbled with his belt and trousers. Despite her dislike for the man and his associates, she couldn't deny the knot of excitement awakening deep in her belly. She felt inside his underwear and pulled out his rigid member. It sprouted before her flushed face, powerful and demanding. Krylov guided her closer. She closed her eyes and opened her mouth, bracing herself. The straining helmet touched her lips. She pulled back slightly, and then the fingers in her hair increased their pressure and she allowed the stalk to stretch her lips and thrust up into her mouth. Her tongue caressed the prominent vein that ran down the underside, until her nose touched the gaping material of his trousers and his springy pubic thatch. He mumbled something in his native tongue above her, and squeezed her between his thighs.

Someone slid quietly out of their chair and squeezed their hands onto her breasts, finding and pinching her traitorous nipples as they stiffened. Someone else peeled her fingers from where they were clamped onto Krylov's thighs, pulled her hands away and held them together in the small of her back, completing her surrender. Now Krylov moved her head up and down, fucking her mouth as she tried to balance on her knees. Perfume wafted over her and feminine lips kissed her hollowed cheek. Soft words encouraged her to suck harder. There was a weight on her back and lips nuzzled into her neck. She had no idea how many hands were mauling her breasts.

Inevitably, a little of Krylov's mounting excitement escaped onto her tongue, a salty harbinger of what was to soon follow, and his cock began to throb powerfully in her mouth, stretching her lips further. His hips started moving up to meet her imprisoned face each time it descended, and then he groaned loudly, and Bonnie felt the rush of his orgasm rise up the length of his penis and gush into her mouth, striking the back of her throat. She swallowed, again and again, clamping his length with her lips as she drew more and more from it, until he slumped wearily in the chair and his arms dangled inertly by his sides.

'Are you wet, little pussy?' Yates whispered in her ear. Before Bonnie could respond Al-Nasseid picked her up and draped her across the poker table, sending plastic chips scattering in all directions. He lifted her stockinged thighs over his forearms, hauled her back towards him as though she was a doll so that her bottom was on the table's edge, pulled the damp gusset of her knickers aside, and plunged his released and erect cock deep into her receptive cunt. Bonnie gasped at the intensity of the exquisite penetration. Her mouth gaped in surprise and her back arched up off the table. She stared, unseeing, up at the ceiling. Her fingers clutched feebly at Al-Nasseid's tailored shirt as he fucked her with total control of himself and her. He still said nothing, but merely stared impassively down at the beautiful object impaled and writhing on the end of his manhood.

Bonnie was vaguely aware of rustling silk touching her cheeks, and then a fragrant warmth enveloped her face. Too delirious to open her eyes, she knew it was Yates. Bonnie instinctively opened her mouth to receive the woman. She used her tongue to pry apart the swollen lips, silky and warm, releasing more succulent perfume and the taste of female dew. She felt the rise of a protruding clitoris, emerging to be worshipped.

Yates suddenly tensed and came with a tiny whimper. She immediately climbed off Bonnie's face and curled beside her, kissing her wet and glistening lips and chin. 'Not bad for starters,' she drooled dreamily. Bonnie opened her eyes and watched Al-Nasseid moving steadily between her raised thighs. His cold detachment only heightened her sense of being used, her sense of humiliation, and her pleasure. Krylov was standing behind him, watching her closely from over his associate's shoulder, once again sipping his vodka.

'He's going to come now, sweet Bonnie,' Yates whispered. 'I just know he is.' She took Bonnie's wrists and pinned them together with one hand on the table behind Bonnie's head.

'Yes please…' Bonnie sighed, and then moaned her frustration as Al-Nasseid pulled out of her. With her hands held captive she could only lay helplessly and watch as Yates reached for the Arab's cock with her free hand, pumped it sharply a few times, and his semen arched into the air and splattered in the concave bowl of her quivering stomach.

Bonnie squeezed her eyes shut, her head in a spin, confused by the man's action. Why didn't he come inside her? Those extra few seconds of penetration would have been enough for her!

As if reading her mind, Yates kissed her again and smiled. 'Ibram only comes inside his wives, my little angel. That's his way of showing fidelity. He wouldn't waste his precious seed in a slave.'

Bonnie closed her eyes and heard them soberly congratulating each other as they straightened their clothing and then left the room, leaving her there, alone on the table, her clothing soiled and dishevelled. She noticed the chill air touching her bare flesh for the first time, her humiliation stoking her anger. She would make those odious lechers pay – of that she was determined.

Once Bonnie explained to Delilah what had happened, she thought she'd have a chance to return to her room and freshen up, or even see Martin one more time, assuming he was still interested. Delilah, however, gently but firmly took her by the arm and led her down to the cellar, not towards the gymnasium and related rooms, but to what she'd always assumed was just another storage room. It was always locked and bolted, and otherwise unmarked. As Delilah fished through the ring of keys on her belt, she nodded with distaste at Bonnie's sluttish appearance. 'Get undressed now,' she said. 'You won't be needing clothes in the hutch. And those are ruined, anyway.'

So this was the hutch Bonnie had heard about in snatched and whispered conversations? She dropped her soiled clothes to the floor and smiled weakly at Delilah, trying to convince herself everything would be okay. Delilah found the right key and opened the door, and ushered Bonnie inside.

Bonnie expected to see the other hares, but she did not expect to see what looked like a wing of a despot's prison. It was long and narrow, and illuminated by harsh fluorescent lighting. The bars of the cages ran from the flagstone floor to the low arched ceiling. The floors of the cages were covered with straw, and there were bowls of water, and food that looked like gruel.

But it was the hares themselves that drew her full attention. They were each in their own cage, naked but for their ubiquitous collars, just like Bonnie. But they were covered from head to toe with paint or make-up of some sort, applied in swirling patterns that looked like camouflage. Zoe and Rafael called to her, but Delilah stabbed a finger in their direction.

'Hares don't talk!' and she took Bonnie possessively by the wrist.

So these were those captives who had been unsuccessful in previous hunts, and now belonged to Victor, Kane, or Paige. Bonnie was amazed that the existence of so many could have been hidden from the apparently tranquil world above ground. She knew there were more hares than just Zoe and Rafael; after all, she'd seen some being exercised by Paige. But she was amazed that she'd been oblivious to the presence of the others. Would this be her fate if the plan failed and she became the property of one of the Castlewells, and then they tired of her? She glanced at each of her fellow captives as she passed them. Some appeared to be sympathetic, and some even seemed as aroused as she was inexplicably starting to feel now; her submissive state, and that of the others, had never before been so

215

blatantly expressed as it was in this claustrophobic cellar. She was beginning to react to it, despite the recent events upstairs.

Delilah led her to an empty cage at the end of the row, nudged her inside and locked the door with a chilling clang. 'Delilah,' Bonnie protested, 'don't I even get to be camouflaged like the others?'

'No. Master Victor's orders. Get some rest now, you'll be up at dawn.' Then she turned and left.

Bonnie reached through the bars in vain. 'Delilah, wait…' but the woman was gone.

Why was Bonnie not to be camouflaged? Her shoulders slumped and she rested her forehead against the cold bars; something was very wrong.

'Bonnie?'

She lifted her head. Zoe was the nearest of the hares to her, though an empty cage still separated them. Her friend was lovely, resplendent in her olive and grey markings, bizarre and alien but nevertheless strikingly attractive. 'Bonnie, what time was it outside? We've lost track in here.'

'Half nine,' she said wearily.

The others were listening, relaying the information. Zoe's gaze remained fixed on Bonnie. 'Why would Victor want you unmarked?'

Bonnie's expression was grim. She shrugged, not wanting to voice her fears, and then tried to take her mind off her concerns and looked up and around, searching, but not finding what she was seeking. But that didn't mean they weren't there.

Zoe's voice dropped to a whisper. 'Have you learned anything that might help us in the morning?'

Bonnie touched a finger to her lips in a conspiratorial

gesture of silence, and said clearly, 'No, Zoe. Absolutely nothing.'

Zoe nodded in understanding, reaching through the bars and into the empty cage as far as she could. 'I wish you were next to me, Bonnie. I wish I could touch you.'

Bonnie nodded, reaching across too, until they almost touched. 'Me too,' she whispered.

They remained like that for a moment longer, then were startled by the abrasive sound of Victor Castlewell's voice crackling from hidden speakers.

'Now that all my hares are assembled and in their proper places, allow me to welcome you to Iniscay's Wild Hunt.'

All the captives looked around, searching for the source of the announcement.

'You should all be honoured that you were selected, for it means you are superior game. Not all of you can triumph, but for those of you who will, I congratulate you now.'

Bonnie sneered, knowing what technology waited above ground to thwart them, but kept quiet.

'But now for the rules,' Victor – or a recording of his voice – continued. 'The rules are simple, as anything not specifically prohibited is allowed. At six o'clock in the morning the first horns will sound, your cages will unlock, and this exit door will rise.' Right on cue a panel in the opposite wall rose, revealing an eerie darkness and a cool draught beyond, before lowering again. 'It gives you access to an underground passage that emerges at a point just beyond the manor gardens. From there you will have two hours to go anywhere you wish. Hide or keep running, but do not try to return to the manor or venture into the ocean. Following your two hours,' the voice droned on, 'the horns will sound again, and the hunters will be released. They may pursue you on foot or horseback, using nets, ropes or their bare hands to catch you. Once caught they will attach an individual irremovable tag to your collars to claim you as their own. Once tagged the hare belongs to that hunter… for as long as he or she decides.'

The captives murmured in their cages, though Bonnie was sure they already understood those stakes.

The voice proceeded, as if having allowed the pause to let the implications of the information sink in. 'Any hare or hares surviving uncaught by noon will be declared the winner or winners. You will know if you have survived when you hear the horns sound for a third and final time. You may then return to the manor and collect your fortune.'

That stirred the hares up, some nodding their approval and smiling, and the general mood in the cellar lightened a little. Bonnie glanced at them through numerous walls of bars, grimacing; ignorance really was bliss.

'That is all, my hares,' Victor's voice concluded, as the lights began dimming. 'Rest now. For better or worse, the most important day of your lives lies ahead of you.'

Bonnie shook her head; he tells them that, and expects them to rest?

The lights went out together, leaving behind an impenetrable inky blackness and a loud silence now their previously unnoticed buzzing had ceased.

'Good night, Bonnie,' Zoe's voice carried to her.

'Good night, Zoe.' Then she risked adding, hoping Zoe wouldn't question her, 'You and Rafael stay near me during the hunt.'

She felt her way to the clump of straw in one corner of her cage and settled down. Her stomach churned; too much could go wrong tomorrow, and the decision of Victor Castlewell to deny her camouflage suggested her plan could be going wrong already.

Chapter Fourteen

When the horns blasted Bonnie was already awake, and had been for hours. But the sudden harshness as the lights buzzed into life made her blink and protect her eyes with a forearm.

She sat up and jumped at the ominous clang of the cage doors unlocking and sliding open. Hares were quickly on the move, clearly keen to get out of the oppressive prison. Bonnie joined Rafael and Zoe, and they made their way to the tunnel, where others were already stooping and scurrying into the black hole exposed by the raised steel door.

Bonnie followed her friends into the drafty abyss, alert and ready for whatever might lay ahead. Its earthen walls and floor were cold, and the way it wound and twisted meant those within would not see the exit until they were almost upon it. Bonnie suppressed a claustrophobic shudder and focused on keeping moving, one foot after the other, occasionally bumping into Zoe or Rafael.

After an interminable period they finally emerged out of the ground. They winced as daylight hurt their eyes, but quickly Bonnie was able to look about, getting her bearings. They were indeed beyond the serenity of the gardens and just into the fringe of the eastern woods.

'Bonnie,' Rafael prompted, with a touch on her shoulder, 'shouldn't we be going, too?'

She nodded. The other hares had scattered, mostly

separately. 'Follow me,' she said.

'Do you know where we can go?' Zoe asked, her voice betraying her attempts at bravado. 'Do you know how we'll survive?'

'How to survive,' Bonnie said, with more confidence than she really felt, 'and how to win, too.'

The manor had been a hive of activity since before six. Everyone was up and about, the hunters dressed in traditional red coats, white riding leggings and black boots, eating breakfast and chatting about the imminent sport.

Everyone but Martin, of course.

He was as alert as the rest, but wearing a simple black T-shirt and jeans. He wasn't intending to leave the house. Indeed, for the duration of the hunt, he wouldn't even be leaving his office. He sat at his desk, his breakfast mostly ignored, the wall map of the island now lit and overlaid with an intricate grid network, marked with letters on each of the horizontal lines and numbers on the vertical. The adjacent monitors were alive, as were the terminals on his desk. He opened a case and removed his headset, not only to be used for communicating with the hunters, but to use the voice-recognition software.

Kane burst into the room, still buttoning up his waistcoat, although he had another hour before he could leave. 'Well, Martin?' he said abruptly, 'can you track them?'

'If I couldn't,' Martin said without looking up, 'you'd have soon heard from me.'

'Show me.' There was an urgency to his brother's demeanour that Martin found amusing, and he was almost tempted to drag things out, just to see him squirm further. But then, Martin didn't want him around any longer than absolutely necessary. He keyed up the transponder codes and numbers appeared, moving slowly across the map in various directions. Kane stared at it for a moment, then turned back to his brother, his face fierce. 'I can't tell which one's which!'

Martin glared back. 'You don't have to – I do. And I relay the information to the hunters, just like it's always been done, Kane.' Martin fixed Kane with a knowing stare. 'And I wonder what makes this hunt different for you?'

Kane ignored his jibes. 'How accurate is the sensor web?'

'Accurate enough.' Martin slammed his palms onto the desk in exasperation. 'Damn it, Kane, I don't question you about being an insufferable jackass, so don't question my work! Why are you really here?'

Kane regarded him for a moment, then said, 'Paige will be out there as well. I want you to lead her and the others away from Bonnie. I want my tag on her collar.'

Martin raised an eyebrow. 'You mean, father's tag, don't you?'

Kane grinned slyly. 'Of course I do, little brother. Just make sure you send Paige as far away as possible.'

'Oh, I'd love to, brother. Believe me. But like I told Paige earlier when she asked me to send you in the wrong direction, father gave me orders against aiding and abetting petty sibling rivalry.'

Kane's grin faded. 'She was here too? And he told you that?'

Martin nodded. 'Yes to both questions. Can't imagine why he'd say that, though. After all, you two love each other so much.'

Kane approached the desk and rested his hands on the edge as he leaned closer, fixing a murderous gaze on his brother. 'Remember this, Martin: the old man won't be around here for ever.'

Martin remained unimpressed. 'Neither will I, so fuck off.'

Bonnie had led them to the pond where they'd been the previous day. She immediately found a patch of mud and began coating her skin with it. She looked to the two of them. 'I could do with some help.'

They complied, hastily kneeling beside her and caking her with handfuls of the sticky goo.

When she was pretty well coated, Bonnie nodded towards a thick holly bush near a fallen log. 'Go and get what I've hidden over there,' she said to Zoe.

'Hidden?'

'Just do it, Zoe.'

As the lovely girl followed her orders, Bonnie's attention focused on Rafael, still running his hands over her muddied body, his fingers straying to her breasts, massaging them until her nipples rose in response. She smiled, then reluctantly moved his hands up to coat her face. 'Not just now, Rafael,' she chided softly. 'Maybe after this is all done.'

'It's a date,' he said.

Just then Zoe returned with a small black burlap sack, tied at the neck. Without waiting for Bonnie's prompting she undid the ties and removed a rectangular box. Bonnie took it from her and opened it, revealing tools like those a watchmaker might use.

'What are they?' Zoe whispered, the tension of the

event making the three of them huddle closely together and communicate quietly.

'The proverbial aces up our sleeves,' Bonnie told them.

'We could get disqualified for this,' Rafael murmured. 'This is cheating.'

'It's no more than what our adversaries are doing.' Bonnie reached for Zoe's collar. She worked at something inside the lining with a pair of pliers, her words faltering with her attention. 'We're being tracked all the time, wherever we are on the island. There are microchips in our collars, as well as a sensor web of cameras, microphones and detectors hidden everywhere around us. Martin follows us from a map in his office, and relays our locations to the hunters.'

Zoe glanced at Rafael, with a stunned expression freezing her features. 'So, none of us ever had a chance in hell of winning the statue?'

'No.' Bonnie pulled back, with a small plastic-coated chip in the pliers' grip. She set it down on the sack. 'That's why they're generous with the head start, and why we're never allowed to remove our collars.'

Rafael turned ashen, despite his natural colour and the additional camouflage. 'How could they cheat like that?'

'Kane once said that honesty is reserved for equals, not slaves,' Bonnie said simply, working on his collar.

'You're removing the transponders,' Rafael said. 'But will that be enough? Can they still track us with the cameras and microphones?'

Bonnie set Rafael's transponder beside Zoe's, then tackled her own. 'Oh, yes, they can still track us.'

'And you're not worried?' Zoe blurted incredulously.

Bonnie glanced up, her transponder gripped by the pliers, just as Tim emerged from the surrounding undergrowth. She waved him over. 'Yes, I'm worried, but I just pray I'm as good a computer programmer as I like to think I am.'

The hunters gathered on the lawn in front of the manor, their horses edgy, responding to the excitement from their riders. The thrill was almost palpable.

As was the annoyance, at least from some.

Paige sided her chestnut stallion close to the steps, where Janine and Isobelle stood, waiting any final commands. 'Where's Tim?' she stormed. 'I can't believe I had to saddle Loki myself!'

Janine and Isobelle looked at each other, unsure to whom the question was directed. Finally Janine, as chief housekeeper, took the proverbial reins, answering, 'I'm not certain, mistress. He was here twenty minutes ago.'

Paige slapped her riding-crop against her thigh, making the horse whinny. 'When I find that idiot I'll leather him to an inch of his worthless life!'

Janine started to reply, then thought better of it; Paige had a habit of taking her frustrations out on those nearest her.

Nearby, Kane ignored his sister's rants, concentrating on adjusting the round weights on the four corners of his net. Like most of the others he preferred the net, not just for its accuracy, but for its psychological power over his catch; a net descending over a pursued hare could easily take the initial fight out of them. But he also carried a lasso. He tapped the earphone on his headset. 'Martin, can you hear me?'

The tinny reply made his inner ear itch. 'A deaf man

could hear you. What do you want?'

'Isn't it time?'

'Have you heard the horns yet?'

Kane bit back an initial retort as pointless. If he didn't need Martin's skills so much... 'Just keep me informed of anything you think I need to know.'

'Of course... wait, there is something you need to know.'

Kane tilted his head, as if listening to the disembodied voice on the wind instead of via the headset. 'Well, what is it?' he snapped impatiently.

'You need to know that you're an obnoxious, arrogant son of a—'

Kane switched off the headset, looked at his watch, then glanced about. 'Father!' he called.

Victor Castlewell manoeuvred his black steed to where Kane sat astride his mount. 'Son?'

Kane noticed the animated gleam in his father's eyes. Only during the annual hunt did he seem to come so alive. 'Are you ready?' he asked.

'The horns haven't blown yet.'

'I'm master of the hunt,' Kane persisted. 'I say it's time.'

Victor glanced into the woods beyond the gardens, as if able to see through the dense undergrowth to the sport that awaited him. 'Very well,' he said, 'if that's what you say.'

Kane switched on the headset again. 'Martin, sound the horns!' He grinned broadly, dug his spurs viciously into Shohan's ribs, and set forth charging.

The hunt was on!

Bonnie was waving Tim away when she heard the horns. Tim heard it too, and rushed off more quickly, while Bonnie returned to Zoe and Rafael who were trying to hide all evidence that they'd ever been there. 'Now what do we do?' Zoe asked earnestly.

Bonnie lifted the sack, collected one more item from it, then threw the sack back behind the holly bush. She set the item into her hair, like a bobby pin, before turning to them. 'At least one, if not all, of the Castlewells will be concentrating on capturing me. You two might be better off on your own.'

'Forget it,' Zoe countered adamantly.

'Yeah, forget it,' Rafael agreed. 'You seem to know what you're doing.'

'Well, let's hope so,' Bonnie said dryly, then started off into the woods towards the western part of the island, her friends following. The ground beneath their feet was mostly soft with dirt and leaves, but occasionally there were sharp stones or sticks that made them wince and stagger.

Close beside her Rafael managed to gasp between pants, 'But... with the sensor web... where can we hide...?'

Bonnie didn't have the breath or inclination to explain why the sensor web was not their greatest problem right now.

The three guest hunters had broken off and moved towards the centre of the island, the better to plan their immediate moves. The three Castlewells, however, stopped at the edge of the southern trail to the cove, and waited.

Back at the manor Martin switched to the all-band frequency as he began reading from the wall map. 'Right, hunters, here's what you've been waiting for. Consult your pocket maps for grid references. Hannah's moving north, currently at reference D11 one hundred feet from the lake, and closing. Francis has stopped in a thicket along the north-eastern trail, at E13. Reason unknown.' He glanced at a monitor receiving camera images from that area, and smirked. 'Looks like she's been caught a little short.

'Siobhan's making excellent progress eastward across the greensward, crossing from F15 to F16. She may either try to hide in the tall grass there, or climb the hill and peel an eye for pursuers. Annette's on the beach in the cove, I13, and William appears to be making his way to the southern lighthouse at L11.'

A heavily accented voice cut through. 'And our *devushka*, Bonnie?'

Martin raised an eyebrow. 'Our *devushka* is with Zoe and Rafael on the north-eastern beach, at C13 to 15. Select your hares, hunters, and contact me for any assistance.' Quickly Martin switched to more selective headset channels, speaking only to his family. 'Hopefully you haven't rushed off to the north-east beach for the grand prize.'

Kane's voice interrupted him. 'Dammit, Martin, what's her real location?'

'She's gone west, staying off the trails with her friends. Looks like you'll bag all three at once. Currently at H7… wait, I mean J8… no, J9.'

'Make up your mind, Martin!' Kane bellowed through the headset.

Martin rose and moved to peer more closely at the

map. Bonnie's, Zoe's and Rafael's transponder signals were jumping about, shifting locations too quickly to account for them being on foot, sometimes appearing together, other times hundreds of metres away. And as he watched his heart began to pound heavily in his chest. All the other transponder signals were behaving in the same way!

'Martin!' Kane's voice threatened to drill into his brother's head. 'What the hell's happening?'

'Something's wrong with the sensor web. I'll try to pinpoint them with the cameras and microphones. Stand by.'

'What the hell else would you expect us to do—?'

Martin cut Kane off, returning to his seat and switching to computer vocal interface, as he supplemented his investigations on the keyboard. 'Computer: audio-visual search program, external sensor web, primary identifix reference Fisher, Bonnie. Secondary references Bashir, Rafael, and Scott, Zoe.'

Even as he began running diagnostic programs to determine the reason for the transponder malfunctions, Martin's mind began to relax a little; perhaps too soon, but he had confidence in the technology at his fingertips. The computer had digitally stored images and voices of all Iniscay's inhabitants, and could search the island to find any or all of them. And all in less time than it would take to voice the commands. Yes, any second now it would locate them.

Yes… any second now.

Any second.

After thirty anxious seconds he glanced up at the monitors, which should have already located the targets. Instead, all nine monitors were diligently focused on

Janine, currently sitting on the toilet in the servant's quarters, reading a magazine and smoking.

'Computer!' Martin barked, growing alarmed and angry. Though he normally wouldn't care if his misbegotten family caught no hare for the next century, he still had a sense of pride in his work. 'Repeat audio-visual search program!'

That drew a response from the computer.

It shut down the cameras and microphones completely.

Martin stared, mouth agape, disbelieving any of this was happening. He'd checked the equipment thoroughly these last few days, and tested the software last week when he had Paige exercise the women on the beach. He examined the results of his diagnostic sweep, and didn't like what he found. Then he switched back to the all-channel headset. 'I have bad news, hunters. The entire tracking and surveillance system has crashed. You're on your own.'

The channels began flooding with replies, none particularly pleasant. Martin filtered out the rest, leaving his family. 'Don't even start on me,' he said defensively.

'Has some hacker jammed his way into the system?' Kane demanded.

'Don't try talking technical, Kane, it makes you sound more obtuse than you already are. Listen, they were first detected at H8, west of the southern lake; that was probably correct.' He paused, wishing he smoked. 'I'll do what I can.'

His father's voice carried, not sounding as angry or disappointed as he expected. 'I'm sure you will, Martin.'

Martin leaned back in his chair, then forward for his cold coffee, which he drank anyway. Hackers indeed;

his brother really was a cretin. Martin was sure he'd explained to Kane many times that the hunt computer was hardened, a stand-alone system inaccessible to outside modems. Only an insider could—

The answer was so deceptively simple and obvious he should have seen it sooner. Indeed, he should have prepared for it beforehand. It was almost as if he secretly wanted Bonnie to do whatever she could to screw things up. But of course, that would be disloyal to the family, wouldn't it?

He buzzed his desk intercom. 'Delilah, could I have another breakfast, please? I let my first get cold.'

For Kane, who desperately tried to maintain decorum no matter the provocation, particularly in front of his father, the debacle had been simply too much, and he was now striking the nearest tree with his crop. 'Damn! Damn! Damn!' he cursed.

Paige, for her part, looked ready to join Kane in the chastisement of the local flora, but instead she tried to steady her nerves and rage by swigging heavily from a silver flask. 'This is so... annoying!' she burst. 'So amateurish! What must our guests think?'

'I don't give a damn about them,' Kane snarled, edging Shohan over and taking the flask from her. 'And neither do you. What about us?' He drank deeply, wiping his mouth on his sleeve. 'How can we track her down without the sensor web?'

Paige recovered her flask. 'Especially in the western woods? You know how dense it is in there. If they're off the trails we'll have to follow them on foot.' She drank again, ignoring the spills she left on her coat. 'Damn Martin and his machines. I wouldn't be surprised if he was lying about the malfunctions, or caused them himself.'

'He didn't,' Victor said simply, his face strangely beatific, untarnished by the unexpected turn of events.

Kane glared uncomprehending. 'How can you be so sure of that, father?'

Victor met the glare with sudden, open contempt, sharing it with Paige. 'Because I was fortunate enough to sire one honourable child among three.'

Both children bristled, Paige recovering first to ask, 'Regardless of the reasons for the malfunction, what are we going to do now?'

Victor steeled himself and drew high in the saddle. 'We are going to behave like true sportsmen, true hunters, for once in a long overdue time. We are going to continue to pursue the game, using our wits.' He cantered between them as he continued along the westward trail. 'Feel free to consult mine, to compensate for your own deficiencies,' he called back over his shoulder.

Kane and Paige glanced at each other like spoilt brats who weren't getting their way, before hurrying along in the wake of their urbane father.

The three hares rested at an outcrop of rock, an oasis of light from above not blocked by the branches of the trees around them. They were sweating, aching, and slightly disoriented, and Bonnie wished she'd thought to include a watch with those tools she'd acquired and hidden away. Still, the sun had made progress into the sky, and was now almost above the level of the treetops.

Not that a watch would have cured the exhaustion in her limbs or the pains in the soles of her feet. Trainers and a watch. And maybe some sweets. Yes, she thought with grim humour, next time she found herself naked and pursued like a wild animal by a pack of sadists, she'd be better prepared.

Rafael had disappeared behind the rock to relieve himself, and now returned. 'Maybe we've lost them,' he offered optimistically. 'Maybe they're hopeless without their tracking equipment.'

But Bonnie shook her head. 'The sabotage I performed on the computer was such that it didn't start until after the hunters were on their way. I couldn't risk the system breaking down beforehand in case Martin spotted it and they delayed the hunt in order to repair it.'

'So?'

'So, they had a good fix on us for the first few seconds. They'll know our general location, and that's probably all Victor Castlewell needs. I don't know about the guests or his children, but he for one doesn't need tracking equipment.' She looked back over her shoulder, listening intently. 'Believe me he doesn't.'

Bonnie was right. Victor had left his mount, found the equipment Bonnie had hidden in the holly bush, and was making his way on foot through the woods, rope wound under one arm, tags on his belt, an intense look on his face.

Behind him Kane and Paige remained on horseback, determined to stay that way, though their progress in keeping up was hampered by the close proximity of the trees encroaching around them. They'd been silent, occasionally glancing uneasily at each other, until finally Kane took the initiative. 'Do you really expect to follow their trail, father?'

Victor tensed, as if woken out of a deep concentration. He glanced over his shoulder. 'I already am, and will continue to do so, if you two would stop making so much damned noise.'

'And if you do find them?' Paige didn't seem to hear or acknowledge the annoyance in her father's voice. 'You left your horse back by the lake, your nets—'

'Thirty years ago I faced a man-eating tiger with little more than what I have on me now. And survived.' Victor returned to examining the trail, the footprints in the earth, the broken leaves and branches.

Kane frowned; had the old man gone senile? 'She isn't a tiger, father,' he snorted derisively.

'No,' Victor muttered impatiently. 'She's far more dangerous.' He winced again as Kane's horse snapped a branch loudly beneath its hoof. The sound seemed to carry through the heart of the wood. He glanced up again. 'You two, head back to the trail, then make your way around and up to the edge of the peat bogs. That's where they'll be hiding. Drive them back towards me.'

Bonnie, Raphael and Zoe were on the move again, stopping, as Victor had surmised, at the boundary between the north-western woods and the bogs. The Atlantic was a choppy salad of blue and white, and the wind an incessant squall.

Bonnie paused, looking back, certain she'd seen figures on horseback. Events were moving quickly now. It was time for phase two. She turned to Zoe and Rafael. 'Time for us to separate.'

'What?' Zoe reached out and touched her shoulder. Her touch was warm and welcome, but Bonnie remained focused.

'We have to,' she insisted. 'It's important for the plan. You two head out to the western lighthouse.'

'There?' Rafael questioned. 'But we couldn't get to it yesterday.'

'Not without messing up our clothing,' she pointed out, and patted his naked bottom. 'But that's not a problem now. Listen, the sensor web will be up shortly, but there'll still be blind spots. That area will be one of them. And you can see anyone approaching.'

'And what about you?' Zoe pleaded, not liking the sound of this at all.

Bonnie couldn't tell her the truth, not without provoking a pointless debate. Instead she said, slightly ambiguously, 'I have some unfinished business.'

Paige finished her brandy and tossed the flask into the ocean; she could always order another. The wind had whipped her hat off and sent it tumbling over and over into a filthy mud hole; she could always order another one of those, too. But now her hair was blowing most unflatteringly in every direction beneath the flimsy protection of her headset.

Paige had suggested to Kane that they stayed together. But he disagreed, and headed off to circle around the woods through the western trail. Good. Let him get literally bogged down while she took the easier route north. But she found nothing! Damn it, she should have brought another flask. Perhaps she should call Martin and have that fool Tim bring her out another one—

Then she saw the movement in the trees – something tall, not a deer—

It was Bonnie!

Paige yelped and charged after her, galloping only a

short distance before foolishly acknowledging that she would probably have to continue on foot. She leapt off Loki, flinging the reins once around a tree to keep him there, and charged ahead. The game was dodging between trees, trying to confuse her. But after a moment Paige noticed something about her prey's progress. It seemed stilted... she was limping!

Paige grinned evilly. With a cry of triumph she charged ahead, the handcuffs attached to her belt jangling as she jumped over fallen logs and elbowed low branches out of her way. Ahead of her, with the distance between them rapidly closing, Bonnie was trying to do the same, fighting her injury. The bloodlust rose as Paige drew closer and closer—

Bonnie turned to face her pursuer just as Paige tackled her, sending them both into a clump of dried leaves with a crash, sending them scattering. They struggled, but Paige had the advantage of being on top and remaining on top. She straddled Bonnie and pinned her wrists to the ground until the girl was near tears.

Paige grinned down at her in triumph. 'Looks like I've bagged myself the grand prize,' she panted, her breasts heaving from the exertion and the adrenaline firing her veins.

Bonnie was breathing rapidly too, her breasts rising and falling, her nipples erect. 'I never... I never knew the chase... could be so... so thrilling...' she managed between gasps. 'Even to be caught...'

'Yes...' Paige purred, gradually getting her breathing under control. 'It is thrilling... especially for the hunter.' She let go of one of Bonnie's wrists, aware of possible further resistance, but receiving none. She removed from her pocket one of her tags, a metal object the size of a coin with a padlock arm. Deftly she reached down and slipped it onto Bonnie's collar, leering as she heard it click into place. 'Now come, father's waiting for you.'

'Wait,' Bonnie pouted a little, 'aren't you going to savour your conquest now… here?'

'What?' Paige was caught by surprise. 'How do you know about that?'

'So it is true,' Bonnie continued, 'that you like to enjoy your prize immediately.'

Paige released her other wrist and sat up straight, the temptation almost overpowering. 'I may have captured you, but you belong to father. If I take you back now I might have time to hunt another for myself… like your friends.'

Bonnie shook her head, eyes aglow. 'They're not as good a catch as me.'

Paige frowned as she regarded her further. 'You're planning something.'

'How can I? You've tagged me, and the tag's irremovable. With that and my limp I'm out of the hunt. I simply want to reward the one who caught me, like a true slave should.' Bonnie reached up and pushed her hands inside Paige's jacket, and caressed the full breasts she found there, still heaving, albeit less violently now, within the confines of a white silk blouse.

Paige made no move to stop her, but continued to look suspicious. 'I should punish you for touching me without permission,' she said, without true conviction.

'You can,' Bonnie conceded, slowly unbuttoning the blouse. 'I…' her voice faltered dramatically, and she looked away as if in shame. 'I have to confess something to you… mistress. I don't want to, but I know I'll never have the opportunity again… or the courage…'

237

Paige looked spellbound, by the gentle hands at her breasts and by the surprising confession coming from the delicious creature lying helplessly between her powerful thighs. 'When you had me chained up in your room, watching Zoe and Rafael make love to you, I wanted nothing more than to join them,' Bonnie whispered huskily. 'Or even better, I wanted to push them aside and have you all for myself. Despite – or perhaps because of – all you'd done to me.'

She peeled open the blouse and kneaded Paige's generous breasts through her white riding bra. Paige closed her eyes and moaned softly. 'I mustn't believe you,' she murmured.

'Paige,' Bonnie persisted, 'though I'll belong to your father, he's a man, a fool like Kane. I'll know that no one can properly dominate a woman like another woman. And no woman can dominate me like you can.'

'How true,' Paige acknowledged, without sarcasm. She bent forward and Bonnie raised her head until their lips met and ground together, their tongues entwining. Paige slowly ground her pelvis onto Bonnie's abdomen, her boot heels digging into Bonnie's thighs, as Bonnie reached up and slipped Paige's breasts out from the cups of the bra.

When their mouths finally parted Paige sat up again, her breasts free beneath the rucked material of the bra, Bonnie reached up and cupped and squeezed the bare flesh, enchanted by the sight and feel of them. 'The worse thing you did to me that night was send me away, after having me grovel before you. I wanted to please you directly, in every way I could. Let me do that now.'

She reached for the fastenings of Paige's riding trousers and started undoing them, but Paige clutched

Bonnie's wrists and shook her head in disbelief or suspicion. 'This must be a trick,' she said.

Bonnie managed to shift slightly until Paige was astride her thighs instead of her tummy, and then guided Paige's hand down between her thighs. 'See for yourself,' she encouraged huskily.

Paige studied the beauty lying beneath her for a while, and then ventured with gloved fingers to probe between Bonnie's moist labia. Bonnie shuddered and cried out, squirming beneath Paige as the woman found the source of her desire, massaging it for a few tense minutes before withdrawing her fingers and finding a delicate web of dew on her gloves. Bonnie looked up hungrily. 'See?' she whispered conspiratorially. 'I told you. The things we can do now. The things we can do after, to ensure your advancement in your father's eyes.'

Paige didn't need any more convincing. She collapsed onto Bonnie as their mouths met again, clamping her fingertips into Bonnie's shoulders and breasts, cruelly enjoying the reaction she evoked from the writhing girl clamped between her thighs. Bonnie genuinely wanted to get Paige's trousers down, and the woman eventually let her up to complete the task. Kneeling beside her Bonnie peeled them and her knickers down to her ankles, but was unable to remove them completely without discarding the woman's boots. But there was no time for that now.

Paige parted her thighs as much as she could within the confines of the material rucked around her ankles and grabbed a handful of Bonnie's hair. 'Now,' she hissed, 'worship the eagle!' and then she jammed the lovely girl's face between her muscled thighs where the tattooed bird guarded her sex.

239

Bonnie drank in the musky aroma of her mistress before gently, almost reverently, spreading the fleshy pink outer labia, then the darker inner folds of flesh, exposing the erect bud of her clitoris and the deep, dark, moist channel of her vagina. And when Bonnie's tongue snaked into that velvety burrow Paige seemed to give up any lingering reservations, clamping Bonnie's head with her sweating thighs, her hands pressing on the top of Bonnie's head, demanding more from her.

And Bonnie obliged, actually beginning to relish the writhing and moaning that overcame the woman as her veneration grew bolder, juices covering her face. Soon Paige was bucking against her face, and she felt the muscles contract around her tongue, the woman's breath escaping in staccato pants.

After a while Paige's passion subsided and she released Bonnie, allowing her to disentangle herself. 'Not bad... slave,' she said wearily. 'Not bad at all...' She opened her eyes, just in time to see Bonnie ducking and dodging away through the undergrowth – without any sign of a limp.

'You fucking bitch!' Paige snarled. She rose inelegantly, looking ridiculous with her trousers and knickers stretched around her ankles. 'Come back here! You're tagged! You're mine!' a few seconds passed, Paige's fury close to boiling over, and then a hint of a victorious smile lifted her lips as Bonnie appeared again from behind a dense bush. 'That's a good little girl,' Paige called arrogantly. 'Come back to your mistress and we'll say no more about your naughtiness.'

But instead of obeying and begging forgiveness, Bonnie fiddled with the irremovable tag, and a few seconds later she held it in the air, and then threw it into the undergrowth.

'What the—?!' Paige roared, and Bonnie slipped silently from view again.

As Paige stood staring after her in disbelief there was a whinny and the sound of retreating hooves. 'Loki!' Paige shouted, swinging round, her breasts swaying beneath the tight bra as her trousers snagged around her ankles and a small bush and she tumbled forward like a felled tree. As her horse deserted her she looked up after it, her face and breasts smeared with mud. 'You can't do this, you stupid horse!' she shouted. 'It's against the rules!'

A short distance away Victor Castlewell, witness to the entire incident, chuckled to himself and moved off after his prey, leaving his daughter to salvage whatever remained of her dignity. 'Rules, indeed,' he said.

Chapter Fifteen

'Father! Kane! Paige! The system's back on-line!'

But Kane wasn't listening. After having to disembark from Shohan for the third time to help her over a clump of rocks and out of a mud hole, he'd furiously thrown his headset and riding-crop into the nearest bog. He emerged onto the narrow pebble beach on the northern side of the island, staying away from the waves on the rocks to his left. Damn Bonnie, damn Martin, damn his father and everything and everyone else. When Kane finally inherited his father's wealth there would be changes.

From the edge of the woods Paige emerged, covered in muddy handprints and minus her horse, waving him closer. She stopped, her head tilted; she was obviously listening to something on the headset.

Kane didn't much care, though. 'Have you seen her?'

'Seen her? The bitch tricked me.'

Kane bellowed with amusement. It was the first good laugh he'd had all day.

'You have to let me ride with you,' Paige sulked.

Kane's laugh calmed into a smirk. 'Kiss my arse, little sister,' he said.

But Paige tapped her headset defiantly. 'Do you want to know where they are?'

Kane's interest was fixed. 'Martin's repaired the system?'

'He says it seems to have repaired itself, at least

partially. The only signals he's picking up are from our three quarries.'

'Where?'

Now it was Paige's turn to smirk. 'Kiss my arse, big brother.'

Kane regarded her for a moment, then reached down to help her up onto Shohan.

They hadn't travelled far before they spied their father, sitting on a huge grey rock overlooking the reedy peat bogs, like a wolf guarding his territory, his coat and headset beside him.

'Father!' Kane called, his voice fighting against the sea wind. 'Martin has a fix on them!'

Victor nodded sagely, still staring into the distance.

'Do you need a ride?' Kane continued. 'Paige can walk the rest of the way back.'

'Fuck off,' she snarled into her brother's ear. 'I owe that bitch something.'

But Victor never even looked down at them as he waved them off. 'You two go on ahead. Catch them if you can. Whoever you find you keep.'

'Even Bonnie?' Kane's eyes gleamed hungrily, and he licked his lips like a lizard as he anticipated his father's reply.

'Even Bonnie.' Victor smiled to himself, adding quietly to himself, 'If you can catch her.'

With a whoop of joy Kane galloped off, Paige clinging to him, already arguing about rights of ownership of their imminent possessions.

Victor watched them disappear from view, then climbed off the rock and jogged into the reeds nearby.

Bonnie had been watching them all from close by. She'd lain hidden, motionless and anxious as she watched Victor emerge from the woods and plant himself on the rock as if pausing to behold the unmatchable power and splendour of the ocean. She tried to control her breathing, to remain calm, waiting for him to move on. Then Kane and Paige appeared, their information regarding the computer's recovery pleasing to her ears. She was, however, suspicious and apprehensive when Victor chose not to follow his foolish son and daughter.

That apprehension was proven well-founded when he leapt from the rock and moved into the reed bed – in her very direction! Had her presence been that obvious to him?

She had no time to consider her situation further, as she turned and struggled to escape the peat bog and rush back into the woods. Victor was at her heels, his speed and stamina remarkable for a man of his age. But he held back, giving Bonnie just enough time and opportunity to stay out of his grasp. He was toying with her, like a cat playing with a doomed bird!

Suddenly he rugby-tackled her around the thighs and they tumbled headlong onto a bed of marram grass. Bonnie struggled, punching his back as he rolled her over and used his superior weight to pin her down as he struggled up her body, laughing gruffly between heavy pants for breath. She tried to pull his hair and even sank her teeth into his arm through his sleeve. He cursed, but she wasn't really able to hurt him. And from the feel of the sturdy column of flesh buffeting against her through his trousers as he moved, he was enjoying the struggle immensely.

And slowly, gradually, so was Bonnie. Her stomach

knotted with simmering excitement and her pussy pulsed for attention. She tried to suppress the shameful sensations, trying to push Victor off her, but without real conviction. He held her easily, his eyes filled with lust as he sensed her turmoil.

'You do understand, don't you my dear?' he heaved. 'You belong to me.'

Bonnie strained her back and managed to sink her teeth into a careless hand. Victor cursed in Italian and rolled her back over, face down, with ease. 'You should learn a little respect for your betters,' he admonished through gritted teeth, and then began smacking her bottom with his bare hand, smacking with such ferocity that Bonnie pressed herself into the grass and earth in a futile attempt to escape the onslaught. And as each blow fell the pain and humiliation was supplemented with a fiery glow that spread through her buttocks to the pit of her stomach and her wet sex. She yelped helplessly, unable to escape the expertly administered barrage of blows.

But as Bonnie shuddered beneath the pain and pleasure of the punishment, Victor stopped, and she groaned her disappointment. He located the rope from where it had fallen nearby during their struggle, pulled her limp arms behind her back, and tied her unresisting wrists together. Then he stood, and Bonnie rolled languidly onto her side and watched as he ceremoniously unbuttoned his trousers, rummaged inside, and then tugged his erection out into the fresh air. Bonnie licked her lips and sighed. Despite Victor's age, his manhood looked magnificent. He stood tall above her, looking down upon her naked and submissive beauty. He was the victorious predator and she the defeated prey.

But he made no move towards her, and just when Bonnie was wondering what was wrong, he said, 'Try to escape.'

'I—' Bonnie was confused.

'Try to get away. Crawl!'

She understood, and tried to do as he ordered. It was virtually impossible with her arms bound behind her, but she valiantly writhed and grunted, managing to cover a couple of feet.

'That's good,' Victor goaded, his voice thick with emotion as he stroked his cock and took a few steps after her. 'Keep going,' he encouraged. 'You want to get away from me.'

Bonnie tried, but she was exhausted, and it was hopeless. Her knees ached and the earth and grass scraped against her shoulders and breasts. 'I can't...' she pleaded. 'I can't go any further...'

'You disappoint me, Bonnie,' Victor said, his fist pumping ever faster. 'Then I shall have to claim you for my own once and for all.'

Kicking her ankles apart, he knelt between them. Hands gripped her hips and pulled them up and back until she was kneeling with her bottom raised and her face and breasts pressing against the ground, her fingers helplessly clutching at thin air. Her soft curls were wet against his trousers. Resting his pulsing cock between her buttocks her ground against her. The stimulation on her clitoris was exquisite. He increased the pressure and intensity and she moaned loudly as she came, her pussy trying desperately to clamp onto his thigh as waves of dizzying heat permeated her.

As her tired senses returned she felt his erection brush

against her inner thighs, seeking its way into her. She shifted slightly to accommodate him, drawing in a sharp breath as he finally found her entrance and sank into her with one long plunge, easily occupying her to the hilt, the literal fulfilment she'd been seeking. They rutted like a pair of mating animals, and she instantly felt another orgasm approaching. His heavy balls slapped against her with every aggressive thrust, while he gripped his delicious trophy with powerful hands, rocking her easily back and forth as though she was merely a vessel in which he could sate his desire. They found a mutual rhythm, the roles of predator and prey momentarily cast aside, each giving, each gaining, her mind and body awash with the delightful sensations evoked.

But soon Victor coaxed their rhythm into a more urgent gallop. She pictured how they might look to an outsider; one utterly submissive, the other utterly triumphant, both caught up in their own pleasures. This image, and an extra deep thrust from Victor as he covered her back, made her climax again with a strangled cry.

Victor came too, grunting, his body spasming on top of her and pinning her arms between them. For a moment his bearing was lost, and he drooled and swore into her ear as his seed pumped into her depths. His words fuelled Bonnie again and another, weaker orgasm made her tense and groan into the earth.

After a time he withdrew and flopped onto the ground beside her, leaving her feeling empty but immensely satisfied.

Relishing her subsiding pleasure, the warmth of spent lust seeping from between her clenched thighs, she turned and kissed his cheek. It was a gesture he seemed to appreciate.

'It's a pity that's over,' he said quietly. 'Subsequent captures never match the first.'

Bonnie's eyes twinkled. 'Perhaps you just haven't been hunting the right game,' she whispered.

Kane and Paige were outside the stables, looking at the closed door. 'Is Martin sure?' Kane demanded.

'Yes,' Paige snapped impatiently, having to listen to one bleating brother while straining to hear the other over her headset. 'Yes, he says all three signals are coming from inside the stables.'

Kane rubbed his hands together and grinned lecherously. 'Good,' he said. With little effort he kicked open the wooden door and shouted, 'You've cheated, my little hares! You're not supposed to come back to the vicinity of the house before the end of the hunt! Your lives are now forfeit to me!'

'And me, Godammit!' Paige added, pushing past him, checking each of the empty horse stalls, stopping once to kick aside bails of hay that might hide a cowering human hare.

And she cringed at what she found.

'Kane,' she said, slowly stooping to pick up the objects she'd discovered.

Her brother, furious at not getting things his own way, spun round angrily, and then his jaw dropped at what he saw. Paige was holding three transponder microchips, at arm's length as though they were cyanide pills.

Kane almost wished they were.

The Castlewell family gathered in Martin's office. Bonnie was there too, although she was not kneeling or supplicating herself in any way. Instead she sat on the edge of the desk next to Victor, watching Kane pace like a caged tiger before them. 'She cheated!' he ranted, pointing an accusing finger at the amused girl. 'She ruined the game for all of us!'

'I don't feel cheated,' Victor informed him mildly.

'She deliberately broke into our computers, removed the transponders from her collar and her friends' collars, sneakily found a way of removing Paige's tag from her collar with a paper-clip, and involved our stable-boy in her conspiracy, and you don't feel cheated?!'

'I should feel cheated if my prey fights back?' Victor questioned, one eyebrow raised. He remained disturbingly placid; something which Kane didn't seem to notice, but which Paige did, hence her subdued presence in the corner, allowing her older half-brother to argue uselessly for the both of them.

Kane stopped pacing, boiling with frustration. 'I want the hunt run again,' he said, his fists clenched.

'I agree,' Bonnie concurred.

'You weren't asked, slave,' he spat at her.

'The hunt will be rerun,' Bonnie repeated, oblivious to his anger. 'But without transponders, without sensors, and without radios.'

'Our guests won't agree to that,' Kane argued.

'They'll agree,' Bonnie insisted, 'they'll have no choice. The footing will be more equal and that, in turn, will add the required spice such a competition deserves.'

'She's right, my son,' Victor added. 'I haven't enjoyed myself so much in years as I did today.' He surreptitiously squeezed Bonnie's thigh. 'I'm sorry you can't appreciate it in the same way.'

Kane smirked contemptuously. 'Why not just put her in charge of the whole damned shooting match while you're at it?'

The Castlewell patriarch smiled broadly. 'Funny you should say that... because I already have. I've made Bonnie mistress of the hunt. And mistress of the house, too.'

'You've what?' Kane and Paige exclaimed in unison.

'Yes, I believe it's better to centralise authority,' Victor continued calmly. 'There's been too much disruption of late from petty rivalries. Bonnie will be answerable to me alone, organising the daily running of the house as well as arranging the hunt.'

'And using the computer to find potential hares,' Martin added. He'd been content to sit behind his desk, having been briefed beforehand of the news by Victor. Now he couldn't help but add to the consternation already gripping the faces of his brother and sister.

Kane turned on him. 'And you're going to just let her take your job away, too?' he sneered.

Martin grinned confidently. 'Just watch me.'

'Martin's destiny lies elsewhere,' Victor informed them. 'I'm certain you'll both wish your brother all the good luck that I do.'

'If you think I'm going to stand by and let you overturn our house,' Paige said to Bonnie with clear menace. 'If you think—'

'Then I'd be right,' Bonnie finished for her, unable to help smiling at the pointlessness of the threat. 'Of course, you can always follow Martin's lead and find your own footing in the outside world.'

Neither Kane nor Paige responded.

Victor looked upon them with disappointment in his eyes. 'No, I didn't think so. Now leave us,' he said dismissively.

Martin waited until Kane and Paige had stormed out. 'Thank you, father,' he said. 'If there's anything I can do—'

Genuine warmth flooded the man's face. 'You can forgive an old man for not letting you lead your own life sooner.'

Martin beamed back. 'Consider yourself forgiven.' He stared at Bonnie, his thoughts ineffable. Then he leaned forward and kissed Bonnie gently on the lips, before turning and leaving.

'I'll miss him,' Victor announced as the door closed.

'I know.' Bonnie stood and faced him, wrapping her arms around his neck and pressing her forehead up against his. 'Still, you'll have me now.'

'True enough,' Victor Castlewell said quietly.

The hares huddled in their cages, naked but for their collars, thick leather with no hidden microchips, their bodies painted by the house staff. Some were anxious, most aroused, all expectant. The rumours they'd heard of this place were true; a lifetime of fortune, or a lifetime of servitude, awaited them all.

The door opened and in stepped the mysterious female who had greeted them when they'd first arrived on the island only days before, the female who had since teased and tempted and tested them to the very limits of their sexual desire.

She was young, shockingly young for the power and responsibility she wielded deftly before them, her chestnut hair a cascade of curls, her almond eyes moving with mercurial temperament over each hare in his or her cage. Her figure was hugged by a black leather outfit, the deep cleavage between her ample breasts displayed from her sleeveless vest, and the curves of her legs by her skintight trousers.

In the course of their short time on Iniscay, some of the hares had fantasised about what she might look like in one of the more revealing corsets of a house slave. But such speculations were quickly dismissed as foolish; the way this beauty strode the corridors of the manor above with confidence, the way she held her riding-crop and exerted authority over the house staff, even over Baron Castlewell's two children, depicted a woman who could never be submissive.

Finally she spoke, her voice smooth and confident. 'Good evening, my little hares. I know I greeted you when you first arrived, but now allow me to truly welcome you, on behalf of Lord Victor Castlewell, to Iniscay's Wild Hunt. And I can safely guarantee you that nothing you may have done before will equal what you will do tomorrow. You may even enjoy yourselves more than the hunters.'

Some laughed nervously. Then one, an innocent looking Asian girl, but with an attitude that prompted frequent beatings on her pert buttocks, broke protocol. 'How would you know?'

Those perceptive hares might have noticed a dreamy expression in Mistress Bonnie's eyes. Then the supreme confidence returned, and she smiled. 'How, indeed?'

Exciting titles available now from Chimera

All **Chimera** titles are available from your local bookshop or newsagent, or by post or telephone from: B.B.C.S., P.O. Box 941, Hull, HU1 3VQ. (**24 hour Telephone Credit Card Line: 01482 224626**).

To order, send: Title, author, ISBN number and price for each book ordered, your full name and address, cheque or postal order payable to B.B.C.S. for the total amount, and allow the following for postage and packing:

UK and BFPO: £1.00 for the first book, and 50p for each additional book to a maximum of £3.50.

Overseas and Eire: £2.00 for the first book, £1.00 for the second and 50p for each additional book.

All titles £4.99 (US$7.95)